I0545909

SLEEPER SPECIES

BY EDWARD J. MCFADDEN III

SEVEREDPRESS

SLEEPER SPECIES

"There are horrors beyond life's edge that we do not suspect,
and once in a while man's evil prying calls them just within our range."

— H.P. Lovecraft

1

Western Ghats, northeast of Munnar, Kerala, India
9:21 AM IST, September 27th, present day

It wasn't the storm of the millennium, but it was close.

Tiger Pugari sat in the back seat of the rented BMW X7 staring through the rain-dappled window at the drenched tropical foliage that packed the sides of the dirt road, the mountains on the eastern horizon hidden in the dense fog that covered the land like smoke. Moisture invaded his body, and his armpits were soaked through, the oppressive heat pecking at his energy and patience.

The incessant *pop* and *tap* of rain filled the car, the windows perpetually smeared, the extreme humidity leaking into the vehicle despite the AC humming at full strength. Pugari was an expatriate Indian antiquities dealer who lived in London, and he had been all around the world and experienced the harshest conditions Mother Earth could conjure up, but the relentless rain was a bit much, even for him.

Raging storms had swirled in the region for weeks. Puddles the size of small ponds filled the road, the jungle underbrush was flooded, and even the largest trees hung low under the weight of saturation. Uprooted palms lay on their sides, their shallow roots unable to hold fast in the quicksand-like dirt. Outdoor activities had been shut down, and persistent fears of landslides drove many to flee their homes in the mountains to the houses of relatives in the lowlands.

The road meandered through the apocalyptic-like town of Marayoor. All the store shutters were closed, the colonial-era bungalows buttoned up tight, the tea museums and vibrant open-air markets closed, and not a single figure could be seen walking the streets.

"Almost makes me want to go home. Almost," said Lucca. One hand rested on the steering wheel, the other propped up her head, her elbow planted on the lip of the door where it met the window. Her dark hair was braided in a rope-like ponytail, which was tucked into her jacket, and sunglasses rested hopefully on her head. "This place…" She shook her head.

Pugari said nothing. He was no fan of India or rain, but when Kiran Beddie called and described a find beyond anything he'd ever seen there had been no question. He had to see it for himself before he decided what to do.

The road transformed into a dirt path that a single vehicle could traverse. In the driving rain, Lucca took it extra slow. There were pull-offs every tenth of a mile or so to allow vehicles to pass each other, but there were no other cars.

"How much further?" asked Pugari.

"Beddie said he'd be waiting at one of the pull-offs with his crew."

Pugari glanced at his watch and saw he was five thousand feet above sea level. The thick greenery on the left side of the road fell away to a misty valley containing a sprawling tea plantation, the rain pounding the fields, thin rivers filling the walking paths between the crops.

Interspersed within the private fields and unfettered forests were Eravikulam National Park and Anamudi Shola National Park, and luckily the find hadn't fallen within either of their boundaries. Like the parks, the surrounding area was comprised of rolling grasslands and patches of tropical forest that were home to various unique types of flora and fauna. Pugari knew little of the people who lived up this way, though he did know the population was a mix of local Keralites and migrants from neighboring Tamil Nadu, and that most who lived up this way were in some way involved with the cultivation of tea.

A large truck that looked straight out of 1950's American central casting appeared out of the fog ahead. Its rounded cab was rusted so badly that its original color was indiscernible, and the trailer attached to its hook didn't look much better. The skid steer atop the trailer looked a little better, but the miniature bulldozer had seen better days, even having been washed clean by days of severe rain.

Pugari smiled as Lucca brought the car to a stop behind the trailer. Rupees were rupees no matter their color, and his contact had come through.

Kiran Beddie was a slight man with a countable number of gray hairs, and they were all pasted to his dome thanks to the rain. He wore a black raincoat, but he didn't have his hood up as he jumped from the truck and charged through the rain toward the BMW.

Pugari figured Beddie didn't want to hide his face, and as he recalled the last time he'd worked with the man his stomach tightened. The retrieval of the Chola bronze statue depicting the Hindu deity Vishnu had gone sideways, and the man had lit out and left him holding an empty bag. Still, Pugari knew he could trust the guy to keep his mouth shut about the find. He shook his head. Scratch that. Beddie's tight lips were tied to the potential financial windfall Pugari could create, and without him, the statue was just a stone carving.

2

The passenger's side rear door opened, and Beddie got in the car. Water sprayed the back seat, and Pugari felt it splash his face. He made a show of wiping the tiny drops away.

"*Sori. Sori*," said Beddie as water dripped from his jacket.

"Speak English," Pugari said. "Please." A less sincere word had never been uttered.

"Certainly, sori… So sorry," Beddie said. "I would apologize for the weather, but God says this is good for the land."

"Far be it for me to question the almighty's watering ability," Lucca said.

Beddie bowed his head and muttered something about Brahman forgiving him.

"I believe you have something for Lucca?" Pugari said.

"Yes. Yes. Of course." Beddie reached into his rain slicker, pulled free a gun, and handed it over the seatback to Lucca.

The gun was a Pistol Auto 9MM, a common sidearm used by Indian security forces. Lucca racked the slide and verified the weapon was empty as a smile slid over her face. The magazine-fed semi-automatic looked used but well-maintained.

Beddie handed over two magazines and said, "They're loaded with 9MM Parabellums."

Lucca stuffed one magazine in a pocket, inserted the second into the gun, and chambered a round.

Gun laws in India were strict. Individuals must obtain a license to own and carry firearms, and this involved a thorough background check, including criminal records and mental health assessments. Only certain civilians, like those with high-security threats, were permitted to own handguns, and if a foreigner was caught with an illegal weapon the penalties were steep.

Lucca opened her window halfway, stuck the gun out into the rain, and fired into the sky. The report thundered through the car as she pulled the gun in and closed the window. "I never roll with a weapon I haven't personally fired."

Beddie shook his head. "Are we ready?"

Pugari nodded, his ears ringing. He wanted to scold Lucca, but the woman had a point, and he had to pick his battles.

The hum of the window sliding down filled the car and Beddie waved to his men as Lucca maneuvered the BMW around their truck.

When the caravan was inching through the downpour, Pugari said, "You were wise to contact me."

"I must again ask forgiveness for my failures on our last campaign. Had I known we were—"

Pugari raised a hand and the car fell still save for the hammering rain. Despite their last mission being a failure, Beddie had supplied much useful information over the years, and overall their relationship had been profitable for both men. "The past. What of the future?"

Beddie nodded vigorously, his wet raincoat throwing spray. "There is an opportunity here that I know only you will see." The man's heavy breathing was fogging the windows despite the air conditioning.

The BMW dove into a puddle so deep the car's engine sputtered as the vehicle plowed through the water, a dirty brown wave crashing over the hood. Behind them, the truck chugged and swayed, but made it through.

To make conversation, Pugari asked, "What is going on with the rain?"

"Monsoon season. The worst in recorded history. The Indian Ocean is a torn-up mess, and the horrible weather is being felt as far as Africa."

Lucca sniffed. "What's the cause? Climate change?"

"That is a piece of it," Beddie said. "The meteorologist big brains say Kerala has received forty-eight percent more rain than average and some regions are experiencing more than double their usual rainfall. Increasing global temperatures and a warmer Indian Ocean lead to higher humidity and heavier rainfall. The topography of the Ghats also makes things worse because of the orographic effect, which causes more rain over the mountains."

"What's all the chatter about the government screwing up?" Lucca asked.

"Yes, that is true, but to a much lesser extent," Beddie said. "There are numerous rivers and backwaters in the Western Ghats prone to heavy rains and flooding, and the poorly timed release of water from several dams simultaneously worsened the flooding. This is what caused sections of the mountainside to give way."

Silence filled the car, and the only sounds were the tinkle of water and the rhythmic tapping of raindrops on the metal roof.

"Three days ago, my contact in the government was surveying the damage by drone," Beddie continued. "He discovered the statue embedded in a landslide."

Beddie ran a tight ship, but people talked, and eventually what had been uncovered would become known, regardless of his efforts to hide it, which was why he needed to act fast. "And this contact has kept his mouth shut?" asked Pugari.

"Yes," said Beddie. "For a fee, of course."

Lucca brought the BMW to a stop as the dirt road abruptly fell away.

4

The cliff face to the east had slid into the jungle below, taking the road and the side of the mountain with it.

"We must walk from here. But it is not far," Beddie said.

Pugari grunted and pulled his hood over his head. Traditional storm attire did little in the driving rain, and water lashed his face as he got out of the car.

Beddie rattled off instructions to the truck driver in native Malayalam, and the rumble of the vehicle's old diesel engine fell still. The party wore boots, but Pugari already felt his socks getting damp as he trudged through mud, the rain coming in dense sheets. Fog limited visibility to fifty feet, and Lucca and Pugari trailed after Beddie like eager ducklings.

The trio had only gone fifty yards or so when Beddie made a hard right, turning away from the landslide. A boulder blocked the way, and their guide disappeared behind the large stone that was wedged into the side of the mountain, muddy water and tiny stones eddying around it.

Pugari came around the rock and his mouth fell open.

"Well, how about that," Lucca said.

Beddie stood aside, a smile creeping over his wet face.

Half buried in mud and stones was a statue of a lizard man holding a tablet.

The monument was chiseled from a single piece of stone, and it stood thirty feet high, its distinct reptilian characteristics also humanoid-like. Its elongated head had prominent almond-shaped eyes, and the entire statue was covered with carved patterns that resembled scales. The lizard man's arms and legs were elongated and ended in claws, and though most of it was buried, Pugari could see the beginnings of a thick tail.

None of this surprised Pugari. There were many documented petroglyphs, hieroglyphs, and monuments of lizard people around the world and some of the ancient civilizations had steles that described similar beings.

But the tablet covered with ancient symbols Pugari had never seen before was something else altogether.

Beddie said, "My people symbolize lizards often and they are linked to various attributes such as transformation, healing, and the ability to traverse different realms, specifically land and water."

"Lizard man theories also include the figures as gods, mythical beings, or ancestral spirits," Pugari said.

"Or they came from space," Lucca said.

"Any clue what type of writing that is? Or what it says?" Beddie asked.

Pugari shrugged. He didn't like saying he didn't know, and he definitely didn't like saying he had no clue, despite obsessing over the photos of the tablet Beddie had sent. He looked over his shoulder and verified that the monument wasn't visible from what remained of the road and said, "Let's get to work."

Lucca broke open a camera case and the duo set out to document the ancient statue.

Pugari was no expert, but he knew when something was old, and the worn stone sculpture was ancient beyond the count of years. Despite being buried until recently, all the lizard man's rough edges were smoothed, and it didn't take much to see that much of the finery had melted away with time and weather.

When the pair was done documenting the find and taking over a hundred pictures of the tablet, Pugari said, "Beddie, tell your men to do their thing."

Beddie nodded and headed back to get his crew. He'd only been gone a few minutes when the skid steer rumbled onto the mountainside and began concealing the monument with fresh earth.

2

Park City, Utah, United States
9:22 AM, October 6th

The door chime buzzed, and Knight looked up from his work. It was early for walk-ins, and he wasn't expecting anyone. Base Camp was the kind of shop you wandered into after a few drinks, and it was early and between seasons.

He signed his name, Lucius Knight, to the proof approval form for Badlands Dinosaur Adventures new print ad in Adventure Magazine. With that done, he slipped the paper into an envelope, turned off the desk lamp, and spun in his seat. The chair squealed as he tapped the keyboard of his computer and brought up the security cameras.

Knight sighed when he saw the man and woman standing just inside Base Camp's main entrance staring at a poster for his most popular tour, hunting for dinosaur fossils in Madagascar.

As if the duo felt Knight watching, Tiger Pugari and Lucca looked up as one and stared at the camera.

He cycled through the exterior security cameras and the antiquities dealer, and his sidekick appeared to have come alone. Not that it mattered. He'd never had anything to fear from Pugari except a bounced check. Things had gotten dull with the end of the summer season, and ski season was still a few weeks off, and Pugari's appearance might be just what he needed.

"Be right out," Knight yelled as he pushed up from his chair. The door to the backroom was open, but there was no reply. He cracked his neck and headed to the front of the shop.

Base Camp was exactly what its name portended it to be: the hub of Badlands Dinosaur Adventures, where the flames of exploration were stoked, plans were made, and the administrative work necessary to run an international business was performed.

The place wasn't much. A thousand square feet carved out of a larger retail space that turned over every three years. Knight leased the entire space and sublet the large part. He'd had grand visions of old planes and cars, dinosaur renderings, and a museum of adventure equipment to help sell the company's motif, but the economic feasibility of the concept hadn't stood up under the light of day.

As he entered the public area of Home Base, sunlight angled through the posters on the front window, each advertising a tour. Dinosaur National Monument in Colorado and Utah, where patrons could participate in fossil excavation, and experience hiking trails, petroglyphs, and scenic dinosaur-themed drives, took up one window. On the other were ads for the Utah Dinosaur Experience theme park and fossil hunts at Badlands National Park, as well as several international destinations.

The shop itself was little more than a conversation pit, with an old flatscreen TV playing videos of past tours, a wall covered in brochures and testimonials, a desk, a few fake plants, a shelf of dusty t-shirts and mugs serving as the gift shop, and a few guest chairs. The joint looked like a real estate office that had been decorated by the same people who styled the Rainforest Café restaurants.

"Are there still slots open for the next trip?" Pugari pointed at the poster promoting an unforgettable life experience hunting dinosaur fossils in Madagascar.

"Hi, Luscious," Lucca said.

Knight hated when she called him by the bastardized version of his first name, though he couldn't deny he was attracted to the woman. Things had been bleak on the dating front recently, and Lucca's leer made certain parts of his anatomy tingle. He said, "You don't call? You don't write?" He hadn't seen or heard from Pugari since he'd helped the man obtain a T-rex skull on a dig in the Badlands. The guy was into all kinds of stuff, some of it shady, but Knight didn't think the man was a criminal, even if he wasn't totally honest.

Pugari smiled but said nothing.

"Missed you, sugar," Lucca said.

"I see you're up to your same old stuff," Pugari said as he motioned at the wall of brochures. "I really thought this little phase would have worn off by now."

It was Knight's turn to say nothing. He could tell when Pugari was lecturing, and he let the man go.

"You're a hunter, like Lucca and me," Pugari said.

"Well, you know. I get my fossils for money and my chicks for free," Knight sang.

Lucca frowned. She wore tight jeans, a white shirt that displayed her ample bosom, and a black sports coat. Pugari wore a dark suit with a white shirt and no tie, and suddenly Knight felt underdressed in his shorts and Jurassic Park t-shirt.

"You being here, doing this, is a waste of talent," Pugari continued.

8

"Please sit," Knight said as he motioned toward the conversation pit and ignored Pugari's compliment. He was a failed archaeology student and a struggling small business owner, not exactly stuff his mother could brag about down at the bingo hall. Like many other males his age, he'd been inspired by Indiana Jones, and after a mediocre high school career enrolled in college. Knight discovered quickly that he enjoyed the hunt more than studying, preparing, and the boring, laborious, and monotonous analysis of what was found.

The trio took seats, a video of a group of tourists hiking through the jungle playing on the TV.

Lucca sat next to Knight and invaded his personal space, and heat spread through him as Knight inched away from the woman.

Pugari sat across from the pair, smiling. "What a lovely couple you would make."

"To what do I owe the pleasure?" Knight said.

Pugari pointed at the poster for the tour to Madagascar. "Did you know there will be an eclipse there on November 8th?"

"Why would I?"

"I don't know," Pugari said. "Lucca, show him the pictures."

Lucca sighed, her ponytail whipping as she pulled three photographs and handed them to Knight.

The first was a picture of a lizard man statue. Everything in the shot was wet, the sky in the background dark, and heavy rain filled the foreground. A second photo showed a closeup of the tablet the statue held, and the third was a picture of a mountainside bare of vegetation.

"It was exposed in India, outside Marayoor to be exact," Pugari said, "where monsoons caused a landslide that wiped away the side of a mountain. We covered it back up, as you can see."

"What the hell is it? How old? Who put it there?" Knight asked as he stared at the picture of the tablet.

"Don't know. Don't know. And don't know," Pugari said.

Lucca sniffed.

Pugari lectured about all the cultures with lizard man statues and petroglyphs in their ancient tombs and cities. Knight had heard most of it before, and he failed to see what was so special about the statue, other than it being a mysterious new find. Pseudo-archaeologists would have a field day when the pictures and monument became public.

Knight said, "I assume since you covered the thing back up, that you have a reason to keep the find a secret?"

"I do," Pugari said. "That tablet. I believe it describes how to reach a secret temple that I believe contains countless riches. Short of that, it could be an incredible find."

Knight looked at Lucca, who pursed her lips. Pugari was the boss, and what he believed, she believed.

"You're going to have—" Knight's phone buzzed, and he felt the vibration on his butt. "Please excuse me. I have to take this." He pulled his phone, swiped, and said, "What's up, Wheat Thin?" Wesley "Wheat Thin" Eakin was Knight's number one man. The ex-Army Intelligence Officer was a rail of a man whose full span of expertise was still undiscovered. On this day he was a van driver.

"Hey, boss," Wes said. "I'm missing one, a Ms. Darma Clay."

"Hang on," Knight said as he scanned his cell, Lucca smiling and Pugari licking his lips.

The tour to the dinosaur adventure park was one of his best moneymakers and all it involved was transportation to the site that was two hours away.

"Sorry, Wes," Knight said. "She called last night to cancel. I forgot to update the guest list."

"No worries," Wes said. "See you tonight."

Knight clicked off and turned his attention back to his guests.

"What excitement," Pugari said. "You're a secretary."

Anger boiled in him, but Knight tamped it down, mainly because the man was right. He said, "I... the business, makes twenty-three dollars a head after expenses for doing basically nothing and it keeps Wheat Thin busy between our real tours."

"Oh, the riches," Pugari said as he pulled at his beard. The man's dark complexion was free of blemishes, but his eyebrows and beard needed a trim, and he reeked of Axe body spray.

"Listen to the tiger roar," Knight said. "If you came here to insult me, I've got things to do." He didn't, but there it was.

"Easy, old friend," Pugari said.

Knight held his tongue and waited.

"I believe this find is of significant value," Pugari said.

"How does it lead to money? That's why you're interested? Right? Why you're here?" Knight said.

"The knowledge, the quest, it all—"

"Let me stop you right there," Knight said. "That kind of bullshit is one of the reasons why I quit archaeology. Definitive answers are elusive. Shit, people are debating what happened yesterday, so what happened eighty million plus years ago is surely up for speculation, and with the 'knowledge is the enemy' crowd, I just don't have the patience."

A self-satisfied smile crept over Pugari's face and Knight wanted to smack the guy.

"What if I had something definitive?" Pugari said.

"How old is it?" Knight asked, knowing Pugari probably wouldn't know.

"It's old. Very old. On the order of one hundred million years, but don't quote me on that, and there's considerable fudge in the numbers."

Knight laughed and tossed the picture of the tablet at Pugari. "I might not be a PhD, but I've never seen symbols and writing like that before. It's gibberish."

"What if it wasn't?" Pugari said.

The gentle roar of a crowd leaked through the room as the promotion video showed a group of children finding a small dinosaur fossil.

"As you might expect, digging old shit up isn't the only business I'm into," Pugari said. "I invest, mainly in things that help me dig up old shit, but technology and its ilk grow tentacles faster than fungus on the side of my pool."

Knight rolled his eyes and waited. Questions would only slow the man down.

"I invested in artificial intelligence early on, and I work with a prof at Princeton who is a leading mind in the field." Pugari paused, allowing Knight to say something, and when he didn't, he continued. "The passage shows signs of Akkadian, though the AI's opinion is the glyphs on the tablet are the base language and led to the creation of Akkadian, not the other way around.

"My expert utilized an AI model trained on sample cuneiform texts. Then she used it to translate the glyphs on the statue's tablet. The AI used all known writing and glyphs, and melded it with a bilingual evaluation understudy BLEU4, a complex algorithm that only the AI truly understands."

"That sounds..." Words failed Knight. That, or he didn't want to offend his guest.

"Crazy. Scary. Impossible." Pugari smiled as he drew out his phone. "The AI substituted modern vernacular for certain unknown parts of the message and filled in gaps using the known parts."

"You mean you're not certain the translation is correct?" Knight said.

"The translation is correct, the interpretation..." He tapped his phone, then read: "In lands where whispers hold the key, down the mountain, winding steep. From here on high, follow the sun as it disappears, down to flat plains where terrible creatures sleep, guarding secrets the ages keep. In the forest's sacred shade, where the ancient songs are made, there will be a monolith of lore. Follow its guide, past the valleys, green and wide, beyond the new river's flowing tide. When the sun disappears from the middle day sky, and life-giving water inundates the land, that which is hidden will be revealed through echoes of a race once seethed, the prize awaits where darkness breathes."

"Is that why you asked about the eclipse?" said Knight. "When the sun disappears?"

Pugari said nothing.

Knight laughed. "As to the rest, the marker stone could be anywhere in India east of Marayoor."

Pugari smiled that knowing smile that Knight hated so much. "The place I seek isn't in India, that is known."

"You're not making sense," Knight said. "I know where Marayoor is, and the message is referring to the direction of the setting sun, but the rest could mean anything."

"Not if I know where, roughly, the monolith is."

Knight said nothing. He was getting bored.

"You've heard of Gondwana?"

"The supercontinent."

Pugari nodded. "It existed in various forms from the late Precambrian to the Jurassic, and around 180 million years ago during the Jurassic period, tectonic forces began to break Gondwana apart. This colossal landmass was comprised of what is now South America, Africa, Antarctica, Australia, and the Indian subcontinent, and it started to fragment due to the movement of Earth's lithospheric plates."

"That narrows it down," Knight said.

Lucca chuckled and put her hand on Knight's knee, and he swept it away.

"As Gondwana disintegrated, the first major split occurred between the western and eastern halves, roughly dividing it into South America-Africa and Antarctica-India-Australia segments. More rifting events further separated these landmasses, and around 135 million years ago, during the Cretaceous, Madagascar began to detach from the eastern coast of Africa due to a rift that formed between the two. Madagascar continued to drift eastward, and this final split set Madagascar on its isolated path in the Indian Ocean."

"Let me get this straight," Knight said. "I'm a bit slow. One hundred-plus million years ago some unknown civilization created this statue, which serves as a guidepost to... what? And now I'm supposed to believe the temple or whatever the hell it is in is in Africa?"

"Madagascar."

"How could you possibly know that?"

12

"Because of this." Pugari displayed his phone, which showed a rock with symbols all over it. "That's the monolith the tablet speaks of. I think we can find it and it will guide us."

"And it's in Madagascar, which is why you came to me," Knight said. "You need Abby and my local contacts there to go after this, whatever *it* is."

"Riches and fame, my boy. Riches and fame."

Knight had to admit he was intrigued.

"Are you in?" Lucca asked.

"I'm still listening," Knight said.

3

Knight had no intention of jumping into Pugari's undertaking without doing his due diligence. Though he'd told Pugari that he was in, and the plan was to meet in Antananarivo, he sent everything he knew to Abby and was waiting for her analysis before making his final decision.

Pugari planned to find the monolith and follow its lead to the temple. The goal was to be in position to see whatever there was to be seen when the eclipse occurred. He was, at best, dubious about the theory that the heavy rain combined with the eclipse would reveal or unlock something, but Knight didn't think those specifics mattered much.

In the meantime, he prepared for his tour to Hell Creek and contacted Matheus Barbo, his main contact in Madagascar, and instructed him to lay the groundwork to hire one helper, gather equipment and supplies, and obtain any necessary permits. When given the final word Barbo would also procure weapons, which was usually how Knight handled things. Though he'd never had cause to use it, Knight usually carried a legal firearm when trudging through the jungles of Madagascar. The country's gun laws reflected a cautious approach to civilian gun ownership, and foreigners typically weren't permitted to carry handguns. But due to the boost he provided to the local economy, in the past, he'd been granted permissions for his team to carry firearms from the Malagasy authorities.

If the expedition was a go, Wheat Thin was joining him, so he was working on finding someone to replace him on the dinosaur theme park runs, which happened every Monday, Wednesday, Friday, and Saturday like clockwork. Wes used several different people to cover for him when he couldn't make the run, so Knight wasn't worried. He'd considered just shutting down for a few weeks. Base Camp would be locked down, but he knew being closed for any length of time would give his competitors an advantage he couldn't afford, so the show had to go on.

None of these details were the real reasons Knight was hesitant. What it came down to in the end was did he trust Pugari. He had worked with a man before, and things had been fine, even if Pugari sometimes exercised what Knight liked to call questionable ethical decision-making. The guy was too casual when others were in danger, and sometimes reckless with the orders he threw around to his people.

But that didn't mean Knight needed to listen to the man, and this was the best lead he'd had in months.

Plus, Pugari was paying his top fee, which he needed. The business was surviving, barely, and he was having trouble funding some of his larger expeditions due to cancellations and reduced down payments. He needed an influx of cash, and unless something astonishing jumped out he and Wes were heading to Madagascar.

Four days later he was out in the Badlands, hiding beneath a pop-up tent as he watched his customers dig in the hardpan when Abby called.

"Can you hear me?" Abby asked. She was over a thousand miles away in Los Angeles.

"Yeah, but it's a bit fuzzy," Knight said. He had high-end satellite service for safety purposes, but the connection was still affected by solar flares and the like. He pushed up from his chair and paced about until the line cleared. "Better?"

"I think so," she said. "Where are you?"

"Out at the formation," Knight said. "What did you find?"

"First, I find it funny that you think Pugari came to you because of me," she said.

"That was one of the reasons. He knows you're an expert in finding unfindable things, and that you're a dog in a fight, and..."

"And?"

"O.K., he might have a thing for you."

She sighed. "Is that going to be a problem if I decide to come on this little venture?"

"It never has been before." Not totally true, but Abby didn't call him out.

"Well, he, you, might not like what I found. As usual, I have a different take than our Indian friend."

Knight waited, the clang of shovels digging in the earth and the muffled chatter of the tourists carrying over the Badlands.

"I have my own AI experts to call on, as you might imagine, and they found a few... potential discrepancies in the translation of the writing on the lizard man's tablet," Abby said. "And... Brace yourself because I'm sure you'll be stunned; it appears that our benefactor has left off an entire line of text."

That was troubling, but Knight stayed silent.

"'In lands where whispers hold the key, down the mountain, winding steep. From here on high, follow the sun as it disappears' clearly refers to going west down the mountainside. 'Down to flat plains where terrible creatures sleep, guarding secrets the ages keep' could be a reference to dinosaurs. There were many species in the area throughout the ages. 'In the forest's sacred shade, where the ancient songs are made' blah, blah. Then it gets interesting. 'A monolith of lore. Follow its guide, past the valleys, green and wide, beyond the new river's flowing tide.'"

"I figured that was a map of a kind," Knight said.

"Solid guess," Abby said, "and based on Pugari's interpretation of Gondwana's breakup, the new river is most likely a reference to the Indian Ocean at its earliest stages of creation. 'When the sun disappears from the middle day sky, and life-giving water inundates the land', the eclipse and extreme water."

"Madagascar, southeast Africa, and the Indian Ocean have been getting pounded by record-setting monsoons," Knight said.

"Yup," Abby said. "'That which is hidden will be revealed through echoes of a race once seethed, the prize awaits where darkness breathes' has two errors, I believe. 'Echoes of race once seethed.' I believe this doesn't mean humanoids, but some unknown race, maybe bestial."

"Why is that?"

"This last part," she said. "'The prize awaits, where darkness breathes.' My AI says the word isn't prize, but hive."

Knight cracked his neck. "Dare I ask why?"

"That last line, which Pugari conveniently left out," she said. "'When the sun is extinguished, and the land weeps, the Salamantis awakens.'"

Abby let that sit out there, Knight's mind churning, his anger growing. After a minute all he came up with was, "That's disconcerting."

"But expected," she said. "Pugari is downplaying the potential danger, or we might not sign up. Treasure is a much more enticing carrot."

"Riches and fame," Knight muttered.

"What?"

"Nothing."

"There's more," Abby said. "I did a deep dive on the word Salamantis, and as it turns out several ancient tribes in the Indian Ocean region have references to a monster in their history. The name Salamantis turned up more than once, and one of the tribes has a direct link to Madagascar."

A child screamed and Knight's head jerked toward the source of the commotion. The kid had found an ammonite fossil. The spiral shells imbedded in stone are among the most frequently discovered sea fossils in the Badlands, and the boy asked why there were sea creatures in the middle of the wasteland. The kid's mother, who clearly had been paying attention to Knight's canned lecture on the drive to the site, said, "Because a very long time ago there was an ocean here."

"Everything O.K.?" Abby asked.

"Yes. Go on."

"An article in the Journal of Human Molecular Genetics claims Madagascar was first settled during or before the mid-first millennium AD by Austronesian peoples arriving on outrigger canoes from present-day Indonesia. The remnants of these people can be seen all over the island, and several splinter tribes can claim Austronesian roots. There is an account of the Salamantis inscribed on an ancient stela outside Quelimane, Africa, and its translation supports my theory that the temple wasn't created to protect and hide riches, but to contain monsters."

This wasn't a new idea, and Knight stayed silent.

"My AI dude translated the writing on the stela," Abby said. "It's grim reading. I know you're aware, but keep in mind these translations are rough. Some glyphs have no comparison or translation, but I think you'll get the picture. 'When the land is flooded, and there is no light to guide the way, take heed of the deadly Salamantis, a creature born of fire and leaf.'"

"Shit," Knight said.

"That's not the half of it. According to legend, the Salamantis was born from the union of two powerful spirits: the Fire Spirit, who danced among the flames of the sacred bonfires, and the Water Spirit, who dwelled deep within the cool, dark pools of the forest. Seeking to create a protector for their beloved land, these spirits combined their essence to give life to the Salamantis, but things didn't go as planned. The last part of the stela reads, 'Dig deep, flee far, for when the beasts awaken no living thing shall survive their onslaught.'"

"Beasts? Plural? As in more than one? Or many?"

Abby said nothing and cold silence filled the thousand-plus mile void between them.

"This is crazy, right?" Knight said. "How has nobody ever seen one of these things? Are we talking Bigfoot here?"

Abby didn't respond.

"It's some big lizard or mutant dinosaur?" Knight said.

"I spoke to Barbo, and he said there's an old Tsimihety shaman that tells old tales down at the local watering hole about a mythical creature called the Salamantis."

"Did you get a name?"

"Narivony Ravelonarivo."

"Did you speak with him?"

Abby laughed. "No phone and Barbo has no idea where he lives, but he's trying to see if the old man will meet with us. When are we leaving?"

Knight had expected Abby's report to seal the deal, but all it had done was raise more questions and concerns. "You're coming with us?"

"What else do I have to do?"

Knight didn't know, but Abby's knowledge, toughness, and fighting skills made her an asset to any expedition, and since Pugari had specifically requested her... "I'll let you know when the final debrief is. Can you handle the team's travel arrangements?" The woman was a hacker and internet wiz, and she could get them anywhere they needed to go fast.

"Sure," Abby said. "Talk soon."

Two days before his fifty-five hour, three layover flight to Madagascar, he held one final meeting by phone with the major players. Knight, Wheat Thin, and Abby holed up in Knight's small office at Base Camp and they spoke with Pugari and Lucca over speakerphone.

"Barbo has hired Volana," Knight said. "You remember her, right?"

Pugari said, "She's his main person, attractive if a little distant."

"And qualified to the teeth," Abby said.

"Of course." Pugari sounded somewhat aggrieved. "Lucca and Tank will be joining me."

"And Abby and Wes will be coming with me," Knight said.

Abby tried to interject but Knight held up a hand. Pugari didn't need to know that Cap would also be on the case watching from afar until needed.

"And all the arrangements have been made? Guns? Food? Tents and such?" Pugari asked.

"I even had Barbo put together some dive equipment," Knight said.

"Yes, very good," Pugari said. "I hadn't thought of that."

"See you in a few days at the hotel," Knight said.

Pugari closed the connection without responding.

4

Royal Grande Hotel, Antananarivo, Madagascar
10:19 PM EAT, October 29th

The hotel had a small bar with some couches, tables, and a stone fireplace. Old wallpaper, brass wall sconces, dim lighting, and white linen tablecloths gave the place a classy timeless feel. A fire burned in the hearth, the endless rain and unseasonably cold temperatures putting a chill into the most hardened Malagasy. The dry season had gone out with a whimper and monsoon season started in late September and only picked up steam into October.

In Madagascar, two seasons are recognized: a hot, rainy season from November to April and a cooler, dry season from May to October, which was when Knight usually brought his tour groups. The eastern portion of the country, where the expedition would be venturing, had a sub-equatorial climate driven by easterly trade winds, which created the heaviest and most consistent rainfall. This produced upwards of one hundred and fifty inches of rain annually, and if the current monsoon season lived up to the early totals Madagascar was on pace to double that amount.

The party of five was seated at a round six-person table beside the fireplace, a bottle of toaka gasy at the center of the group. Conversation was subdued, and Knight kept one eye on the entrance as he sipped the ginger and orange-infused Rhum Arrangé.

All heads turned when Narivony Ravelonarivo blew into the room. The fire cracked and popped as the man looked around, and when he found Barbo he raised a hand and started for the table.

Ravelonarivo looked like a cross between a priest and a goat herder. He wore black boots, dark, dirty jeans, and a red cotton lamba wrapped around a blue flannel shirt like a huge scarf. The shaman wore a hat of woven straw decorated with beads and feathers, and several chains with odd charms hung around the wizened man's neck. A brown leather Gandalf-like pouch hung from his belt, and Knight knew it most likely contained herbs, roots, and other natural elements used in healing practices. It didn't take a genius to see the man was uncomfortable, the hotel outside the man's normal habitat.

Barbo said, "Ravel is of Tsimihety ancestry, and his people are known for their wisdom and deep connection to the land. To this day they are led by ombiasas, revered shamans, who are believed to commune with the spirits of nature and their ancestors. Ravel is one of these shamans, though he enjoys modern conveniences like drink and smoke. Though he'd never be caught dead in a place like this. Too snooty and expensive."

The group stood when the ombiasa arrived tableside.

"*Izay mihevitra fa mahalala ahy no miantso ahy* Ravel," the shaman said.

"He says 'Those who think they know me call me Ravel,'" Barbo said.

"Can you speak English?" Pugari asked. "Our... other guests aren't as culturally diverse as I."

"Yes, my apologies. I have studied the holy books," Ravel said.

"My name is Knight, and this is my advisor Abby, the cultured Mr. Pugari, his associate Lucca, and you know Barbo."

Ravel grunted and rubbed his gray beard, the glow of the fire painting shifting shadows on his face. A cup sat upside-down before the only empty seat, and the man wasted no time sitting, turning the cup over, and filling it to the brim. He closed his eyes as he took a long pull of the flavored rum and released a contented sigh as his snake eyes slid open. "I'm not surprised that you have come to me," Ravel said. "The rains say it is time and the sun will soon disappear."

Knight knew, as did everyone else, that on November 8th, much of Madagascar would experience an eclipse, but he held his questions.

"You want to know of the Salamantis?" Ravel said. He finished his toaka gasy and poured himself another.

"Any information you can provide might prove helpful," Pugari said. "Like have you seen the monument stone?"

Ravel nodded. "Many moons ago, though I think I could find it if the gods willed it thus."

The fire spat and hissed as everyone waited on Ravel, who seemed more interested in the rum than the five people hanging on his every word.

"Long ago, before Madagascar became a destination, the Tsimihety people thrived nestled within the lush, emerald canopy of the rainforests," began Ravel. He took a long pull of toaka gasy, looked each of his audience members in the eye, and continued. "When the world as we know it was still young and the spirits of nature walked among us, our ancestors stumbled upon a hidden stone structure deep within the heart of the forest. It had been raining for over a year, and on this day the sun disappeared from the sky.

"This tomb, which was what the warriors thought the place to be, was ancient and forgotten. It is said the place held great secrets and treasures from a bygone era and some claimed it was the entrance to a vast underground city. Driven by curiosity and the promise of untold riches, a group of brave Tsimihety warriors ventured into the depths of this mysterious place."

Knight and the others listened in rapt silence, their faces illuminated by the dancing flames and faint overhead lighting. Ravel's eyes gleamed as he continued, his voice carrying the weight of millennia.

"Legends say that to reach this place, one must become something else, and the entrance door is said to have symbols unknown to man."

"Have you ever heard mention of a lizard man?" Pugari asked.

Ravel paused with his cup halfway to his mouth. "Yes. How is it you know this?"

"Lucky guess," Pugari said.

Barbo quickly filled the shaman in on the statue uncovered by a landslide in Kerala, India.

"Yes, I see," Ravel said. "The Tsimihety somehow gained access to this place, and as they descended into the darkness, the air grew cold, the silence thick. The walls—"

"Wait," Lucca interjected. "You don't know anything about how the warriors gained access?"

The ombiasa hiked his shoulders and said nothing.

"Great," muttered Abby.

"Please, go on," Knight said as he shot Abby a 'shut your piehole' look.

"The walls of the corridor beyond were adorned with strange pictographs and carvings, telling the story of a powerful being known as the Salamantis. According to the ancient inscriptions, this creature was a guardian of the natural world, a being of immense power and ferocity, capable of controlling both fire and foliage. It was said that the Salamantis had been sealed away by the gods themselves, imprisoned in this tomb to protect the world from their wrath."

Silence pressed in on the group, and it appeared that the two patrons at the bar, the bartender, and everyone sitting at tables were also listening to Ravel's tale.

"The Tsimihety came upon a massive stone door adorned with intricate carvings of flames and leaves, the symbols of the Salamantis. With great effort, they managed to pry the door open, unleashing a wave of searing heat that scorched the air around them." Ravel's voice grew hushed, and everyone at the table leaned in. "As the door creaked open, a blinding light filled the chamber, and from within the depths of the tomb emerged the Salamantis.

"Its body was a fusion of fiery hues and vibrant greens, its limbs long and slender like those of a mantis, yet its skin shimmered with the iridescence of a salamander. The creature's eyes burned with an intense, otherworldly light, and its movements were both graceful and terrifying."

Suddenly Knight felt very cold despite the heat of the fire.

Ravel's face creased with sorrow as he recounted the tragic fate of his forebearers. "The Salamantis hungered for food, and the flesh and blood of man satisfied its cravings. Though they tried to flee, the beasts unleashed their fury upon the warriors, and they fought valiantly, but my kin were no match for the creatures and much blood was spilled. Many were slain in the chaos, and the echoes of the past say only three of the warriors made it home to tell the tale.

"The survivors, realizing the danger they unleashed, retreated, their hearts heavy with guilt and fear. They fled the tomb, sealing the stone door behind them in a desperate attempt to contain the beasts. With great effort, they managed to seal the entrance, hoping that the Salamantis would remain trapped within its subterranean prison for all eternity."

"That would explain why nobody has ever seen one of these things," Pugari said. "But all this sounds a bit... big."

"You don't believe?" asked Ravel.

Pugari pursed his lips, and said, "Old legends die hard."

Ravel finished his rum and poured another.

Knight followed suit. He considered pressing Pugari for leaving out the information about the Salamantis, but decided against it, seeing nothing to gain.

"Generations of my people have guarded this secret," Ravel concluded, "passing down the story of the Salamantis as a warning to never disturb the tomb again. The spirits of our ancestors watch over us, ensuring that the creatures remain sealed away, protecting us from its wrath."

Knight coughed gently.

Abby stared at her drink.

Lucca gazed wistfully at the fire.

Pugari spun his full cup on the table before him as he licked his lips.

Barbo stared openly at the shaman, his face tender with sympathy.

The fire crackled softly as the ombiasa's words settled.

Ravel's voice, now gentle and reassuring, broke the silence. "Remember the lessons of our past. Respect the land and the spirits that dwell within it. Our ancestors paid a great price for their curiosity, and it is our duty to honor their sacrifice by living in harmony with the world around us." The shaman leaned back in his chair and sipped his toaka gasy.

"If your people didn't build this temple, or city, or whatever it is, who did?" Barbo asked.

"Ah, now you get to it," Ravel said. "My people do not know. Long ago, before the invisible bones of the beasts who bring the *vazaha* here existed, another people contained the creatures."

"But then your ancestors unsealed the tomb, and then resealed it?" Knight asked.

"Yes, and when the monolith stone was found, which leads one to the tomb, my people used it as a reminder to all that the site should not be disturbed."

"Do you still believe this?" Pugari asked.

Ravel sighed. "I have no desire for riches and fame, but if you intend to go to this place, I must accompany you to ensure..." The old man sipped his drink.

"To ensure we don't muck things up?" Lucca said.

Ravel smiled.

Pugari dropped a picture of the monolith on the table, the huge boulder covered with petroglyphs and decorated with vines and dirt. "You said you think you can find this?"

"I do."

"Will you show us?" Pugari asked.

Knight bit his lip. The last thing he needed was another passenger. Especially one who looked like he might fall apart if he walked more than a mile.

"I will," Ravel said, his eyes bloodshot but still burning with something Knight couldn't identify.

"Until the morrow then," Pugari said.

When goodbyes had been exchanged, a meeting place for the next day set, Pugari said, "What do you think?"

"Why would he show us where the rock is if he doesn't want us messing with the site?" Abby asked.

"I was thinking the same thing," Lucca said.

"What do you think, Dusky?" Pugari said.

Silence fell over the table and Knight felt his face grow hot. He knew they called him Dusky behind his back sometimes. It was all in good fun, and he had to admit the moniker was quite clever. It was a balance between his first and last name: Lucius Knight. He was considered a rational, middle-of-the-road type of guy. Lucius meant light, and Knight meant darkness. So dusk, or Dusky, something in between, had become the joke.

Knight let the jab roll off him. "I think we need to be cautious, but I didn't hear anything that makes me want to run home. Every ancient culture has stories like this. The leaders of old used them to control their subjects and keep the masses away from places they didn't want them to go."

"This seems like a little more, no?" Barbo said.

"Maybe," Knight said. "Are we ready to leave in the morning? Do we have enough supplies for an additional person?"

"I'll see to it," Barbo said. "And yes. I've arranged for us to be picked up at dawn and transported to the trailhead along with our gear. There'll be five ATVs waiting there for us, two of which will be 6x6s with trailers that have built-in gear boxes."

"And the weapons?" Lucca asked.

"They're secured in the weapons lockers on the trailers along with the ammo. I think you'll be pleased."

"We always are, Barbo," Knight said.

"Anything else?" Pugari said.

The fire creaked and cracked and Barbo coughed. All eyes turned his way.

"Barbo? If you have something to say, now would be a good time," Knight said.

"Your locally flavored opinion is one of the reasons you're here," Pugari added.

"It's just..." Barbo looked pained, deep fissures cutting across his face, the bags beneath his eyes turning a shade blacker. "If the old man speaks it true, perhaps whatever is out there should stay hidden."

Pugari laughed as he pushed to his feet and slapped Barbo on the back. "Food for thought if we actually find something."

Goodnights were shared and everyone retreated to their rooms for a final night in a bed before hitting the trail.

As he stared at the dark ceiling of his room Knight's stomach twisted with the unique mix of nervous energy and anticipation that proceeded any venture worth doing. He recalled Barbo's words, but he was too tired, and before he could make a list of pros and cons, his brain shut down for the night.

5

The caravan of ATVs sounded like a bunch of broken bassoons as the party pushed through the torrential rain that pounded the forest. A culvert filled with rushing water ran alongside the trail, and thick vegetation hung low, causing the group to slow to avoid hitting branches overloaded with wet elephant ear leaves. In the driving rain, the team had met the rental agent just off RT6, and after packing supplies and checking their weapons, the party struggled through the flooded dirt roads to the trailhead nestled on a hillside south of Amber Mountain National Park.

From the trailhead, the explorers headed north on a track that was barely a path. Ravel and Tank led, the mountain of a man driving one of the Can-Am quads with Ravel sitting on the jumpseat behind him. Next came Lucca and Pugari, Lucca driving one of the 6x6s, which had gear trailers as part of the rear assembly. Knight and Abby followed, also on a 6x6, and then Wes with Barbo and Volana serving as rearguard. To say that morale was already low would be decorating the situation with extra rose water. It was the damnable rain. Knight already felt soaked through, and it wasn't even lunchtime on the first day.

In addition to the gear boxes and ammo cases in the trailers, each Can-Am Outlander was outfitted with a ROTOMAX auxiliary fuel tank clipped to its load rack. The ATVs had 1000R engines with a fuel tank capacity of 5.4 gallons. This meant that on average the machines could travel sixty miles on one tank of gas, but the auxiliary tanks each carried five gallons of fuel, which doubled each unit's range.

The forest undergrowth was thick with huge ferns and periwinkle, splashes of pink and white peering out like tiny eyes from the greenery. Thick shrubs with spiral rosettes of long, narrow leaves were packed tight with scrub evergreens. Beyond the raging culvert, the forest floor was a dense carpet of mosses and leaf litter, and an earthy aroma permeated the air despite the rain. Evergreens towered above it all, their trunks straight and covered in rough, grayish-brown bark.

To the east, the jungle fell away revealing a hillside of rugged boulder-laden terrain that transitioned to gentle slopes covered in verdant forest. A spray of magpie-robins exploded from the greenery, a chaotic mess of glossy black plumage and white and brown feathers. The beasts squawked and argued as they drove through the mist, the ATVs cackling, the wind pushing the rain sideways.

Knight called a halt beneath a massive Baobab tree that towered over the forest like a sentinel. Its large, umbrella-like canopy provided extensive cover from the rain, and only tiny drops leaked through the dense, open hand-shaped leaf clusters.

The ATVs fell still, and the party dismounted, stretched, and broke out rations of food and water.

"How's your back?" Abby asked.

Knight grunted.

Pugari and the others sat next to the trunk of the great Baobab tree. Everyone other than Tank. He was wandering the perimeter of the semi-dry area beneath the tree, rivulets of water leaking over dead leaves.

Ravel said, "It is possible my ancestors of old planted this tree. See how there are no others of its kind around? Excellent shelter in… What is it you say? A pinch?"

Knight said nothing.

The group went to work eating, resting, and disappearing to address bodily functions, Tank's proclamation concerning his plans being the most colorful. "I'm going to fertilize nature."

Knight leaned in close to Abby and said, "Did you hear Cap before?"

Abby's eyes shifted to the others as she whispered, "Not sure. I think I heard an ATV in the distance a few times, but I can't be certain."

Knight's gaze strayed to Pugari. "Do you think he suspects anything?"

She chuckled. "Doesn't he always suspect something?"

"Good point." Knight pulled his Glock 19, checked the weapon again, tucked it back under his raincoat in its holster, and buttoned the holster flap. He bit his jerky and took a long pull of water. Despite his rain gear, his hands were shriveled like he'd been in the water for days, and moisture was fighting its way into his boots.

Pugari pushed to his feet, wiped dead leaves from his butt, and went to Ravel.

The shaman sat cross-legged, hands on his knees, eyes closed as if in prayer.

Lucca coughed but got no reaction from the old man. When she gagged, the ombiasa's lizard eyes slid open.

"Do you have a sense of where we are?" Pugari asked the shaman.

The old man nodded almost imperceptibly, a steady drip leaking through the leaves and pelting his shoulder.

"Care to share?" Pugari asked.

Ravel shrugged.

"Share," Pugari said with the tone of a command.

"There is a great cleft in the land, and into the rift falls a river," Ravel said. "There I will get my bearings."

"A waterfall?" Knight asked.

Ravel nodded.

"How much farther?" Wes asked.

Ravel lifted his shoulders again.

Anger burned through Knight. All his concerns about the shaman leading the party away from the monument stone and not toward it resurfaced like a corpse.

Barbo said, "I think I know the rock formation he means. It's about ten miles from here through rough terrain that will take us northeast into the mountains."

Birds cooed gently from within the cover of the tree canopy, and Knight jumped when a giant dragonfly buzzed his head and landed on the tip of Barbo's ATV's handlebars. The thing's wingspan was ten inches long if they were an inch. Its elongated body was segmented and covered in a tough exoskeleton, and its head featured large, multifaceted compound eyes that dominated its face, its powerful mandibles cycling as if tearing apart an invisible morsel.

Knight stared at the dragonfly as he ate, the fly's wings moving so fast they were a blur.

Abby filled her canteen as the strange insect took flight and buzzed away, almost bouncing off Tank's head as it did so.

"Did you get anything to eat and drink, Tank?" Knight asked.

What little Knight knew of the man wasn't good, unless he was on your side. He'd been dishonorably discharged from the Marines for incapacitating his superior officer during a raid in Iraq. He'd received a purple heart for the same mission. Though success usually trumped indiscretions, this didn't hold in the military, especially when said superior officer was a whiney college graduate who understood the history of every battle tactic ever utilized but had no practical experience to back up the knowledge. This inexperience and hubris had put his men in unnecessary danger, and that was something Tank claimed he just couldn't abide.

No plan survived implementation. Knight knew that. He had lived it, so the ability to adapt, to make changes to carefully thought-out plans regardless of the budget impact or whose face might get smeared with dirt was paramount to the success of any mission. So it was that he respected, but didn't trust Tank.

The big man said, "I could eat."

"Go ahead," Knight said. "I'll keep an eye out." For what, he wasn't sure. There was plenty of dangerous fauna in the area, ranging from catlike fossas to the Malagasy Giant Hognose snake, to bees and an entire army of insects that would puncture, bite, and scrape anything with tender flesh and warm blood. But the larger animals rarely attacked unless provoked, and the heavy rain had forced most of the forest's inhabitants into their shelters for the foreseeable future.

Tank nodded his thanks but looked to Pugari for approval before heading for the food chest.

Wes, Barbo, and Volana joined Abby, and Tank joined Lucca and Pugari, the team split into two groups like little kids on the playground as Knight stood, gun ready but in its holster.

"Barbo, how are you feeling about all this so far?" Knight asked. He trusted the local more than anyone else because he had the most experience in the jungles of Madagascar, and as far as Knight was concerned, their guide was Barbo, not Ravel.

The shaman sat alone, back in his trance-like position, eyes closed.

Barbo hiked his thin shoulders, his brown face wrinkling in consternation. "The place he speaks of isn't well known, and I have never been there, and I know of no one who has. But don't worry. There are spots fifty feet from roads where no human foot has ever tread, and the dense greenery can hide even the largest of anomalies, but if Ravel says he can find it..." Barbo smiled.

"Any idea how far we have to go?" Abby asked.

Barbo licked his lips, and glanced at the shaman, but said nothing.

The party followed the trail for two days, the path dipping in and out of flooded depressions as it climbed steadily upward only to drop precipitously into a shallow valley filled with sharp stones and evergreens. A stale breeze redolent of earth and decaying leaves carried through the forest, and the quads moaned and chortled as they clawed at the muddy dirt, every crack and hollow in the path filled with brown water.

Ravel ordered the procession to leave the trail when the team reached a fork in the path, and there was a brief debate. Since Ravel was the only one who knew where they were going, Tank took the lead, Ravel sitting behind him as the pair slowly picked their way between trees, the thick-knobbed tires of the quad rolling over the waist-high underbrush of ferns and weeds.

Knight felt the claws of unease scratch at the underside of his skin.

The group was leaving a clear trail through the vegetation, so getting lost wasn't a concern. They could always backtrack. Knight was more concerned with the lack of sightlines, and the idea that a fossa or other creatures could be hiding in the brush.

He snaked his hand into his jacket and felt the holster flap that protected his Glock from the rain. Knight would have been more comfortable carrying the weapon at the ready, but the gun wasn't military grade, and he didn't trust it to fire when drenched, though the gun's maker would insist the weapon could be submerged in water and still fire. He was old school and still believed gunpowder and brass didn't like H2O.

The underbrush grew sparse, and the ground turned to stone as the company entered a narrow ravine with notched gray rock walls. Torrents of water poured over the edge of the sheer walls in several spots, spilling into the crack in the land that looked like a pulled-apart puzzle.

Vines and plants clung to the sides of the ravine like unruly green hair, the cliff faces a symmetric pattern of square edges and rectangular protrusions that Knight thought would fit together perfectly if the land was pressed back together.

Ravel waved excitedly, and the company pressed on, using the stream that meandered through the canyon as a path. The gorge narrowed and the quads gurgled and popped as the caravan climbed from the ravine into a broken country of stone slabs covered in vines and weeds that could pass as exotics in any formal garden.

Tank and Barbo were forced to trailblaze through virgin jungle, and progress had slowed to a crawl when the party came to a cluster of tremendous boulders that forced the company to adjust their direction.

As Ravel requested divine intervention, and Lucca and Pugari tried to get their position on the satellite GPS, Wes took hold of Knight and Abby's jacket sleeves and tugged.

Knight turned casually.

Abby spun like a fossa had slunk from the cover of the forest.

Wes licked his lips as he shifted his attention to Pugari and the others, then tossed a quick nod toward his feet.

An arrow made of stones pointed east.

Knight bit his lip and sucked in a deep breath as he casually scattered the rocks with his foot. If any of the others saw the arrow, they gave no sign.

Wes and Abby prepared to leave, and relief flooded through Knight when Ravel pointed east between a huge stone shaped like a shark tooth and a mesa-like boulder with a miniature version of the surrounding jungle covering its top. Streams of water flowed through every gap, and deep green moss covered many of the stones.

Thunder cracked, and the glow of lightning momentarily painted the dark clouds white.

Back in Park City, everyone would be getting ready for the invasion of skiers and boarders and the circus they brought with them. Every house would be rented, every hotel maxed, and the restaurants and pubs would have already started recruiting out-of-town help. Not to mention it would probably be dry as a popcorn fart, but as Knight pulled his hood tighter, he knew there was really no place he'd rather be.

6

Ravel grew excited when he found the remnants of an animal path. The line of bare hardpan cut through the center of a thicket of rhododendron-like bushes, and the party dismounted and threaded single file to a precipice that looked out over a wide valley filled with rolling hills covered in tropical forest.

"It is down there," Ravel said. "I am certain of this."

Knight looked to Barbo for guidance, but the local shrugged.

With dense vegetation packing the lip of the valley, it was decided that looking for a better way down was at least worth a try. Rain fell sideways, and gusts of sharp wind stripped leaves from trees as the group trailblazed around the edge of the valley, avoiding obstacles, the ATVs rolling slowly over underbrush like miniature snowplows.

The convoy came to a spot where the cliffside had given way and a rough slope of tumbled stones fell away to the valley floor. Knight called a halt and consulted Pugari. Both men agreed they weren't likely to find a better way down. On foot, the descent down the incline would've been a nightmare, but on an ATV it was just a bone-rattler.

Food was eaten, water consumed, and the vale below was scanned with binoculars. The valley floor was a carpet of green with an occasional hardwood tree rearing its head above the vegetative fray, and the rough stone walls were covered in creepers, weeds, and trees fighting for purchase.

"Anything?" Pugari asked Ravel.

Lucca disappeared into the jungle to take care of personal hygiene, and in the distance an ATV roared, then quickly fell still.

Knight bit his lip, but nobody else appeared to have heard the sound.

When Ravel didn't answer Pugari, Barbo said, "There are three spots we should check. I think." He looked to the shaman for support.

Ravel pointed.

Pugari took Barbo's field glasses and Knight accepted Volana's.

Following Ravel's line of sight was impossible, but Knight saw the tall stone covered in vines that the old man was referring to. It took a couple of minutes, but he was also able to locate two smaller monoliths of green-covered stone, though Knight wasn't certain any of these was the boulder they sought. It was far away, it was pouring rain, and the rocks were covered with vegetation, so it was impossible to see if there were carvings in the stones, even utilizing the high-powered binoculars.

The ride down the scree pile was a bumpy, spine-jarring affair that ended in a patch of vine-like shrubs with stiletto-sized thorns. ATVs rumbling softly, the rain a chorus of splashes and taps, the party waited for Barbo, Tank, and Wes to cut a path through the thicket with machetes. There were no animal trails, no signs at all that anything bigger than chipmunks prowled the valley floor, though the secluded location was sanctuary-like for creatures with wings. Birds of every shape, size, and color darted about beneath the tree canopy, their cries and titters barely audible below the arguing storm.

It took over three hours to reach the first monolith which appeared before the party in the greenery, hidden by vines and years of dirt and grime.

Gear boxes were cracked open, and the team worked with shears and knives to clear the vines and used brushes to wipe away dirt. The heavy rain helped, and the top half of the stone had already been scoured. All the washed-away sediment had built up at the base of the stone, and the folding shovel was utilized to move a yard of dark dirt that would've sold for a thousand dollars back home in Utah.

Knight studied the monolith as the find was documented with video and photos.

The stone was a large granite boulder, approximately twenty feet in diameter, and it was adorned with over one hundred geometric and zoomorphic pictographs and petroglyphs. Carvings depicting rivers, terraces, ponds, woodlands, and tunnels covered the rock, all interconnected in a complex and intricate design that suggested a sophisticated understanding of water and its flow. The intricate network of channels and basins flowed with fresh rainwater that spilled into a large basin at the center of the stone.

Pugari said, "This level of detail and accuracy would have required careful planning and a complex understanding of the material properties of the stone, the behavior of water, and the surrounding terrain."

"Whatever culture made this used advanced tools," Barbo said. "Despite its wear parts of the carvings look like they were cut with a laser. Clearly, water was a vital element in their cosmology. Like Ravel, for most of the local tribes water symbolizes life, fertility, and purification."

"Or it's a warning that when the rains come…" Abby's voice trailed away.

The intricate carvings on the monolith appeared to depict a map. Triangular engravings symbolized trees, channels illustrated rivers and hollows of missing rock served as ponds. It all ended in a basin surrounded by tall trees that was the centerpiece of the stone. There were arrows in spots clarifying the directional flow, and the labyrinth had several smaller pools where rain would have collected during a normal storm, but these were overflowing, and water poured down the face of the stone.

Representations of zoomorphic figures such as frogs and serpents surrounded the water highlights, and below the large basin, which spilled over with accumulated rain, there were a series of disturbing images.

A large creature Knight presumed to be a Salamantis looked down upon an ordered series of pictographs that reminded Knight of an ancient comic strip.

The creature was five times the size of any of the other figures depicted on the monolith, and its lithe, elongated body was covered in round notches that Knight figured represented smooth, glossy scales. Its triangular head resembled that of a mantis, and it featured large eyes and a pair of long, serrated antennae. Two hinged, mantis-like forelimbs, equipped with scythe-like claws extended from below the beast's head, and though its forelimbs were long and jointed, the creature's midsection was more reminiscent of a salamander. The beast's four shorter, more robust legs behind its forelimbs ended in webbed, clawed feet, and a series of ridged protrusions ran along the creature's spine and down its tail which was long and tapered to a point.

Below the Salamantis pictograms showed trees, a frog, and what appeared to be a humanoid standing beside a calm lake. Etched lines streamed from the human's mouth as if the figure was talking or screaming. The next frame showed the Salamantis, but only parts of the creature were visible. Knight thought the image represented the monster blending into its environment like a salamander.

Death and mayhem filled the next two frames as the creatures attacked the stick figures. The final pictographs at the end of the row showed a round opening with unintelligible writing beneath it.

Pugari stepped forward and traced what looked like a pile of rocks with his index finger. "Treasure? Gold?" he said.

"It does appear that the… thing is guarding that pile," Lucca said.

"That pile could be anything," Abby said.

"A pile of turds," Wes added.

"Is that what you think?" Lucca asked.

Silence fell as the group stared at the stone, thousands of years of history depicted in the simple carvings.

"What now?" Barbo asked. The local was looking at Pugari, but the question was really for Knight. Politics were politics, and money was money, even in the forgotten forests of Madagascar.

"Knight?" Pugari asked.

"I think we need some time to match the symbols to an actual map," Knight said.

Pugari nodded vigorously.

Thunder cracked and Knight jumped.

Abby slapped him on the back and said, "Are you O.K., boss?"

"We need to document this thing better," Knight said. "Get good pictures of all the symbols."

"What if the typography has changed?" Tank asked.

That was a good question. Knight glanced at his watch, and it read 5:19 PM. "Let's find a place to camp. We'll eat, refresh ourselves, and see if we can make sense of this."

With orders given, the party set out to find a dryish spot, though Knight saw no caves notched into the sides of the valley. But there were several stone outcroppings that jutted from the walls of the gorge. Pugari chose one and the team went to work stringing up tarps, assembling tents, and setting up the cooking gear.

There was debris and twigs scattered about the dry area, though tiny rivers ran across the rock-encrusted hardpan. Though there wasn't much wood, there was a fair amount of branches and forest trash that had drifted beneath the overhang, and it was enough for a fire. Dark smoke filled the alcove as cooking stoves were ignited, and a pot of premade stew was put on.

When the party's rock shelter was buttoned up, each member of the team grabbed a cup of stew and seated themselves around the tiny fire.

As he ate Knight was tormented by the illustrations of the Salamantis. Even without color, the images depicted a formidable creature. He'd seen nothing that convinced him the creatures were protecting something. Several of the symbols on the stone looked like stop signs. Though not octagons, but hexagons, the symbols appeared to have a human hand facing outward. If this didn't mean 'halt', Knight didn't know what did.

Then there were the four pictographs that showed stick figures staring up at a sky without a sun or moon.

Still, thousands of years had slipped away since whatever the monolith warned of had walked the Earth, and finding the site would surely bring the much-needed influx of cash he was counting on. His gaze shifted to Abby, who had her head buried in her stew. Wes fidgeted, clearly uncomfortable, his eyes cycling toward the jungle every few seconds as if he saw Cap hiding in the bushes.

Cap had left no other signs that Knight had seen, and he felt bad about the guy having to camp on his own out there somewhere with no

34

help. He brushed the thought away. Slinking through the forest alone was what Cap lived for.

When dinner was done, the pots and cups cleaned, the group sat in Pugari's large tent, a topographic map of the region laid out on the floor between them. A bottle of wine was opened, and as Knight sipped, he stared at the small black X that marked their position on the map.

"With Abby's help I transferred the major markers from the monolith to the map using the arrows and our current position as starting points," Pugari said.

Abby nodded. "I think we've got something."

Knight's stomach burned with anticipation.

"The forests and glades of specific types of trees are represented by different tree symbols," Abby said. "The tunnels and rivers are shown via actual channels where rainwater flows to the main basin."

Pugari said, "Though placing some of the landmarks was impossible given the change in topography, it all does appear to lead to a very distinctive feature in the jungle."

The party waited as Pugari and Abby exchanged a smile.

"Barbo, Ravel, have either of you ever heard of a deep, round karst sinkhole filled with water in the jungle?" Abby asked. "It would be roughly in this area." She pointed at an area on the map roughly fifty miles northeast of their current position.

"Karst sinkholes are depressions or holes in the ground caused by the collapse of a surface layer into an underground cavity," Pugari lectured.

Barbo and Ravel looked at each other, smiled, and then said in unison, "Tsimi's Tear."

An owl hooted as darkness pressed into the tent, the rumble of thunder and the static of raindrops the only sounds.

Ravel cleared his throat and said, "The Tsingys rise abruptly from the forest floor. Towering limestone pinnacles and rugged formations, their ancient surfaces etched and sculpted by millennia of erosion and dissolution, their sharp, needle-like peaks creating a natural fortress."

The owl hooted hard as if asking Ravel to continue.

Barbo said, "Some of the limestone pinnacles are over a hundred feet high, and interspersed within this labyrinth of dry stone are shimmering pools of water that glisten like emerald jewels."

"Or tears," Ravel said.

"And there's a large central round sinkhole?" Pugari asked.

"I don't know," said Barbo.

"Yes, I believe so," Ravel said.

"It will take days to get there at the rate we've been traveling," Barbo said. "Should we pull out and regroup?"

"It's O.K. We've got time," Pugari said. "The eclipse is still several days off."

Knight nodded.

Later, when he was zipped up tight in his bag, his companions snoring and wheezing, Knight stared up through the ceiling of his tent at the movement on the underside of the stone outcropping. Bats. The fire was nothing but a gentle glow, and the beasts were stirring.

Knight recalled Ravel's story of the Salamantis killing his kin, and the monster he'd seen on the stone. His nerves clawed at the underside of his skin, but he was exhausted, and as he fought to order his thoughts his eyes slipped closed, and sleep took him.

7

The camp was silent, save for the driving rain and the distant call of nocturnal birds. Shadows danced around the embers of the dead campfire, their shapes twisting and contorting with each gust of wind as it pushed into the cleft at the base of the cliff face. Knight sat on a stone, headlamp on, his nerves jumping as he reviewed images of the monolith on his datapad. The stone was covered with intricate symbols, the water rushing through the channels and spilling from the pools a blur, but one image entrapped the eye. A pictograph larger than the rest. The Salamantis.

Knight's eyelids grew heavy as he stared at the pictures, and his mind drifted, reality blurring with the whispers of the jungle. He closed his eyes, took a deep breath, and when he opened them, he stood before the monument again, rain beating his jacket, thick drops falling from the brim of his hat.

The pictographs seemed to come to life, their lines shifting and writhing as if trying to escape the stone. Knight watched, fear poking at his rationality, his eyes stinging. The image of the Salamantis moved, its wet scales glistening under the glare of Knight's headlamp. Dark eyes locked on him as the creature's head pushed from the stone, its long, serrated antennae crackling as they twitched from the rock and probed.

With an explosion of stone, the Salamantis broke free of the monolith, its enormous body unfurling.

Terror rooted Knight's feet to the rain-soaked hardpan, his heart pounding in his chest, the creature locked in the headlamp's beam.

A low hiss carried through the rain, the call turning into a shriek as the beast's triangular mantis-like head rotated, its antennae swaying hypnotically. The creature's jointed forelimbs cycled about, the claws at the ends of each clicking and snapping, its long tail lashing out like a whip.

Knight's mind raced as he recalled the legends Ravel had told him about the Salamantis. It was said to be a guardian of the ancient forest, a protector of the secrets hidden within. But why had it come for them? What had they done to incur its wrath?

The monster lunged forward, its claws slicing the air.

Knight dropped and rolled, and he felt the brush of wind from the claw as it passed an inch from his skin. He jerked his utility knife from its ankle sheath and brandished the weapon before him as he got to his feet.

The Salamantis recoiled, blending into the rain as the pattern of its skin shifted and changed.

A horrible thought assailed Knight: what if the Salamantis could change the color of its skin? The adaptation involved pigment cells called chromatophores, which contained different pigments. These cells could expand or contract to change a salamander's skin color.

Desperation fueled Knight's movements as he waved the knife in a lame attempt to drive the creature back. Shouts and screams filled the night as the other explorers joined him, Abby on one side, Wes on the other, the remainder of the party forming a defensive line behind them.

The Salamantis hissed, its antennae twitching in agitation, and it didn't retreat.

Gunshots rang out as Pugari and Tank fired on the beast.

Rock cracked and popped, and a hail of splintered stone sprayed the area. The air hummed with energy, and the Salamantis paused, its crimson eyes shining through the rain.

The monolith began to glow, and as the light intensified it enveloped the party in a fog-like luminescence.

As if burning under the light's harsh glare, the Salamantis roared in defiance, its body wavering, its form flickering, rear legs cycling wildly, forward claws reaching out. With one final, mind-piercing cry, the Salamantis was sucked back into the monolith, its body merging with the stone. The light dimmed, and all that was left was the chanting of the rain, the darkness, and his companions yelling.

Knight came awake with a start, darkness leaking into his tent. There was screaming and yelling outside, and the thump of pounding feet. He had a fleeting thought as he climbed from the temporary death of sleep. Perhaps the Salamantis was afraid of light? Or maybe it hurt them?

He tried to vault to his feet, but he was wrapped in his sleeping bag, and as he fumbled with its zipper the screaming outside the tent intensified. Free of his cocoon he was faced with his next obstacle; unzipping the tent door in the dark. Knight made fast work of this task and dove through the opening into chaos.

Flashlights cut through the inky darkness, a wall of rain boxing in the cleft in the cliffside. Ravel's tent was aglow like a green Easter egg, and Knight saw the man's shadow within. Tank, Wes, and Lucca stood in a row, weapons up as they stared into the dark recesses of the overhang.

There was a shallow tunnel where the cliffside met the giant slab of rock that gave way to the forest floor. Barbo and Volana stood in its opening, gazing into the darkness, their guns at the ready.

Abby emerged from her tent and asked, "What's happened?"

"I don't know." Knight did a fast mental inventory and came up one short. Pugari.

Abby ducked back into her tent and came out with her Glock.

Knight did the same.

"I don't see anything," yelled Barbo. He wore boots and underwear.

"Me, either," shrieked Volana. The woman's long dark hair roamed free, and she wore her sleeping attire; shorts and a t-shirt.

Knight and Abby joined Wes and the others. "What are they looking for?" Knight asked.

"There was screaming. We think it was Pugari, and Volana saw a fossa run into that tunnel," Lucca said.

"A den, maybe?" Abby said.

A gunshot rang out, but none of those present had fired.

Like a group of kids who had heard the ring of the ice cream truck's distinctive bell, the group surged into motion, everyone running toward the curtain of rain that separated their rock veranda from the harsh waterlogged world beyond.

Knight was the first to break free of the shelter and what he saw made him skid to a halt and raise his weapon.

Cap stood at the edge of the jungle with Pugari. Another man, whose back was to Knight, was eyeballing a fossa as it darted into the foliage. Cap and Pugari were arguing, and as Knight got closer, he saw that the third man was Kamal Khan, one of Pugari's enforcers.

Flashlights cut through the rain, and a low growl came from behind Knight.

He spun, along with his companions, and a bobcat-like fossa darted from its hiding place, its muscular, elongated body covered in coarse, reddish-brown fur. Small black cheetah-like spots marked the beast's skin, and frothy saliva flew from its mouth as it ran.

"Hold your fire!" shouted Knight. The fossa was in the crosshairs, but any misses or slugs that went through the beast would pepper their camp.

The beast fled into the cover of the forest.

Back under the overhang, the air thick with the scent of smoke and gasoline, his heart pumping double-time, Knight said, "What the hell happened?"

Ravel had crawled from his tent, and the others stood in a circle around Knight and Pugari as if there was going to be a fight.

"I was taking a leak. I went out into the rain because I didn't want to bother you all with the smell. I was almost attacked," Pugari said. "If it wasn't for Kamal, I might be dead."

Kamal towered over everyone except Tank. The man was wrapped in a rain slicker, but under its hood his black turban could be seen, his dark eyebrows overgrown and hanging over suspicious eyes.

"That's ten kinds of bullshit," Cap said. "I was watching. He came out into the rain to meet his man. That's when the beastie found them." Cap wore forest camo and black boots. His bald black head gleamed with moisture, his eyes red with anger, his weapon still in his hand.

"First you leave out a chunk of the translation on the statue and now we discover Kamal has been tailing us?" Knight said. He was unable to keep the anger from his voice despite the retaliation he knew was coming.

"And how did Cap get here? By magic carpet?" Pugari said.

That seemed to take the spice out of the gumbo, and the patter of the rain and the chortling wind drained away Knight's anger. He wasn't surprised at what Pugari had done. He had committed the same infraction. "Look, I'm shot. We can work through this in the morning. Who wants the first watch?"

"I got it, boss," said Cap.

"I'll join him, sir," said Kamal.

Knight sighed as he headed for his tent.

The next morning, the weak light of the rainy day leaking under the overhang, Pugari and Knight had a heart-to-heart. Both men had withheld information and kept secrets, and they both felt justified. Since there'd been no harm, it was easy to overlook the fouls, and Knight introduced Cap and Pugari presented Kamal Kahn, though both Knight and Abby knew the man.

"Cap here was a Captain in the Army. Back home he's got a chest salad of ribbons and medals," Knight said.

Nobody spoke or looked up from their task.

"He had 119 confirmed kills in Nam," Abby added.

Kamal and Lucca looked up from their work, their gazes shifting to Cap. They both looked him up and down with newfound respect but said nothing.

"You know Kamal," Pugari said. Wes, Cap and the locals didn't, but apparently, the man didn't care.

Knight nodded at Kamal, but the giant made no sign.

"At least we have two more ATVs," Pugari said. "I'm done riding bitch."

A wheezy chuckle escaped Cap's lips, but the mercenary didn't speak.

"Let's saddle up. Abby, fill our new arrivals in about where we're heading," Knight said.

Pugari and his team huddled up, and Ravel sidled up to Knight as he checked the gear to make sure everything was tiptop and ready to move. "You were screaming in your sleep last night. Before the commotion," Ravel said.

"Yeah?" Knight said. "What did I say?"

The old shaman stared at him, his eyes like searchlights, but he didn't speak.

"What is it? So I had a bad dream."

"Why must it be bad?" Ravel asked.

Knight felt Abby watching him.

"Heed what dreams tell you," Ravel said. "They are often insights into our future, and failing that, provide clues otherwise not found."

Knight sucked on his lips and nodded. He didn't believe in fate, or divine intervention, or that there was an entity in the clouds judging and weighing everything he did. Was it all over when one shuffled off their mortal coil? Perhaps not, but what lay beyond was above his pay grade and his level of mental gymnastics.

The rumble of the ATVs sparking to life pulled Knight from his reverie and he found Abby staring at him.

"Are you really O.K.?" she asked. "You've been acting a bit... I don't know. Un-you-like."

"I'm fine," he said as he zipped his raincoat and pulled its hood drawstrings tight. He wore gloves, and rain gear covered his pants. None of it mattered. By lunch he would be wet and chafed, his sweat doing just as much damage as the humidity and precipitation. Knight mounted the Can-Am, started the motor, and goosed the throttle.

Abby climbed onto the seat behind him, and it felt good having her pressed to his back. They'd explored a romantic relationship once, and both agreed it had been a complete disaster. Their kisses had been awkward, like a brother and sister, and they discovered quickly they were much better friends than lovers. But they'd tried, and now they could both say they had no regrets, though that didn't help in the deep of night when he was alone. She wrapped her arms around him as Knight thumbed the throttle control and pulled out from under the cover of the overhang into the perpetual, unforgiving, life-sucking rain.

8

The four-day trek to the karst sinkhole would have been enjoyable had it not been for the rain, and as a tour operator, Knight thought he could get big bucks to retrace their route. As Pugari and Lucca consulted the map, the cackle of the ATVs bounced off the limestone spires that protruded through thick vegetation. Small pools appeared in the undergrowth and the knot in Knight's stomach loosened. They were getting close. He didn't need to consult a map to know that.

Tank led, and Ravel sat in the jumpseat. As the caravan pushed through head-high weeds the jungle fell away, revealing a dark crack in the land that led into a narrow ravine. The gorge was only five feet wide, and its entrance was guarded by two thin spires of limestone.

"See! See!" yelled Ravel as Tank shut down his ATV and everyone else followed suit.

Knight dismounted and wiped water from his face with the back of his hand. It felt like the skies had cleared because the rain had let up a bit, though it was still teeming. The thick cloud cover was less black, and the jungle seemed silent without the incessant tapping and dripping.

"These were once guardians of the passage," Ravel said.

"This?" Pugari pointed at a section of the map very close to the water-filled karst.

Though their features were barely discernible due to weathering, and a thick covering of vines, Knight saw the ghosts of carvings in the thin spires of limestone, the faint outlines of times long past.

"Shamans," said Ravel.

Though of different heights because they were molded from existing spires of stone, the faces of both figures had softened to smooth, unexpressive visages. Their facial contours were gentle slopes, the noses reduced to subtle ridges, the mouths merely suggestions. Headdresses, which might have once been elaborately decorated, were now crowns of indistinct rounded limestone that blended seamlessly into the spire. The arms, once raised in gestures of invocation or blessing or restraint were nothing more than stumps. Though still broad and imposing, the torsos had lost all their detail, and the robes and symbols that once told stories of the shamans' deeds were reduced to faint lines and cracks.

"I'm standing ten feet away and they're hard to see," Abby said.

"Am I to assume they're guarding what's beyond?" Pugari said.

"Who's to say?" asked Ravel. "I believe they guard the valley not just as ancient protectors, but as symbols of a culture that revered the natural world."

"Yet before we studied the marker stone you didn't know they were here?" Cap said. "That right?"

Ravel said nothing.

Knight studied the shaman's face and thought the man had known about the statues. It made him wonder about what other things the old man might be withholding.

"If I had to guess," Abby said, "I'd say their right arms were raised, maybe palms out in the universal sign of stop."

Ravel shrugged, and if he had any thoughts on the matter, he kept them to himself.

There was barely enough space for the ATVs to pass through the ravine, and the caravan took it slowly. Vegetation packed the narrow valley floor, but the sheer rock walls were mostly free of greenery. Knight's skin itched, claustrophobia gnawing at his rationality. They could be trapped in the canyon or ambushed, and if the rain picked up and the gorge flooded the party, and all their equipment, would be swept away.

But nobody was watching them, so there would be no ambush, and his fears of getting washed away in a flood disappeared as the party exited the ravine and entered an alien landscape.

Limestone pinnacles and rugged rock formations, their ancient surfaces etched and sculpted by millennia of erosion, rose abruptly from the carpet of green. Their sharp, needle-like peaks created a broken crown around the water-filled karst, which was hidden by teeming foliage.

The team powered down the ATVs, and with Barbo leading the way and bushwhacking, the companions worked their way to the water's edge.

Rain-dappled crystal clear water reflected the lush green foliage, the towering trees, and the dark sky. Knight estimated the karst's diameter to be a thousand feet, but its depth was difficult to predict. The edges of the sinkhole were lined with steep, jagged limestone cliffs covered with a variety of vegetation from tiny mosses to larger ferns and vines that clung to every available surface. Small caves and crevices, home to bats and birds, punctuated the cliffs, the call of the creatures that lived therein echoing off the walls.

"Is the water drinkable?" Cap asked.

Barbo said, "I would think so, water filters well through limestone, but we'll filter it anyway."

Due to the lack of sunlight, the water appeared greenish, the vegetation below swaying slowly as gentle eddies and an array of insects disturbed the water. Though he saw no fish, that didn't mean none were hiding in the greenery.

The air was thick with the scent of wet earth and rotting vegetation, and with the rain a faint pitter-patter, the sounds of the jungle took center stage. Back was the constant hum of insects, the distant calls of lemurs, and the rustling of leaves as creatures that had been hiding from the deluge ventured out to hunt.

Thick jungle encroached to the water's edge, and roots and branches dipped into the karst. The cliffs were more exposed in other areas, the limestone dark.

"How deep do you figure it is?" Wes asked.

"Hang on," Lucca said. She pulled her cellphone, which had no signal, and she bent and took a picture of the watery surface of the karst. Then she stood and tapped at her phone like a spasmodic chicken. "Based on my app here, which analyzes the picture using points of depth for reference and an AI algorithm says the karst is fifty-six feet deep."

Knight whistled. He'd dived plenty of times, but he knew special gear and preparation were needed for any dive over sixty-five feet. He'd known from the moment the sinkhole became their destination that diving to the bottom of the thing would be necessary, but the basic gear they had could only handle the most rudimentary of dives.

"I think we're O.K.," Cap said. He was a divemaster.

"What about the bends?" asked Lucca.

"And we only have four dive setups, and they're not much. Masks and mini-scuba units," Barbo said.

Cap nodded. "First off, we don't need to concern ourselves with the bends. Decompression sickness typically occurs when a diver ascends too quickly, causing dissolved gases, mainly nitrogen, to form bubbles in the body. For shallow dives, thirty feet or less, the risk of the bends is very low, especially for quick dives. When you get deeper than sixty feet more caution is needed, though the risk of DCS is still very low."

"We can ascend slowly and make a few safety stops if needed," Knight said.

"What about the four-unit problem," Abby said. "I don't know about the rest of you, but I can't free dive sixty feet."

"What's the deal with the mini-scuba?" Pugari asked.

"The units provide about ten minutes of air," Barbo said. He opened one of the gearboxes and pulled a sample unit free. The cylinder was blue and the size of a standard wine bottle with a black mouthpiece at its top and a control valve beneath it. "As you can see, they can be shared."

"We're all doing this?" Wes asked.

It was a good question, and as Knight sized up all the ATVs and gear, he wondered if someone should stay behind.

Reading his mind, Pugari said, "What about the gear?"

Barbo shrugged. "Someone or someones could stay behind to watch our backs. Assuming we discover something down there, but I don't think it's necessary. Having the extra person below will be more useful. Plus, we're in the middle of nowhere, in a spot people haven't explored in years, so unless more folks are following us—" Barbo glanced at Cap and Kamal, "I think the equipment will be just fine. We'll cover the ATVs, lock whatever we don't take in the storage boxes, and hide everything in the vegetation."

"Plus, we'll take the keys," said Kamal. It was the first time the man had spoken on this day.

As the party packed the weapons, ammo, food, water, and other supplies in dry bags, Volana and Cap prepared to be the first divers in the water. A section at the edge of the sinkhole had been bushwhacked, and Volana and Cap sat on a stone with their feet dangling in the water. After a brief discussion, it was determined that the pair were the most experienced divers, and both claimed that in a pinch they could free-dive up to sixty feet. Proving the claim wasn't necessary because of the scuba gear, but it was agreed that, if anything was found, the pair would secure a lead line for others to follow. This would make the dive much less difficult for the less experienced among them.

"I'll come back up with Volana's scuba unit," Cap said.

Ravel coughed and all heads turned in his direction.

The shaman was by far the oldest of the party, and sixty feet deep was no joking matter.

Pugari said, "Do you want to stay behind, Ravel?"

The old man glanced at the smooth surface of the karst but said nothing.

"See you down there," Volana said, and she jumped into the clear water.

Cap followed.

The party watched as the pair descended into the depths, their images wavering slightly as they went deeper, bubbles exploding on the surface.

Knight cracked his neck, the lead line playing out through his fingers as the two divers dissolved into water. The rope was a hundred feet long, and it went slack when about half the line had disappeared into the sinkhole.

Three minutes slipped away before Cap's dark shadow appeared in the water again, and soon the man was on the surface. "There's a tunnel that leads to a grotto with air," he said while treading water.

"Who's up?" Pugari said.

Wes and Abby stepped forward, clipped their drybags to the lead line, and jumped in. Everyone waited for the mini-scuba units and facemasks to be cycled back topside via the lead line, and next went Kamal and Pugari, then the rest.

When Barbo and Knight were the only ones left, they checked the hidden gear one last time before Barbo tied the lead line around his waist and the pair slipped into the water.

Knight held the mini-scuba in one hand, the gauge showing that the cylinder was still more than half full. He pushed all the air from his lungs, and his oxygen-starved body sank through the clear water like a stone, Knight using the guide rope to quicken his pace.

The tinkle of water and the murmur of bubbles were the only sounds. Green algae and plants clung to the sides of the sinkhole, but Knight saw no fish or other creatures. Visions of giant crocodiles slithered in his head as his lungs burned, and tiny stars appeared behind his dive mask.

When he could take the pain no more, he inserted the mouthpiece and sucked air through the regulator as he used the guide rope to pull himself to the bottom.

The clear water darkened as he went deeper, but he could still see the shadows of long kelp-like plants on the bottom wavering in the gentle current. Knight didn't see the entrance to a cave, but he was able to follow the rope.

Rocks and a layer of debris; branches, decayed leaf matter, and sand coated the floor of the karst, and the yellow rope led into a dark maw hidden in watery shadows.

Knight had been slowly releasing his air, and when he pushed the last of it from his lungs, he took another pull from the mini-scuba before attaching the unit to the guide rope. Then, using both hands, he used the line to propel himself onward.

The dark ragged jaws of a tunnel mouth stood in sharp contrast to the undulating greenery and headlamp beams cut through the murky water and painted heaving shadows on the narrow cave walls.

Ears stinging with pain, his eyes burning cinders, muscles aching, Knight made one final push, kicking his feet as he pulled on the rope. He emerged from the tunnel at the bottom of a clear pool and as he stared up through the light-filled water he saw Barbo, Abby, and Wes staring down at him, their headlamps blazing from the darkness.

9

Knight's imagination painted a vivid fantasy as he emerged into the subterranean chamber. It was like being reborn. He poked his head cautiously above the rippling surface of the water and found his companions staring at him in amusement.

"Give me your hand, boss," Wes said as he helped Knight climb from the pool.

Barbo crawled from the water behind him and rolled onto his back, his breath coming in ragged bursts. He let his mini-scuba fall to the stone floor as he said, "I... didn't usshhs ...any of it."

A vast, echoing cavern raced away into darkness, the headlamps of his companions creating a cloud of light in the blackness. The air was rich with the earthy scent of minerals and the tang of damp stone.

The cavern walls rose in flowing shapes, sculpted by millennia of water erosion. Stalactites hung from the ceiling, their surfaces glistening with the moisture that perpetually dripped into the placid pool. The water in the grotto was strikingly clear, a rippling mirror reflecting the cavern ceiling and making the space feel both small and large. Knight felt a sense of timelessness as if the cavern had remained unchanged for eons.

In the harsh light, Knight's senses heightened. He noticed the lack of rain, though water dripped everywhere. He'd just crawled from the pond, and moisture filled the air, though he felt drier than he had in days.

Upon closer inspection, the party found that there were two large cracks in the wall opposite the pool. One was tall and narrow and slanted at a thirty-degree angle, and the other was wide but only four feet high. A nasty stench of rot and decay wafted from both caves and all around the openings hexagons with hands palm out at their center were chiseled into the stone.

Weapons were dug out of dry bags, locked and loaded, and water was consumed. Everyone slipped on their booties and dry shirts, and the scuba gear was stowed along with the food and water supply. Each member of the team carried a dry bag, but despite this much of the supplies had to be left topside. Knight estimated that, if the group rationed, they had roughly five days of food and water, though he didn't think finding water was going to be an issue.

The air was heavy with moisture, but Knight had no issues breathing. Everyone in the party, including Ravel, had completed the swim without incident, and it was time to decide which way to move forward. Nobody suggested going back. The thought flashed through Knight's mind but was quickly dismissed.

Pugari shined his flashlight into the tall tunnel. The cave sputtered out after about thirty feet, the crack getting smaller and smaller until it faded into nothing.

Knight checked the other natural cave, and it ran on into darkness. At four feet tall and six feet wide, any explorer venturing into the tunnel would have to crawl.

The party was silent, the drip of water and the distant whisper of the breeze playing the cavern like a flute.

Cap sighed and said, "I'll go."

No one protested. Cap knelt before the smaller tunnel, angling his headlamp inside. The blackness peeled away, nothing but bare stone twinkling with tiny eyes of quartz that stared back at him through the emptiness. He sat and pulled off his boots, the rest of the party watching intently.

Cap made two short strips by tearing thin threads from his wet t-shirt, and then he used the ties to secure his booties to his knees.

"That's a good idea," Abby said.

"I've got some bands we can use so we don't have to tear our clothing," Barbo said. "If he had asked I cou—"

"Give me the other end of that," interrupted Cap as he pointed at the length of the rope that Barbo still had tied around his waist.

Barbo nodded as he handed the end to Cap, who tied the lead line around his waist. Then with a mock salute to Knight, Cap crawled into the tunnel, Glock in hand, dry bag slung over his back.

The rest of the party prepared to follow by protecting their knees and trussing their dry bags.

Knight was securing his kneepads when Cap yelled back to the group. "Come on in. Everything widens up in here."

One by one the party followed.

The tunnel came alive with harsh LED light, the explorers' shadows dancing on the black walls. Rubber squeaked on rock as Knight felt the rough texture of the stone beneath his fingers and the coolness of water on his skin. He coughed and sputtered, the air thick with the sharp scent of mold and decay. The ceiling rose into darkness and the folks in front of him pushed to their feet.

Headlamps clustered thirty feet up the tunnel, and Knight breathed deep, calming himself, his mind reminding him he was seventy feet underground, but the primal side of his brain was having none of it. He was excited. Exhilarated, and his heart beat hard and fast as a determination to explore drove out all rational thought.

A sharp pain knifed up Knight's spine as he got to a knee, and then to his feet. When he reached his companions, a discussion was already underway as his companions peeled booties from their knees and replaced them on their feet. The tunnel split into three separate natural caves.

"The center one is the largest by far," Kamal said.

"But what about these." Abby strode forward and laid a finger on one of the stop sign symbols. The hexagon with the outward facing palm at its center was carved into the stone on both sides of the center door.

"Let's break. Eat, and we'll reconnoiter all three tunnels and see what's what," Knight said.

The suggestion of food was met with total support, and as the group refreshed themselves Kamal, Cap, and Wes probed the three tunnels.

"Look at that," Ravel said. The shaman was drinking from his canteen and pointing to a rusted soda can.

Abby retrieved the can and said, "It's old, but not that old."

The can's top and bottom were rusted, but the words Clicquot Club in yellow block lettering ran across the top, and below that Flavor Aged in red script. Thick white lettering stained with patches of rust read Ginger Ale, and the face of a baby wrapped in fur adorned the bottom of the can, but it was mostly rusted away.

Knight said, "That's proof that people have explored this cave in modern times, though the lack of other signs tells me it was a long time ago."

"That can is upwards of a hundred years old," Pugari said.

Kamal returned first and reported that the cave ended at a slab of stone where the tunnel ceiling had collapsed many moons ago.

The right tunnel was explored by Wes, who returned after fifteen minutes to say the cave petered out about two hundred yards in, and there was nothing to be seen except the tracks of rodents.

Knight wondered what the vermin ate, but the thought fled when Cap returned from the center cave.

"There's an archway. A circular doorway, really. What's that called? A portal?" Cap asked. When nobody responded he continued. "It's blocked, and there are symbols…"

"Blocked?" Pugari asked.

"Come see for yourself. It's not far," Cap said.

Headlamps blazing, the party shuffled single file into the center tunnel. They left their belongings behind at the intersection, intending to return, but the party carried their guns.

As promised it wasn't far, and as Knight exited the tunnel into a large natural chamber his breath caught.

The stone wall ahead was sheer as if the rock had been carefully hewn by human hands, and a round doorway, twenty feet in circumference, was chiseled from the stone. A series of wide slashes surrounded the portal, and they got smaller the closer the decorations came to the opening.

Knight licked his lips, an image forming in his mind that made the scent of rot settle in his nostrils and stir his stomach. The doorway looked like an... anus.

The opening exuded motion, yet was perpetually frozen in stone, as if at one point in the geological history of the cave it had spewed something capable of dissolving rock, like lava. Or maybe water had flowed through the opening for a very long time.

A deep pile of rubble sealed the portal, the ceiling and top portion of the doorway having collapsed.

"Look there," said Barbo. "See those grooves?"

"The overhang above the doorway was purposefully chipped away," Abby said.

A faint shriek carried through the stone and the conversation died.

"Now what?" Tank asked. The mercenary looked like he'd already had enough. Sweat covered his dome, and the underarms of his shirt were dark.

"Now," Pugari said as he picked a stone off the pile and tossed it aside. "Now, we work."

Kamal and Tank began clearing the stones, the rest of the party watching Knight.

"There are some big ones in there," Wes said. "How are we going to move them?"

"Have faith, my boy. Have faith," Pugari said.

"Be careful not to shift the pile," Knight said.

Barbo, Volana, Wes, and Lucca went to work moving stones as Pugari backed off and watched.

Abby whispered, "I've got a really bad feeling about this."

Knight nodded. He understood why. There were stop symbols etched into the stone all around the opening, and many of the rocks that blocked the doorway were adorned with a hexagon, the hand at its center. There were no signs of the Salamantis or riches of gold and jewels. "You're saying we should turn back?" Knight said, knowing there was no way she could, even if that was what she wanted. Abby was cut from the same cloth as he was, and they'd come too far, discovered too much, to just walk away.

Abby harrumphed but said nothing.

"What? I'm asking."

"Should we go back?" she asked. "Yeah, we should. Am I going back?" She waved a hand dismissively like that was the dumbest question in history.

An hour later after several scrapes and bruises, the group had cleared away all the small stones and rolled away some of the larger rocks. But as predicted, there were several large boulders remaining that couldn't be moved by brute force.

The portal was still blocked.

"All we need is a small spot to crawl through," Pugari said.

Knight sighed and looked at Wes, and then at Abby. They agreed without speaking. None of them saw a way to create that crawl space.

Pugari and Kamal chatted as Abby said, "Is it odd the opening doesn't have a door that can be closed?"

Knight hadn't noticed that, or if he had, it hadn't registered. "You're right," he said. "The circular opening wasn't designed to be closed, so whatever the tunnel beyond led to it wasn't a vault, or any other type of sacred place that would have required that it be secured."

Pugari appeared at Knight's side. "May I have a word?"

All eyes turned in their direction as Knight nodded.

Abby crossed her arms over her chest and waited.

"Kamal has a bit of flashbang," Pugari said. "I was going to save it for an emergency, but…"

"Flashbang? Do you mean explosives? Are you crazy?" Knight said. "We could bring this entire place down. I don't…"

Pugari put up a hand to stop the assault. "We've got some C4, and Kamal knows how to use it."

The big man nodded, his black turban swaying along with his head. "Plastic explosive is stable and is known for its high detonation velocity. It can be easily molded into different shapes to direct the explosion," Kamal said.

Knight's stomach, which had been churning with nausea, settled a little.

"See the spot at the top there," Pugari said. "If we could just move that rock at the top, I think it would cause a tumble, and we could wriggle through."

Knight saw what the guy meant, but his concerns hadn't been alleviated. "What if you bring the ceiling down?"

Kamal shook his head. "That will not happen. The force of the explosion will be centered on the stone."

"You're saying it's not possible to cause a cave-in?" Ravel said. The shaman hadn't spoken in some time, the old man simply watching with burning eyes.

"We can retreat to protect ourselves," Cap said.

Knight pursed his lips and looked at Abby, who hiked her shoulders and nodded. If they wanted to try, he figured he couldn't stop it, and his biggest worry wasn't for their safety anyway, but that they might block the opening further.

The party retreated to the junction where the cave split into three passages as Kamal set a small charge of C4. Several minutes slipped away before Kamal arrived, his cellphone in his hand.

"Calling your mom?" Wes asked.

Kamal said nothing as he worked his phone.

"Bluetooth connects to the detonator," Pugari said.

"Are we ready?" Kamal asked.

The companions moved away from the central tunnel opening and pressed their backs to the rough walls.

"Three, two, one," said Kamal.

A second passed, and then a loud *thump* reverberated through the cave. Rock dust and smoke poured from the central tunnel, and a loud crack was followed by the grumble of tumbling stones.

Knight followed Abby into the cloud of dust.

10

Headlamp beams cut through the clouds of dust and smoke, and small stones chinked and snapped as the rock pile settled.

"Bingo!" yelled Cap.

The large stone at the top of the rubble pile had split and a gap had opened at its pinnacle.

Again the lead line was utilized, but this time Kamal was the canary in the coalmine.

The big man secured his weapon, tied the rope around his waist, and gingerly climbed the rock pile. Stones shifted and fell, but the large rocks served as steps. Kamal reached the top and peered through the three-foot-wide opening, using his headlamp to see what lay in the chamber beyond.

"Pull the rope taut and give me some tension," Kamal said. "I can get through. If I tug hard on the rope pull me back."

Wes and Barbo took up the rope as Knight anchored its end around a stone.

Grunts and the crack and pop of shifting stones filled the cavern as Knight's heart thumped.

Several anxious minutes passed before Kamal's turban-covered head appeared in the opening atop the blockage, the harsh lights making his brown sweat-slicked face shine. "It's O.K. I'll anchor the line on this side," Kamal said, his voice carrying through the gloom.

The party packed up and stowed weapons in dry bags, and like ants crawling over a narrow tree branch, the companions climbed the rock pile and crawled through the opening.

Knight, Barbo, and Volana were the last three, and as Barbo untied the lead line Knight mounted the rock pile. His muscles ached, and he regretted not using his booties as kneepads as he crawled through the opening created by the C4. The cool stone was unforgiving, but he was soon through, and headlamp beams drove away the darkness. Wes and Cap helped Knight get his feet under him as Barbo and Volana climbed down the rock pile.

Light splashed around as the chamber wrapped Knight in a cool, damp embrace, the air heavy with the earthy scent of ancient stone and the faint echoes of unseen flowing water.

An array of natural formations filled the wide cavern, each telling a story of water's patient erosive dance. Stalactites protruded from the ceiling like crystalline daggers, droplets of mineral-rich water glistening in the dim light as they leaked into shallow pools. Stalagmites climbed from the cave floor, reaching towards their counterparts above, their surfaces carved into statues of animals and lizard-shaped forms standing erect. The statues had melted under the perpetual drip of water, the surface rain penetrating deep underground.

Limestone made up the vast cavern walls and it showed layers of sedimentary history in bands of varying hues: subtle gradients that shifted from creamy whites to soft grays and occasionally streaks of ochre or russet. These colors, painted by the minerals carried in the water that sculpted the subterranean world, were overlaid with the faint imprints of ancient fossils, reminders of a time when the cavern lay submerged beneath primordial seas, inhabited by creatures long extinct.

But none of that was what drew and held Knight's eye. Black and gray stars, the size of a full-grown human hand decorated every surface, and as Knight stared, the images began to move.

"Cave spiders," Tank said.

The creatures had eight legs, each striped black, their bulbous torsos mottled gray. Two large black eyes sat above two medium-sized eyes, and below that a row of four small eyes, and Knight felt every one of the dark orbs locked on him. Hollow fangs used to inject venom hung over dark, hairy skin, and sensory appendages near the creatures' mouths cycled around as if manipulating unseen prey.

The creatures covered the walls, floor, and ceiling.

"Are they poisonous?" Lucca asked.

"No," Barbo and Abby said in unison.

Abby chuckled.

Knight added, "Most species of cave spiders possess venom effective against their prey, such as insects and other small arthropods. While they will bite if provoked, their venom is typically not harmful to humans."

Abby finished, "Bites might cause mild irritation or a reaction similar to a bee sting, but serious medical issues are rare."

"The light doesn't appear to affect them," Pugari said.

"They're probably stunned. Let's see what happens when I do this," Cap said as he broke into a slow run, stomping the ground and screeching as he covered and uncovered his headlamp with his hand creating a strobe effect.

The spiders closest to Cap scuttled away, and soon the entire party was yelling and stomping on stone.

Like flowing water, the spiders retreated as if controlled by one mind, the creatures disappearing into a crack that zigzagged across the floor.

It was then Knight saw the remains of the carnage Ravel had spoken of.

Clouds of dust created by the retreating spiders filled the air, and Knight sneezed. All about the floor there were the remnants of the Tsimihety warriors, but there wasn't much. There were badly deteriorated shields and spears, and within the remnants of loincloth-like garments there appeared to be decayed bones.

Dark brown splotches covered the floor and walls, but the only evidence of whatever had killed the warriors were small piles of thin bones that looked like a ball of tangled fishing line.

None of this was surprising. If what Ravel said was true, it had been eons since his ancestors fought the Salamantis in this hallowed place.

There were bench seats carved from the limestone walls that made the place look like a public hall. At the opposite end of the chamber stood another imposing doorway, but unlike the one the party had just come through, it was secured.

The crack in the floor that the spiders had disappeared into cut across Knight's path. He stepped over it, wondering how deep it went. The fissure was a testament to the constant shifting of the land, and there were several smaller cracks in the walls and ceiling.

As the group gathered before the doors, Knight felt an underlying tension seeping from his friends. An anticipation in his companions, expectations beyond the achievable.

Rough rock walls joined seamlessly with carefully placed rectangular stones that formed a square opening secured by two large slabs of door-like stone. Runes and pictographs encircled the doors and, on both sides, stood a lizard man statue, each imposing figure holding a pike that didn't end in a point or blade, but with what looked like a bee's stinger.

The doors themselves were decorated with two large trees, a trunk on each door, their canopies joined above the depiction of what looked like a map of an underground city. Stop symbols were painted over the rough surface with the same brownish substance that covered parts of the floor and walls.

A pile of thin bones protruded from beneath one of the massive stone doors as if one of the creatures had been crushed as it was closed.

There was no obvious way to open the doors.

"Kamal, get the C4 ready," Pugari said.

"Tsy misy!" shrieked Ravel. *"Tsy misy!* No! No!" The shaman opened his leather pouch, pulled free a worn notebook, and consulted it.

Pugari hiked his shoulders.

"Let's not rush this," Knight said.

"Do you find it odd that we've seen no references to the eclipse?" Abby said.

Knight glanced at his watch. The eclipse was still three days off. "I see nothing to indicate that light from the surface ever reaches this place."

"You're saying there isn't going to be some grand opening on the 8th when the sun disappears?" Tank said.

"Did we ever believe that?" Knight asked. What he left unspoken was he thought the eclipse had something to do with the Salamantis.

"Then C4 it is," Pugari said. "Why wait?"

"This!" Ravel said. He pointed at his notebook and then at a series of symbols that ran next to the vertical edges of both doors.

Knight traced the symbols with the tip of his index finger. "They're raised, and each one is on a separate stone."

"Like buttons," Barbo said.

Each row of symbols had nineteen characters, and though many of the symbols appeared to be letters, he didn't recognize any of them. There were shapes of all types with lines running through them, some thick, some thin, and there was a variety of pictographs that separated each series of runes.

Pugari laughed. "An ancient combination lock?"

Knight shrugged.

Cap inched forward and pressed against the doors. "These things are thick, very heavy, but look up there. See those gaps? My guess is there are pins in there that serve as hinges that allow the doors to open via a counterweight."

Pugari gazed up into the darkness, then made a show of examining the walls next to the doorway.

"Do you have an idea?" Knight asked.

Pugari licked his lips, the glare of his headlamp momentarily blinding Knight. "I was just thinking about what might happen if the wrong code is entered."

Images of a giant stone ball chasing Knight and the others through the tunnel filled his mind but quickly fled.

All eyes turned to Ravel. The shaman sat on the stone floor, cross-legged, as he read his notebook.

"Is this what we need right now?" Pugari said as his anger bubbled over.

"Easy, let him be," Knight said. "That is unless you've got another idea that doesn't involve blowing shit up?"

Pugari sighed but said nothing as his team fell in behind him as if there was about to be a rumble.

Knight said, "Show me the pictures of the marker stone."

"The marker stone." Pugari's eyes grew wide as he fumbled for his datapad.

Knight didn't recall seeing any of the strange symbols on the marker stone, but perhaps he'd missed something.

Pugari swiped and tapped. A minute slipped away, two, and then Pugari's eyes grew wide as he yelled, "See! See!"

The party crowded in, Knight peering over Pugari's shoulder.

Pugari focused in on a section of the marker stone's map, and as he zoomed in a line of symbols so faded they were barely visible appeared. There were chip marks and gouges all through the symbols as if someone had tried to scour the images from the stone.

"That has to be it," Knight said.

Barbo said, "But the markings don't match up."

"And I can't read those middle two," Kamal said.

"But they do match," said Pugari as he pointed at the picture of the marker stone. "These are sacred numbers. Right, Ravel?"

The shaman didn't look up from his notebook.

"Nineteen, nine, six, and four. Also, see the large dot with squares around it? The Tsimihety used that symbol to signify security and friendship." He pointed at the spots where the symbol appeared next to each door.

"No way," Abby said. "Speak friend and enter?"

That saying was stuck somewhere in the back of Knight's mind, but he brushed the thought away. "We've got one symbol, but what about the numbers? As Barbo said, the runes don't match."

"I believe the friend symbol is only part of the code. A friend would also know how to read this," Pugari said as he expanded the picture and focused on a line of symbols that looked like Roman numerals. "Between the friend symbols the marker stone lists several numbers, none of which are listed here." He pointed at the doors.

"I don't see how—"

Pugari held up a hand. "Based on ancient Tsimihety writings, I believe we total the numbers, and we'll find that number between two of the friend symbols." A self-satisfied smile crept over Pugari's face.

"I just did some fast math and—" Abby said.

Pugari held up his hand again. "The number six, represented on the marker stone by six slashes, is an evil number and never used. Think of it like the number thirteen in your culture. Therefore, it wouldn't be included in the total."

"Like Pugari said, what if we're wrong?" Cap asked.

To that, nobody had anything to say.

Several uncomfortable seconds dripped away before Ravel spoke. "Let me do it."

The odd sense that he couldn't trust Ravel leaked through Knight again, his stomach growing hot. Memories of his concerns resurfaced. Questions about why Ravel would lead them to this place if he thought it should remain hidden. But that was nonsense. He just didn't want Pugari to blow the place to smithereens.

Everyone except Ravel retreated down the tunnel away from the doors. Knight thought about what would come next if the doors didn't open, and he saw an argument with Pugari.

A shriek carried from beyond the doors. Or was it the breeze playing the cavern like a broken harmonica?

"Ready?" Ravel found the symbols he was looking for between two friend runes. Moving right to left, he pressed on the first friend symbol, and it retracted into the wall, the scrape of rock on rock carrying through the cavern. The number rune took a bit more effort, but it also disappeared into stone without fanfare.

Like the last bolt on a wheel that needs to come off, the final symbol wouldn't budge. Ravel stood and kicked at it with his foot. Nothing.

"Hold up," said Barbo. The local fished a rock hammer from his bag and passed it forward.

The echo of metal hitting stone rang through the cave, and then a loud snap as the stone button released and Ravel pushed it in.

For several long seconds, nothing happened. Then a loud click reverberated through the chamber, and a blast of dust and stale air wafted over the area as the doors cracked open, the shriek of scraping stone filling the cave.

Ravel backed away, his eyes locked on the doors.

The rest of the company pushed forward, Pugari and Knight at the head of the group. Headlamps danced on the walls of a corridor beyond and there were several shields, spears, and what looked to be the ancient remains of several warriors scattered about the floor. Sconces blackened by fire lined the passage and the murmur of rushing water and the rank scent of rot permeated the air.

Knight said, "Ravel, you weren't kidding about your warrior kin. I think—"

It was then Knight and the others realized Ravel was gone.

11

Ravel climbed the stone pile at the opposite end of the chamber, his headlamp bouncing around, his gasping breaths chanting through the cave.

"What the hell is he doing?" Knight said. He turned on his Maglite, and the cave transformed into whiteness and dark shadows.

Ravel had something in his right hand, and he used his left to aid him in his climb. When he reached the top he yelled, "I am sorry. Truly. But I know you will never stop. You Anglos... You just don't know when to quit. And you, Mr. Pugari, well, we all know what drives you." Ravel wormed into the opening at the top of the rock pile.

"What are you talking about? We ca—" Knight was cut off by Kamal.

"The C4 is gone from my bag!" Kamal shrieked.

The scratch of metal on nylon filled the chamber as guns were drawn.

"Hold your fire! The C4!" screamed Abby. "It's stable but an intense shock or impact, like a bullet, could cause it to detonate."

"Bullshit," Lucca said as she opened up. The crack and pop rang through the confined space and Knight's ears filled with static.

The shots peppered the stones around Ravel's feet, which still protruded from the opening, and the man screamed as he disappeared.

Pugari was the first to realize their dilemma and he broke into a run, gun up but not firing.

Knight's desperation took hold a moment later and then he was running, chasing the shaman. The companions ran across the ancient chamber, Pugari leading the way, their footfalls kicking up dust and grit, the melted stalagmite sentinels slick with water.

Womp.

A sharp crack and a prolonged, thunderous boom pounded through Knight's chest as a blast of hot air followed by a blinding white-orange flash filled the cave.

Knight fell back, the shockwave knocking him from his feet as rock fragments and sand stung his exposed skin. Larger fragments smacked the walls and floor around him, and a searing wall of heat pressed through the chamber, the sharp, acrid odor of chemicals filling the air. Smoke and dust billowed through the cave, and a stalactite broke free and speared the floor with a deafening *smack*.

Eyes stinging, vision blurred, Knight pushed to his feet, his ears ringing with a high-pitched whine that drove out all other sounds. The taste of dust and grit settled in his mouth, and the unpleasant scent of chemicals filled his nostrils. Pugari and the others still lay prone on the tunnel floor, but Knight threw himself forward, rock dust filling the air. He hit a stone and tripped, but managed to keep his feet as he skidded to a stop.

Dark figures raced past him in the haze, headlamp beams jumping. Then Kamal was yelling, and Cap was ranting about trust and loss and how screwed they were.

Knight found his companions huddling together gazing at the destruction.

The explosion had taken out the tunnel's ceiling, and the walls had caved in, demolishing the doorway and blocking it under tons of stone. Rocks snapped and argued as they cycled down the rubble pile, two giant stalagmite statues of a turtle and lizard holding back the tide.

"Back up, everyone. This thing is still shifting," Abby said.

Hard LED light lit the cavern revealing deep fissures in the floor, ceiling, and walls of the cave. The explosion had rattled foundation stone that had never been disturbed. Knight wondered what other damage had occurred that might impede them when... what?

They were trapped.

Retreating, the party reached the open doorway, where each companion dropped to their butt in exhaustion. As the adrenaline fled, and the roar in his head dulled to a crashing ocean, Knight sucked on water and scolded himself for not pushing his concerns about the shaman.

"I had a feeling he was going to run out on us," Pugari said, voicing Knight's thoughts.

"Didn't we all?" said Barbo.

"Knight was the one who questioned the man's motives," Volana added.

"What does it matter now? We all saw the signs and chose to ignore them," Abby said.

"We should have watched him closer," Tank said.

"Yes, YOU should have!" Pugari said.

"What now?" Barbo asked. "I'm afraid we're outside my wheelhouse."

"There is no wheelhouse for this, my boy. There is no steering this ship," Pugari said.

"You think we should continue?" Wes said. As hired help, he didn't sound very convinced.

"You saw that pile, Wes," said Knight. "I see only one way at the moment."

"Forward," Pugari said.

The party stared at the open doors, the remains of the shaman's people scattered about the dust-covered floor beyond.

"Should we all go? Maybe a scouting party first?" Cap said.

"Split up?" Kamal said. "What if the doors close?"

"We can wedge the doors with a stone so they can't close all the way," Barbo said.

"And what difference would that make?" Pugari and Abby said as one.

Abby looked at the floor.

"Do you want to be trapped in that antechamber?" Pugari continued. "There's probably plenty of air, but…"

"We should stay together. Saddle up," Knight said.

Whatever fight the party had was under tons of stone, and nobody questioned Knight's order. He knew they were all wrapping their noodles around their situation, and it would take some time for the shock of their dilemma to fully transform into acceptance. The group repacked dry bags; the blue cylinders of the dive gear, the spare ammo, water, and foodstuffs visible through the clear plastic.

"At least he left his bag," Cap said. "Ravel."

At the sound of that name, the cavern fell still, the whispering breeze and the constant sound of flowing water echoing through the chamber.

Beyond the open doors a square tunnel, hewn from the sedimentary stone, stretched into the distance, a mesmerizing marvel of ancient craftsmanship and natural beauty. The walls, ceiling, and floor showed a subtle gradient of hues, shifting gracefully from creamy whites to soft grays occasionally marred by vein-like streaks of red. The sharp angles and clean lines of the passage created a sense of order amidst the pointy natural stone the party had experienced thus far, and the walls rose to a uniform height, meeting the ceiling in perfect angles.

Ancient runes and pictograms adorned the walls, and most were integrated into the tunnel's structure, their outlines barely discernible against the backdrop of sedimentary layers. Fragments of columns, archways, and bas-reliefs were scattered sporadically along the walls, suggesting that the tunnel was not merely a passageway but part of something grander.

Cap and Kamal pressed forward, followed by the crew.

"This is amazing," Pugari said, his voice reverberating off the smooth walls, each footfall and murmur amplified.

Knight shined his flashlight on an alcove next to the doors which housed a series of rock pins and tumblers that made up the lock mechanism. "Looks like you were right, Cap." The gaps at the top of the door's inner edges had pins that connected with slots and counterweights.

A shriek, like a large bird being strangled, carried down the passageway.

All heads swung toward the sound, the undercurrent of flowing water like static.

"What was that?" Cap asked.

Knight shined the Maglite down the tunnel. Nothing but gray ending in a square of blackness.

Pugari started down the passage, gun up, his headlamp panning around as he examined the faded runes and pictograms.

Lucca, Kamal, and Tank followed.

Barbo said, "We shouldn't split up."

"I know," Knight said. Anger burned his chest and face. He didn't like it when others took control of his life and made decisions that put his people in danger. But he saw no other option and he wasn't going to find another way out sitting on a pile of rocks. "Heads on a swivel," he said because he couldn't think of anything else.

Knight eased down the tunnel, the glow of Pugari's headlamp nothing but a faint white cloud in the distance. Amidst the drawings and runes, there were holes, some no more than half an inch in circumference and others as big as a bottle top. Knight pictured spears, flames, or acid jetting through the holes, a last line of defense to protect what lay beyond.

As if its builders were intentionally trying to trick the eye the tunnel got subtly wider, and the dark stripes in the walls got wider and straighter as the top of the tunnel gave way to a natural ceiling of stalactites. Two waterfalls overflowed from spouts on the walls that looked to have once been visages of faces, but were now nothing but lumps of worn stone.

The fellowship pushed ahead and the smooth walls gave way to notches and a labyrinth of narrow tunnels and passageways that were meticulously carved into the rock. The walls and ceilings of the tributary tunnels were rough-hewn, bearing the marks of ancient tools. The chambers open to the main tunnel were of varied sizes and shapes, the recesses lost in shadow.

Abby said, "This looks like the start of a city. I see potential living quarters, kitchens, and storage rooms, and look at the ventilation shafts.

Though they're pouring with rainwater now, those most likely aided airflow."

The rooms had low doorways, and many had niches carved into the walls for storage, while others contained stone benches and tables.

"Is it just me, or is it colder?" Pugari asked.

"No, it's not you," Barbo said.

The main tunnel ended in a communal space. Huge stalactites and stalagmites met, forming pillars that were carved with symbols and pictographs. The images were blurred by the build-up of the mineral-rich water that perpetually dripped from the ceiling, and four more waterfalls spilled from the walls, filling pools that didn't overflow.

Knight paused by one of the pools, his headlamp painting its surface shimmering white. "There's a drain at the bottom regulating the flow."

A large archway lay straight ahead, and several winding side corridors disappeared into blackness. The sound of rushing water filled the space, the sharp scent of moisture and wet stone filling the air.

"Which way, Barbo?" Pugari asked.

"As I said, this is all way out of my wheelhouse. I've got no clue," Barbo said.

Volana said, "I'm starving and exhausted."

"Me also," Wes said. The man had been in clam-mood for the last hour, his eyes wide as quarters, his face red with over-exertion and lack of fuel.

"Yes, perhaps we should take advantage of the rooms and get a little rest before we go on," Pugari said.

"Might be a good time to send a recon group ahead," Cap said.

Kamal and Tank grunted.

"Let's give it a few minutes," Knight said.

Pugari said nothing as he backtracked into the main tunnel and chose a notch with a large stone table.

Knight and his people chose the next apartment over. Every horizontal surface was covered in a thick layer of dust and grit, and the group cleared the top of a large table-like stone and an area in a corner where they could rest and have their backs to the wall. Headlamps were shut down to preserve battery life, and the camp stoves came alive just long enough to take the chill out of the rations.

"What do you think of the water?" Knight asked the group. A steady flow was leaking from a spout in the wall into a basin that was draining via a hole at its bottom.

Volana grunted.

"If we boil it, sure, but…" Barbo said. No need to state the obvious that the cookstoves had limited fuel.

"It's mineral-rich, for sure," Abby said. "My guess is folks on Park Place would pay big money for it." She put her cupped hands below the flow of water, and when they filled, she drank. "Tastes fine to me."

With that proclamation, everyone emptied their canteens and refilled them with mineral water. A latrine of a kind was designated, and though Knight's watch showed it was only 9:16 PM topside, he was done for the day. Judging by the drawn faces of his companions, they felt the same and nobody protested when he suggested hitting the rack—stone.

A watch schedule was set, and mylar blankets were broken out, and with his stomach squeaking and heaving like he'd eaten a bushel of beans, Knight's eyelids collapsed, and sleep took him.

Knight was driven from sleep by the screech of Abby's panicked voice. He pressed to his feet as he drew his weapon, his head ringing, eyes still foggy, his brain ranging between reality and a dream.

A screech worse than nails raking over glass peeled through the complex of chambers and tunnels, darkness pressing in from every direction.

"Volana!" shrieked Barbo from the blackness.

Knight surged forward, the chamber coming into focus, the glow of headlamps pushing away the shadows.

Abby stood at the edge of their apartment where the open portion spilled out into the main cavern.

"What's happened?" Knight asked.

"Volana was on watch," Abby said as her headlamp swung in his direction. "I think something took her."

Pugari and Lucca arrived. "Where are the rest of your people, Knight?" Pugari asked.

"I…" Knight didn't owe the man an answer, especially one he didn't have. "I just woke up. Volana is missing."

Seconds of tense nothingness slipped away, every muscle in Knight's body campaigning for action. Do something. He drove back the thought. A great way to get shot was to go running around in the dark with a bunch of angry, armed people searching for their abducted companion.

There was yelling and shouting from the main tunnel, and the glow of approaching headlamps faded in and out. Shadows writhed on the walls, footsteps thudded on stone, and a gunshot cracked through the confined space, then another.

A bestial wail rose over the ever-present sound of trickling water and a flashlight beam cut across the passage separating the stone rooms as a huge shadow fell on the far wall, a drawn-out mantis-like body ending in a triangular head. Antennae shifted and swayed, and a pair of forelimbs reached out toward the light. The shadow's crest ran to a long tail, and legs cycled about in a dark blur.

"We need to get out of here. Now!" Abby said.

As if in answer the sound of hard beetle-like legs cycling over stone carried through the chamber.

12

More gunshots, three staccato bursts followed by screeching and exploding stone.

"We're going to shoot each other!" someone yelled. Knight thought it was Kamal.

Knight corralled Abby as he took several steps backward and pressed his back to the wall, Abby beside him.

Pugari and Lucca did the same, the four companions huddled together, their headlamps illuminating the small chamber. Light arced across the dark open end of the space, and the sound of nails scuttling over rock drowned out the hum of rushing water.

A stench akin to rotten eggs wafted through the space, and a low hiss like a car tire slowly deflating carried through the room.

Two glowing eyes appeared in the darkness beyond the chamber. They hovered in the blackness for an instant before disappearing.

Knight brought up his gun but didn't fire.

"I've got her!" rang Wes's voice through the tumult.

"Wait here," Knight said as he pushed from the wall.

Pugari nodded after him and Lucca fell in behind Knight as he eased out of the chamber into the main passageway, gun up in a doublehanded grip.

There was a cloud of light in the direction of the large communal area. He broke into a run, his heart hammering, sweat dripping down his face. When he reached the light all Knight's worst nightmares were realized.

Tank, Cap, Kamal, and Wes stood around the fallen woman, Barbo on his knees, Volana's head in his hands.

"Oh, shit," Lucca said, and looked away.

Volana's right arm and left leg had been severed, and muscle, gristle, and shattered bone stuck from the stumps. The corpse lay in a pool of blood, Volana's long black hair splayed about her head, her eyes already staring into the next world. Her stomach had been torn open, and entrails spilled onto the stone. The remaining limbs were twisted at odd angles, and slash marks cut across the corpse as if the woman had been cut repeatedly with a sharp blade.

Cap laid a mylar blanket over the body as he tried to separate Barbo from his fallen friend.

Barbo was having none of it, and he clung to his dead partner like she was a life raft and he was alone on a tumbling sea.

A roar blasted from one of the side tunnels and the call was answered by another.

"Screw this!" Cap yelled. The ex-soldier darted toward the sound, his gun out before him, rage painting his face red in the harsh LED light.

"Cap, wait," said Knight.

The soldier for hire didn't listen, but he didn't get far.

A creature appeared in the tunnel mouth before Cap and the mercenary skidded to a halt.

The Salamantis reared back, its triangular head angling up as it lifted its cycling forelegs, claws searching. It filled the tunnel, though Knight had a passing thought that the beast looked thin.

With a shriek that made Knight's nerves claw at the underside of his skin, the beast surged forward, a fluid mass of arms and legs all churning in a chaotic, yet smooth motion that propelled the monster forward at astonishing speed.

Cap fired four times. The first two smacked into the Salamantis's head and severed one of its long wavering antennae. Green and white goo splattered the wall, and with a *splat,* the third shot blew apart the creature's midsection. The crack of breaking exoskeleton reverberated through the chamber as the monster doubled over and broke in half, its thick rear legs still churning. Due to all the motion, the fourth shot missed its mark but still managed to smack into the beast's tail.

The Salamantis shambled forward a few more feet before crumbling to the stone with a final sigh of hot air that pushed a nasty blood cloud over Cap. Like a deflating balloon, the creature's body sagged, and within moments it was nothing but a mound of skin, cracked exoskeleton, shattered bones, and blood-speckled goo.

Pugari eased into the cloud of light along with Abby.

"Dang," Abby said.

"It smells... bad," Pugari said. He put a hand over his nose as he knelt to examine the dead creature. "Your Salamantis, Mr. Knight."

The creature's lithe, elongated body was covered in smooth shell-like skin that shimmered with hues of deep emerald and iridescent blue, and as light hit the creature the colors appeared to fade. As Knight stared, the skin color shifted to a light gray-black that blended into the surrounding rock.

All along the monster's spine, there was a series of ridged, spiny protrusions that appeared flexible, and its tail was long and tapered to a fine point, making the appendage capable of rapid, whip-like movements, which Knight figured could be used for balance and as a weapon. The creature's large, multifaceted eyes still gleamed with an eerie intelligence, and its remaining serrated antennae twitched.

But it was the jaws filled with sharp teeth that drew Knight's eye.

A chortling series of inhuman calls carried through the cave.

"It sounds like there are many," Kamal said.

"We should gather our stuff in case we have to... move," Wes said. The man looked whiter than ever, and though he was trying to control it by pressing the weapon against his leg, the gun he held was trembling.

Knight glanced at his watch. 2:31 AM. He'd slept for almost five hours. "Did everyone get some rest?"

Nods and general grunts of agreement.

With day and night cycles no longer an issue, Knight saw no reason not to press on.

"Do you want me to scout ahead, boss?" Kamal asked.

Pugari pursed his lips and looked at Knight, the glare of his headlamp obscuring his face.

"Given the danger, and that we have no idea which secondary tunnel to explore first, I can't see how it could hurt to do a bit of recon," Knight said as he shuffled forward, still half in a daze. He paused over Volana's covered body. "We need to do something with her or..." What would happen didn't need to be voiced.

The party gathered at the center of the communal area at the end of the main tunnel, the waterfalls roaring, the dark opening of the unexplored archway looming ahead. There were seven other side passages, and they all twisted through the sedimentary stone into blackness.

"There's nine of us lef... nine of us now. Kamal, Lucca, and I will take the main tunnel," Pugari said.

"I don't like splitting up," Knight said. He looked at the floor as he considered. "But I guess we don't have much choice, or we'll never get out of here."

The rest of the team naturally divided: Barbo, who was still weeping over Volana's body would stay back with Wes, and Knight and Abby and Tank and Cap would explore the side passages.

"We'll get everyone's gear together and bring it here," Wes said.

"Good," Pugari said. "How far should we go before we turn back?"

"Use your judgment," Knight said. "But I'd say no more than twenty minutes."

"That could be a long way," Abby said.

"Fine," Knight said. "Ten minutes. And don't get lost. Leave markers on the walls, and when in doubt, come back. Take no chances.

There'll be plenty of opportunities for recklessness in the future I'd guess."

To that, nobody had anything to say, and the company went about checking weapons, cinching up shorts, and tightening bootlaces.

"Wes, you'll help Barbo with..." Knight said.

Barbo sat on the floor with his head in his hands, Volana's covered corpse before him.

Wes nodded. "I'll try and gather some stones and cover her. I can't think of anything else."

Knight nodded but said nothing. What was there to say? Burying her was out of the question and burning her seemed like a task that could cause more problems than it would solve. He had as much respect for the dead as the next guy, but Volana was gone, and if he didn't get his act together, and fast, he and the others would be joining her.

Cap and Tank disappeared down one of the tunnels, Pugari, Kamal, and Lucca headed down the main passage, and Wes went to work gathering the company's gear. When Abby and Knight were the only ones left with Barbo, the glow of the other folks' lights fading as they delved deeper, Knight said, "I'm sorry, Barbo."

The man looked up but said nothing.

"We'll see she gets a proper burial. You have my word," Knight said.

Barbo chuckled and then began to laugh, hard, a manic unhinged cackle that rose above the hum of rushing water. "None of us are getting out of here!" he screeched. "Don't you see?"

Knight bit his lip and put a hand on the man's shoulder. "Get hold of yourself or you'll make your proclamation come true. Here, get up." Knight put his hands under the man's arms and jerked Barbo to his feet.

Barbo sputtered and wept but didn't protest.

"Go help Wes," Knight said.

With one last look at the silver mylar blanket covering his friend, Barbo nodded as he pulled his eyes away and traipsed off into the darkness, his headlamp trained on the floor.

Knight and Abby eased into the cave directly to the right of the one Tank and Cap had chosen. The walls were smooth, but there was no doubt that the passageway wasn't natural. Like the large main tunnel, right angles marked the passageway's joints, though there were no pictographs or runes on the walls.

Side shoots appeared on both sides of the tunnel, many of which led into chambers similar to those carved into the sides of the main cavern. Table-like stones filled some of the spaces, and piles of brown dust and the faint remnants of wood, cloth, and fossil-like bones spoke of habitation in the distant past.

70

Knight stayed in the main passage, heeding his advice. Despite not taking any turns, he still used a rock to scratch Xs into the passage walls every hundred feet or so, just in case. Though he didn't want to think about it, there might come a time when he wouldn't have the luxury of the headlamps, and wandering around the tunnels in the pitch-black without anything to guide him worried him more than the Salamantis.

His head pounded as he walked, gun up, though he heard nothing except the flow of water. The tunnel turned sharply left and the LED light pushed away the blackness, but just beyond its glare, a field of eyes settled in the darkness. Claws scurrying over stone filled the cave and several creatures peeled themselves from the darkness, rushing forward into the light, a tangle of arms and claws, jaws agape, antennas swaying.

Knight and Abby opened fire. The snap and crack of expanding gunpowder, the whiz of bullets streaking through the air, and the thwap, crack, and pop as shots tore into the creatures filled the tunnel. The beasts at the front of the pack collapsed and crumbled, which slowed the creatures behind them.

When his gun clicked empty Knight screamed, "Fall back." He and Abby had been walking for roughly five minutes, so they'd only gone a quarter-mile or so.

Abby emptied her weapon and Knight heard her fall in behind him, the scrape of metal on metal as she inserted a fresh magazine reminding him to do the same. With the howl and shriek of the creatures spilling up the tunnel behind him, the clatter of claws rattling on stone turning his stomach into a boiling painful stew, he pulled free the empty magazine, pocketed it, and slammed a full one home. As he chambered a round he spared a glance over his shoulder.

A fist of monsters surged through the cave, a rolling knot of limbs, claws, teeth, and tails.

Knight squeezed off three shots as he ran, but the beasts didn't slow. A Salamantis fell before the onslaught as Knight's shots struck home, but the creatures surged over their fallen mate.

Suddenly aware of the company's limited supply of ammunition, Knight turned his attention back to the path ahead. Abby hadn't slowed, and her headlamp bobbed in the distance.

Wind chanted through the cave, pain lancing his chest, his knees threatening to come unhinged. He dove from the tunnel into the vast junction and found Abby, Tank, and Cap waiting on him. As soon as Knight cleared their line of fire the trio let loose, filling the tunnel Knight had exited with lead.

The shrieking and bellowing of the beasts got louder, and creatures poured from the other tunnels and crawled from every crack.

Barbo and Wes stood at the center of the chamber, back to back, creatures pressing in on them.

"We need to get together and find cover. If we don't—"

"Knight! Knight!" It was Pugari. He, Kamal, and Lucca were holding down an alcove at the base of the main tunnel. They were surrounded by rock on three sides, and the trio had their guns trained outward, an occasional shot keeping the curious beasts at bay.

Knight and Abby ran for Pugari, the Salamantis horde scuttling over every surface, the rotten egg stench overpowering.

Cap and Tank served as rearguard, and the foursome selectively shot any Salamantis that got too close. When Knight and the others reached Pugari they backed into the alcove and were soon joined by Barbo and Wes.

With all the remaining members of the group pressed into the small space their sweat turned sour, and Knight's eyes stung as he aimed his weapon at the growing army of beasts building before the alcove.

Soon the monsters were several rows deep, their claws clicking and snapping, their red eyes aglow.

Tank, Cap, Wes, and Kamal kept the creatures back with carefully placed shots, but the beasts were pressing each other forward and becoming more aggressive.

"If they come at us in a wave…" Kamal said. No need to state the obvious. They didn't have enough bullets to kill all the beasts and couldn't reload fast enough even if they did.

"Jackpot!" screamed Barbo. "One of your air vents, Abby."

In the far corner, a stream of water cascaded into the chamber from a rectangular hole in the ceiling. There was no basin beneath the opening, which told Knight the hole hadn't been intended to supply water. The opening was two feet by three feet in size, roughly the dimensions of a modern industrial duct.

"You think we're going to crawl through there?" Kamal said.

The guy had a point. Knight wasn't sure he'd be able to fit himself.

"I've got another idea," Lucca said. "Someone give me a lighter."

72

13

The gunshots in the confined space were like thunder, and the air was thick with smoke.

Knight held out his lighter.

"Hold it a second," Lucca said.

A Salamantis broke through the line of defense and crashed into Wes, knocking him to the floor. The creature stood over him, its triangular head darting forward, teeth bared.

Cap placed the tip of his gun to the beast's temple and pulled the trigger.

The green and black head exploded, and blood and goo splattered the cave wall as the beast crumbled. This gave the rest of the creatures pause, and Wes vaulted to his feet and retook his position holding the line at the edge of the chamber where it opened into the vast city-like cavern beyond.

Lucca dropped to a knee, opened her dry bag, and pulled free a cookstove. She pulled her knife, snapped it open, and went to work on the stove's regulator which was attached to a small propane cylinder.

The shrieking and clicking of the beasts reached a fever pitch, the creatures at the forefront of the horde leaping forward, probing their limits. Carefully placed shots kept the monsters back, and a wall of dead, mangled creatures was forming.

"What are you doing?" Abby asked, her eyes shifting from Lucca to the commotion outside the alcove.

"I see what she's up to," Knight said. "Give her a minute."

"The more important question is where are we going to run to?" Pugari screamed.

"I saw that some of the domiciles on the main cavern have rear passages," Barbo said. "If we could get to one of those, maybe…"

"What about the tunnels we've explored?" Knight said. "Did you guys find anything?"

"Nothing!" screamed Cap from where he stood holding back the creatures.

Pugari said, "The main tunnel opens up and splits, but there's not much there except bones that turn to dust at the slightest touch or motion of the air."

"And it pitches down badly," added Kamal between shots.

Knight didn't like the sound of that last part at all. He wanted to go up, not deeper.

The foursome holding back the onslaught had gotten adept at covering for each other as they reloaded, and the floor was covered with brass. Wes stepped back to get a better angle on a shot, rolled over the spent cartridges, and almost went down.

"O.K.," Lucca said as she stood. "Everybody locked and loaded?"

Nobody spoke, and as Knight's gaze ranged over his team, he thought they looked anything but ready. They were dirty and wet, and the dry bags slung over their shoulders looked like they weighed a thousand pounds each.

"Right or left?" Lucca shouted.

Knight gave the question a momentary thought. Right led to the large chamber and the outflow of paths, including the arch and the continuation of the main tunnel. Left would be committing to an unknown, but that escape was closer and felt more doable. They could keep stone to their backs, which would provide some protection.

"Left!" shouted Knight.

Pugari licked his lips as he glanced at Kamal and Tank. Neither man even looked in his direction.

Lucca eyed her boss, but when Pugari stayed silent she stepped forward until she stood behind the front line and held out her hand to Knight. "Lighter, please."

Knight handed the lighter over and said, "The flame on that stove isn't very big."

"I know," Lucca said. "It's going to be mainly a diversion. Get ready to run and shoot anything that moves… well, not everything."

Knight and Abby took up positions to Lucca's left, while Pugari and Barbo positioned themselves to her right.

Lucca checked her gun, sealed and slung her dry bag, and rolled her shoulders.

Almost as if they sensed the coming attack, the knot of creatures at the entrance doubled their efforts, screeching and bitching as they cycled over one another like ants trying to get to a fallen lollipop.

Lucca eased the stove's control knob to the on position and flicked the lighter. A spark burst from its top, but no flame. She thumbed it again. And again. Still nothing. Lucca shook the plastic device, closed her eyes, chaos raging around her, and tried again.

A weak flame rose from the lighter, flickered, and went out.

"Shiiitttttt!" screamed Pugari.

Knight had to admit his frustration was growing faster than his courage.

Lucca thumbed the lighter and it came alive briefly, just long enough to ignite the thin stream of propane jetting from the stove's modified regulator. When a steady flame was pouring from the stove, Lucca darted forward and placed the stove upside-down on the stone just beyond Wes and the others as they fired.

"Back up!" Lucca yelled as she fell back.

Flames billowed around the upside-down stove, the paint peeling from the fuel canister as fire climbed up its sides.

Knight shielded Abby as he turned toward the wall.

A *womp*, followed by a prolonged shriek-hiss, cut through the chaos as the propane cylinder took off like a rocket, a rooster tail of smoke and flames trailing behind it. The makeshift rocket's tail set several of the creatures aflame, and the beasts scampered about, fire dissolving their bodies.

The uncharred monsters watched as flames licked the dead beasts, the explosion freezing the horde in place for a two count.

That was all Knight and the others needed.

The foursome on the frontline all fired at once as they surged from the alcove and feinted left, driving back any eager creatures.

A huge Salamantis reared up before Knight, but he dispatched it with two shots.

Abby and Knight jumped over the fallen creature, and Pugari came next, Lucca taking up the rear.

The companions didn't need to go far. Knight barely had time to register his position before Kamal and Cap led the group into another notch in the cavern, a large table-like stone at the center of the space, square rock stools strewn about.

Kamal and Cap took up positions at the back of the chamber on each side of a narrow tunnel. Tank and Wes ushered the others on, and the knot in Knight's stomach released when he and Abby entered the passageway.

It grew colder at once, the strong breeze pushing up from below chilled by the flow of water and cold stone. Unlike many of the other passageways in the underground complex, this one was a natural cave, nothing more than a crack in the bedrock where a weak section of sedimentary stone had split. The floor angled down at a thirty-degree angle, and Abby and Knight slipped and slid through the tunnel, the strangled cries of the rest of the team carrying through the cave.

Headlamp beams painted the tunnel in surreal black and white, the calls and scuttling claws of the Salamantis horde fading as the sound of rushing water took hold once more.

75

Knight didn't know how far he ran, but as the minutes ticked away and the sound of the raging beasts faded, he slowed to a jog. "Are you alright?" he asked Abby.

"I think so," she said.

The roar of rushing water got louder as the passageway emptied into a natural grotto. Thin waterfalls spilled into a large basin that had hewn stone steps on its sides.

"A bath? Water supply?" Abby murmured, her tone caught between a question and a statement as she and Knight trundled to a halt.

Barbo, Pugari, and Lucca were the next to arrive, followed by Cap, Kamal, and Wes. The group stood in stunned silence for a time, staring at the dark maw of the tunnel they'd just exited, everyone waiting on Tank.

Pugari breathed a loud sigh of relief when the big man tumbled from the tunnel holding his right leg where a red patch covered his jeans.

"One of the bastards got me," Tank said. "But I'll be fine."

"Lucca," Pugari said.

"Got it," Lucca said. "Sit here."

Tank complied as if Lucca was his mom.

As Lucca dressed Tank's wound using supplies from the first aid kit, she said, "Should someone keep watch up the tunnel?" Knight noted that the woman hadn't volunteered, but he didn't hold it against her. If it wasn't for Lucca, they all might still be trapped.

The clatter of the beasts had diminished but was still there, like low static.

"We're not going to be here long. Hurry," Pugari said.

As Lucca worked the company drank water, reloaded, and repacked their dry bags. They'd lost Ravel's bag, and much of Tank and Abby's stuff had been lost in the rush, but they still had food and ammo.

A loud shriek emanated from the tunnel the party had exited.

No orders were necessary. With the echo of the cry still hanging in the air, the party surged into motion like a herd of sheep and followed Barbo, who seemed most eager to move on. The dark bags under the man's bloodshot eyes glistened with unshed tears, but his fast movements reflected a desire to stay alive.

Knight thought of Volana, and how quickly her death had been driven from his mind. Fighting to survive could do that.

There were several passageways running from the grotto, a series of natural cracks that spidered away from the basin as if the depression had been created by some massive explosion. Knight knew the cause was much slower and less exciting. Water. It dripped from the ceiling and flowed through cracks in the walls, and there were puddles on the floor.

As the party followed Barbo into one of the tunnels the local said, "Look at the rock dust mixing with the water. This tunnel hasn't been wet in a very long time."

Knight's mind spun backward. "When the sun disappears from the middle day sky, and life-giving water inundates the land, that which is hidden will be revealed through echoes of a race once seethed, the prize... hive awaits where darkness breathes." He glanced at his watch. The eclipse was still thirty-six hours off, so what the disappearing sun had to do with the sleeper species awakening, he didn't know. But the water. There was plenty of water.

As the companions ran on the sounds of the monsters faded. After a time, the tunnel bulged and split into eight passages and the group paused to drink water.

Knight calculated the company had traveled at least half a mile from the main city cavern, but they'd seen no other chambers or living spaces.

"It appears that the bane of our existence is choosing between random unknown paths," Pugari said.

"I don't like the smell of the two on the left," Kamal said.

Knight agreed. The rank stench of rot and stagnant water wafted from the tunnels.

"The center paths appear to slant upwards," Kamal said.

"Ummm," muttered Pugari. He was eyeing a wide tunnel that plunged precipitously downward.

"I want to head up and out," Knight said.

"Out?" Pugari said. "What have you seen so far that lends itself to the existence of a back entrance?"

"There's always an escape route," Wes said. The man had regained some of his color, and his hands no longer shook.

"Wes has a point, though most likely any such escape hatch would be blocked or destroyed," Knight said. "And based on what I've seen—"

A Salamantis rocketed out of a tributary passage, forearms outstretched and rear legs churning in a blur. Its claws were splayed, jaws wide, and rows of teeth glittered under the harsh LED lights.

The group scattered as weapons were raised.

"Hold your fire!" screeched Knight. In the confined space, with the harsh glow of the headlamps creating dancing shadows across the walls, the risk of hitting a teammate or someone catching a ricochet was too great.

Kamal threw his dry bag at the beast as he moved in close, gun in one hand and a knife Knight hadn't seen the man pull in his other.

Pugari, Tank, and Lucca ducked into the tunnel nearest them.

Wes fell in behind Kamal, gun up as he waited for the opportunity to put the creature down.

The Salamantis jerked and writhed, its long body arcing up and down, the snapping of its claws and the thump of its tail smacking the walls driving out all other sounds.

Cap darted into the tunnel nearest him, and Knight and Abby followed.

Gunshots pierced the chaos, and the maelstrom of screaming creatures and yelling rose around the echo of the shots like frothing water.

Knight, Abby, and Cap plowed forward, and the tunnel went on and on, the shriek of the creatures chasing after them.

When Cap stopped running Abby bumped into him.

"What is it?" Knight asked.

"Turn off your headlamps," Cap said.

"What? Tur—" Knight started.

"Do it!"

Knight and Abby complied, and the tunnel fell into blackness.

"Let your eyes adjust," Cap said.

Knight counted the seconds, but his thoughts were lost in the sound of the wailing beasts.

"Do you see that?" Cap asked. "In the distance."

Knight peered down the tunnel, his eyes stinging. At first, blackness stared back at him, but then slowly, like a digital image taking shape, the gray outline of a rough rectangular opening appeared at the far end of the tunnel.

"Is that... daylight?" Abby stammered.

"As close to it as this island has seen in months, but yes, natural light. And see the curtain of rain?" Cap said.

Knight didn't, but he said nothing.

"An exit," Abby shrieked as she bolted past Cap and disappeared into the blackness.

Knight double-timed it after her, Cap on his heels. Doubt clawed at him as he ran. If it was an exit why hadn't the beasts escaped into the jungle? Maybe they had, came the answer. As the rectangle of gray gloom grew larger so did Knight's hope.

14

Hope is a fickle bitch.

There was an opening, and it was filled with natural light and the shimmer of falling rain, but there was no exit.

The tunnel opened into a natural sinkhole, its sheer walls of smoothed stone two hundred feet tall if they were a foot. Roots and vines snaked their way down in search of moisture, but Knight didn't see many crags or cracks. So many waterfalls cascaded into the hollow that it was hard to tell how many there were, or whether they were permanent or merely overflow from the continual deluge. The group stood on a pile of stones at the mouth of the tunnel that had broken free when the sinkhole was created. Rain beat on tropical foliage that withered to light-deprived brush as Knight's eyes swept right.

"Is this on the map?" Knight asked.

"I think so," she said. "If my memory serves, it's a standard *lavaka*, a sinkhole that formed as the limestone bedrock dissolved, a process driven by relentless tropical rains, I might add."

"My guess is it's often hidden from view due to its depth and the angle of the sunlight," Cap said. "Based on the vegetation, I'd say straight ahead is north. Look at how sparse the greenery gets to our right."

"Can we climb out?" Abby asked.

It was then Knight realized the rest of the party hadn't arrived. He turned without answering Abby as he flicked on the Maglite and trained it into the tunnel.

The harsh light pushed away the darkness until it faded. Nothing moved and the sounds of the creatures had died away.

"Should we go back?" Cap asked.

Knight loved the way the man said "we" as if he wasn't hired help. Of course, he was much more than that. He'd known the man for years, and the ex-soldier had never failed to come through for him. Knight said, "Let's wait here a bit. We can look around, but I want to give them some time." He dropped his dry bag and Cap and Abby did the same.

Thanks to the abundance of water, the party drank their fill, ate power bars, and took turns relieving themselves behind a boulder.

Nobody else arrived.

"How are you feeling, Abby? Need a rest?" Knight asked. "I'm going to take Cap with me and look around a bit. See if there is anything to be seen. You're welcome to come with us, but you know what they say about three being a crowd, and why risk three when two will do?"

"Plus, if the others arrive it would be good if at least one of us was here," Cap said.

Abby looked at the gun in her hand and said, "Don't go far." Her gaze strayed to the tunnel mouth, which was dark and soundless.

Knight nodded.

The sky was black, whatever starlight and moonlight there was hidden by burnt cotton candy. Despite there being no animal paths, the micro-ecosystem within the sinkhole was teeming with life. Small rodent-like tenrecs and reddish-brown mouse lemurs darted about in the underbrush, and unique plants Knight didn't recognize were packed beneath a covering of huge ferns. The humidity was palpable, fostering the growth of mosses and beards of lichen that hung from many of the trees.

"Let's head east to where this mess thins," Cap said.

"How big is this thing?" Knight asked. "I'm not as diligent as Abby, but I don't recall seeing it on the map."

"It was there," Cap said. "I'd say it's at least five times the size of Tsimi's Tear. Maybe three miles across. It looks damn close to a perfect circle."

Knight nodded as he trailed after Cap. The sinkhole did look almost unnaturally round like it had been driven into the Earth with a huge hole puncher.

The vegetation encroached to the sides of the sinkhole, and without a machete, it was slow going. Rain pattered on huge leaves, and after half a mile Cap sat on a stone, tipped back his head, and opened his mouth to catch the rain. The jungle before them had thinned as the duo had come east, but there was still a tangle of tight undergrowth beneath the huge ferns and thick trees with spiked bark.

"We're screwed," Cap said as he stared up into the rain. "At least it's warm. The rain, I mean."

Knight hadn't put on his rain gear. It was stuffed in his dry bag which was back with Abby. His hat was long gone, but he still gripped the Glock in his hand, a full magazine at the ready, a round in the firing chamber.

"I didn't want to talk about it in front of Abby, but... Is there any way we're climbing out of here?" Knight asked. He'd climbed a bit and knew the basics, one of which was it took skill to climb a sheer two hundred-foot cliff face with a hundred feet of rope.

Cap grunted. "If we had a lot more rope, five dozen pins, a bunch of carabiners, maybe a belay device." He shook his head. All we've got is one length of rope, three bingers, and one five-piece set of pins, three of which are so small I doubt they'd hold Tank or Kamal's weight."

"But it would hold your svelte ass?" Knight said.

Cap laughed, and it was a welcome sound.

The laughter abruptly cut short when a bellow carried from the jungle.

As he slung his dry bag over his shoulder Cap pushed to his feet, the echo of the odd call still hanging in the air.

To the north, the jungle canopy rustled and shook, and leaves fell as branches snapped.

As fast as the commotion in the forest began, it stopped. Birds shrieked, the rain argued, and thunder mumbled in the distance.

Knight stood open-mouthed, staring, his heart hammering.

"We better get back to Abby," Cap said.

On the trek back the pair didn't speak. Their excursion had yielded no new information. If anything, more questions were raised. Upon leaving the tunnel Knight had no intention of backtracking. But as thoughts of Wes and the others clogged his mental stream, he couldn't get around the idea that he couldn't leave Barbo, Wes, and the others behind. Their local guide had already lost a good friend, and the best Knight could hope for was that Volana would be the only one to pay the price for Pugari's, and his, hubris.

"Knight! Knniiigggghttttttt!" It was Abby.

Cap and Knight doubled their pace, which was still slow. Though they'd trailblazed a path along the base of the cliff face, to call it a path was an insult to paths.

Knight scrambled over stones and flattened vegetation, ants, centipedes, and a myriad of beetle-like insects fleeing before each of his footfalls, disappearing under rocks, and into deep puddles and thick mud.

Gunshots cut through the rain and muffled screaming.

Cap shouted Abby's name, all his pent-up anger bursting free as he launched off a rock in an attempt to avoid a pool of water. He slipped, fell ass-over-teakettle, and landed face first, a deluge of water surrounding him as he sputtered and fought to right himself.

Water streamed from the cliffside, the tall rock wall angling inward slightly as if looking down on the chaos from above. Knight helped Cap up and the two men struggled on.

Abby had gone silent and there had been no more gunshots.

Knight heard the Salamantis before he saw it, a low hiss that sounded reptilian. A tangle of fern leaves blocked his view, and he fought through them.

Abby stood atop the tiny scree pile, her back to the cliff face, the dark opening of the tunnel to her right.

The Salamantis looked newly born, its skin translucent, its claws only partly formed. Clear slime hung from the creature, and its head jerked around as if the beast's brain was still learning how to control its machine.

Abby fired and the bullet passed through the creature and smacked into a tree.

Cap yelled, "Over here."

The Salamantis stepped back, but its movements slow and erratic as its triangular head turned in Cap's direction. Despite the gloom, the beast's eyes sparkled like garnets, and Knight felt the creature appraising him.

Cap raised his Glock in a twohanded grip, planted his feet, and aimed.

Abby dove into the tunnel mouth for cover.

Cap fired three times in fast succession, the gun barking and barely moving in his hand.

Exoskeleton cracked and popped, pieces of the beast's soft shell shattering and peppering the ground. One of its forelimbs was severed, but the other two bullets pierced the beast's head, and it burst, spraying the area with goo and translucent skin. The Salamantis took one more step before falling to the ground in a tangle.

The rain eased, nothing more than a thin teeming mist that felt as dry as the desert after the constant downpour.

Abby exited the cave mouth, gun up.

"Are you O.K.?" Cap yelled.

"Yeah," she said. When Knight and Cap reached the woman's side, she added, "It… It surprised me."

Knight and Cap said nothing.

"I was watching," she said.

Cap and Knight waited.

"It just… appeared, like it had been invisible, which of course it wasn't, but…"

"It blended into the greenery so well you didn't see it until it started up the escarpment?" Cap pushed.

"It was the darndest thing," Abby said as she nodded. "The undergrowth became… transparent is the only word that fits. Then the thing crawled into being like it was being birthed by the forest."

Cap turned and examined the pile of goo, bones, and cracked shell. Though the Salamantis was nothing more than a pile of mush, its skin was still alive and hadn't gotten the news that the creature's brain had given up the ghost. As he watched, the skin of the Salamantis turned gray and blended into the stone.

"It's those specialized cells called chromatophores again," Abby said. "Until the skin dries and dies, they'll produce and reflect the various pigments and colors around them."

"Right," Cap said. "I recall the lecture."

The rain picked up again and the team retreated inside the tunnel mouth. As the sky turned a less dark shade of black, and the sun rose beyond the cloud cover, none of the other party members arrived.

"I don't see how we can plow forward," Abby said. "You didn't see any paths? No way through this thick jungle?"

Knight shook his head. "As you can see from here, the vegetation thins as one travels east, but it's still a tough go."

"That last interchange had how many tunnels? Nine? Ten?" Cap asked.

"Eight," Abby said.

"Some of them have to terminate here, right?" Cap said.

That question brought the conversation to a standstill. He and Cap hadn't gone far, but they'd seen no signs of other tunnels emptying into the sinkhole.

"It just doesn't feel right to…" Abby hiked her shoulders.

"I know what you mean," Cap said. "But wouldn't they be here by now if they took the same tunnel?"

Knight had to agree. Wherever Wes and the others were, they wouldn't be traveling the same route he and his partners had. "They might not be together," Knight said.

"Or someone could be hurt and they're waiting around for us," Cap said.

There it was. The nail in the proverbial coffin. "Saddle up," Knight said. "We're heading back."

Cap grunted.

"I don't like it any more than you do, but…" Knight said.

"Yeah, but." With that, the wind left Cap's sails and the big man got to his feet, checked his weapon, and glared at Abby and Knight.

The hardest journey to finish is the one never started, but that motivational poster, which hung on his office wall back in Park City, now seemed like ten kinds of bullshit. But he motioned for Cap to lead the way, and the trio shuffled back the way they'd come, their headlamps lighting the cave.

Knight's Xs, still freshly carved into the stone, seemed like children's drawings, their lines crooked and uneven. The companions had only retraced their steps about two hundred yards before the shrill cry of a Salamantis carried down the tunnel.

All three headlamps went dark, and the tunnel was plunged into impenetrable blackness.

Knight heard the ragged breathing of his partners and smelled the harsh scent of their body odors. The strangest thoughts flitted through one's head in times of fear and danger, and Knight tried to calculate the last time he'd bathed, not counting the dive in Tsimi's Tear. "The hotel?" he muttered.

"What?" Cap said.

"Nothing."

The trio stood in the darkness, waiting… for what Knight didn't know. A sign? A sound that told him he wasn't doing the stupidest thing he'd ever done in his life; crawling back into a confined space with apex predators roaming around and looking for food.

Food? What did the beasts eat? Though the sleeper species rarely awoke, all living things needed sustenance, and if the creatures had been trapped within the ancient city for eons, what did the beasts eat? How long did they live? Due to the extraordinary length of time, there were little to no remains left of the creature's last awakening… if that's what he could call it.

"Knight! Wake the hell up," whisper-yelled Cap. "Orders?"

Cap's frustrated bark pulled Knight from his reverie and brought him back to the here and now. He rolled his shoulders, cracked his neck, and said, "We go on because that's what Wes would do." I think.

Knight slipped past Cap and continued through the blackness, his headlamp off.

15

Pugari clicked on his headlamp as he ran, the thunder of gunshots and the screech of Kamal ringing in his ears. His muscle had hung back to deal with the Salamantis, but Barbo ran ahead, and Lucca and Tank trailed after him, the big man limping on his wounded leg. He spared a fast thought for Dusky—Knight, and the others, but what was he to do?

The tunnel ran straight and true, the floor even, the walls slick with water. Gunshots, screaming, and the shrieks of the Salamantis carried through the cave, driving Pugari onward. The faint heat of guilt seeped through him as he ran, though he pushed the mild tremor away like a weak thought. He hadn't been the only one who wanted to continue when it became clear the legends about the Salamantis were closer to the truth than his vision of riches and glory. Still, no one had protested. Knight and Abby were eager to discover what lay in the ancient subterranean city, and even with the deadly creatures on his heels, Pugari didn't regret the decision he'd made.

Funny thing, regret. It didn't hit you like a brick until it was too late to duck.

Torrents of water spilled down the sides of the cave, waterfalls that drained into large cracks in the floor. The ceiling was dotted with tiny white stalactites, and a steady flow of water dripped from each point.

Pugari ran, his dry bag slung over his back, his gun in his hand, his knees aching.

There was an inrush of air and the tunnel floor collapsed.

Pugari was consumed by dirt and water as he flailed about, his fingers clawing for purchase, his headlamp dark with muck. He screamed and sucked in mud as Lucca gripped his shoulder for a moment before it was torn away.

The companions didn't fall far. After a ten-foot drop, the trio landed in a heap, water, rocks, and mud pouring onto them.

Barbo was the first to free himself and he helped Tank.

Lucca and Pugari untangled themselves and pushed to their feet, mud still pouring onto them.

Tank and Pugari's headlamps had gone dark, but the remaining lights tore away the darkness.

Pugari's breath caught in his throat. He wasn't a brave man, he knew this. He hired others to be courageous, but he was no coward. He'd fought and shot his way out of many situations, more than one with

Lucca by his side, and it took a lot to rattle him. His stomach soured, his mind stuttering as he tried to process what he was seeing. Pugari wiped the mud from his face as he stared, his skin crawling with equal parts fear and excitement.

The chamber was roughly rectangular, and at its center, there was a hole that spiraled into the floor as though it had been created with a giant drill bit. Water spilled into the cavity despite the debris and mud from the caved-in ceiling, but none of it was what drew the eye.

Against the walls, in rows like stored soldiers, Salamantis were encased in cloudy semitransparent cocoons. Their red eyes stared out, but Pugari sensed no awareness, no intelligence.

"They're still… sleeping," said Lucca.

Pugari walked along the line of dormant creatures, and under closer inspection he saw that some of the beasts were moving, small incremental actions that appeared to have no purpose.

A splat, like a piece of skin being torn, rose over the sound of rushing water. All heads rotated toward the noise.

Like a crab shedding its shell, a Salamantis was emerging from its cocoon. The creature appeared bloated with water, and its exoskeleton was cracked along its jointed lines. As if roused by the LED light, the creature's movements became more deliberate and strained as it began to extract itself. The beast's carapace inched through the thick slime that encased the animal, its forelimbs, claws, and legs still cemented in goo. The process was painstakingly slow as if the beast had all the time in the world.

Water poured onto the creature, filling its chrysalis, but there was no movement in the ruby eyes.

Barbo said, "This doesn't look like any hive I've ever seen."

"Hives are strange things," Pugari said. "Have you ever seen a tiny bee's nest not far from a big one?"

"Sure," Barbo said.

"Of course you have. It's normal," Pugari said. "The presence of small bee hives near larger ones is often a result of the natural behavior and reproductive strategies of bee colonies. One reason is because of a process known as "swarming," where a single colony divides to form two separate colonies. Normally, this occurs when a hive becomes overcrowded or resources are abundant, prompting the colony to reproduce and expand. The original queen, along with worker bees, leaves the large hive to establish a new colony, forming a temporary cluster nearby while scout bees search for a suitable permanent location."

Tank grunted. "We've sure seen the creatures swarm. Am I right?"

"Do you think these things have a… queen?" Lucca asked.

Pugari ignored both questions and continued his lecture. "Not that the Salamantis horde has a choice, but it's very common for a new bee cluster, or small hive, to remain close to the original hive during its initial stages.

"In our case here…" Pugari sighed. "Clearly environmental constraints and habitat availability are factors and in areas with limited nesting sites, bees may settle close to the original hive. When ideal nesting sites are scarce, new swarms may establish their hives near an already successful colony, capitalizing on the known availability of resources and favorable conditions. In the case of the Salamantis, these restrictions might have driven a rebel Salamantis to attempt to create a new hive."

"Makes sense, I guess," Lucca said.

"I didn't even mention the major unknown," Pugari said. "Bees use pheromones and other signals to communicate about food sources, dangers, and to defend the hive. Being close to another hive allows the new colony to tap into an existing network of information about the local environment, enhancing their chances of survival."

"Do you think that's the case here?" Tank said. "At times, the creatures do appear to coordinate their efforts."

Pugari had seen that as well and it made him cold.

A crackle, like a leg being torn from a roasted chicken, made the group turn their attention back to the Salamantis that was wriggling in its prison.

The beast's exoskeleton was fully visible as it pressed against the slime, but it was much paler and softer looking than the creatures the party had seen thus far. Pugari did recall the one beast that had attacked them, how its skin had been translucent, its claws only partly formed. Did these creatures live one cycle? Or did they hibernate for thousands of years at a time? Based on what he'd seen, it was either a combination of the two, or the Salamantis growth rates were akin to the blue whale, which can gain more than two hundred pounds a day when young.

As the Salamantis continued to struggle free, it appeared almost alien, its body expanding and contracting as it breathed.

Pugari's head hurt. Was the Salamantis an alien race?

"I hate to be the soldier here," Tank said. "But are we going to wait around for these things to wake up? Or…" He raised his gun.

Tank had a point. While the creatures were contained in their chrysalises, they would never be more vulnerable.

"Look," Lucca said. "The color of its shell is deepening, taking on the hues of the stone walls." She reached out, her index finger poking the rubberish coating surrounding the Salamantis.

The beast's claw thrust from the cocoon, the hiss of its breath filling the chamber. A loud splat, followed by a tearing sound as the creature pulled itself free, thick slime dripping from its frame, a loud pucker echoing through the room.

Lucca avoided the creature's strike but fell onto her ass.

Tank fired twice. The bullets went through the creature with wet thuds and punched into the wall as the Salamantis eased back into its cocoon.

Like zombies emerging from a long sleep, a multitude of forelimbs broke through slime, and many of the creatures began to stir, their chrysalises undulating and bulging as the monsters came awake.

Tunnels ran away into darkness at both ends of the rectangular chamber, and Pugari went for the righthand passage. He tapped his headlamp, and it didn't come on, but still he ran as if fire chased after him.

Shrieks, growls, and low murmurs filled the space, as claws reached for him, but the beasts were still waking, and they were slow and confused.

Lucca squeezed off a shot, but when the bullet ricocheted and almost thumped into Barbo, she held her fire.

Barbo was helping Tank, blood running down the big man's leg as they scuttled between the emerging creatures.

A tail broke free of the slime and struck Barbo and Tank. The blow drove the duo across the room toward the waiting forelimbs of the beasts breaking free on the opposite side of the chamber.

Barbo slued and avoided the hole in the floor as he reached out to Tank in a vain effort to help the man. He fell to a knee, his legs slipped out from under him, and he tripped Tank.

The big man hit the floor hard, a loud gasp followed by a groan leaking from his lips. He rolled onto his side and avoided the strike of a claw.

Barbo's arms shot back as his butt hit stone, and he surged to his feet in one smooth motion that drained the last of his energy reserves. He'd been going hard, and without a continual supply of free radicals and nightly rests in a feather bed his body was beginning to protest its foul treatment.

A claw darted from the slime, its knife-like edge not fully developed, but still sharp. With a screech, the claw impaled Barbo's right side.

Barbo doubled over, blood spilling from his mouth, his intestines spilling from the gash in his stomach.

Pugari saw all this in an odd slow motion as he ran for the nearest tunnel entrance, his peripheral vision distorted by the lack of light.

Barbo wailed as he hit the floor, a dark puddle forming around him.

Pugari considered going back, but why? Barbo, even if he somehow managed to survive the attack, would be a dead man walking, his injury far beyond the skills of any in the party to repair, even if they'd had more than a basic first aid kit.

Tank wailed as he fired, bullets bouncing around the chamber, sparks flying.

Pugari spared a glance over his shoulder as he entered the tunnel, and the last thing he saw before the darkness engulfed him was the sight of Tank standing over Barbo's prostrate form.

Two more creatures burst from the tunnel, and they were both on Kamal before the big man could get a bead on them with his gun.

Wes fired and turned the first beast into pulp, but before turning his attention to the newcomers he searched for Knight and the others. He saw that he and Kamal were the only ones left, and the glow of LED light leaked from two of the tunnel mouths.

Kamal screeched as the two new arrivals attacked from both sides, their claws raking stone as they reached for the big man.

The creatures were eight feet tall, their thin torsos casting long shadows on the dark walls. Antennas swayed, claws scratched stone, and four glimmering orbs of molten light burned through the gloom. Tails thwapped against the walls as the beasts came on, two fists of fury, teeth, blood, and bone.

Wes caught the whiff of mold, the rank scent of rotten meat, and dry-heaved. How long had it been since he'd had a proper meal? He shook his head and aimed the Glock, but Kamal and the creatures were a knot of muscle, undulating anger, and frustration. Sweat dripped down his face as he lunged forward, looking for a way to separate the creatures from his partner.

Kamal bucked and heaved, trying to shake free, but the monsters gripped and tore his clothing as he fought them off, unable to aim his gun. He shrieked as one of the creatures slipped under a punch, its jaws latching onto his shoulder as teeth sank into flesh.

The shrieks and calls of more beasts rang through the cave as Wes double-tapped the beast biting Kamal. The creature's head disappeared in a hail of bloody mist, and this gave the remaining creature pause.

Ears ringing, Wes spun on his toes as he swung the Glock, bringing it to bear on the last Salamantis.

But the creature was big, fast, and agile. It disappeared for a heartbeat, its skin fading to a dull gray-black and blending into the stone.

Wes fired blind, aiming at where the beast had been.

A shriek exploded through the chamber and blood splattered the floor. Wes kept firing, bullets ricocheting around, sparks fluttering through the severe LED light.

Then the beast was there again, the color of its skin shifting, its momentum carrying it forward. The creature hit Wes, driving him off his feet, and his headlamp smashed as he hit the floor and the chamber fell into darkness, the shriek of the creature rising above Kamal's ragged breathing and the tinkle of water. With a yell of rage, Kamal finished the beast.

The stink of the corpses made Wes cough, and as he gagged his vision blurred. He got up and rubbed his eyes.

Kamal sat with his back pressed to the wall.

Wes sat next to the guy. No words were necessary. They needed to rest and wait.

Wait they did, and when nobody returned, Wes began to despair.

Kamal's injury was worse than it initially had appeared, and the big man was in a lot of pain. Time stretched out and with no medicine or ice or bandages all Wes could do was clean the wound with water.

Hours slipped away, and Wes was about to suggest scouting the passages, when a faint light appeared in one of the tunnels.

There were eight tunnel mouths before Wes, and the third one from the right glowed gray.

Wes got to his feet and helped Kamal up. The guy was dazed, but he still held his empty Glock.

Suddenly the subterranean chamber felt very cold and quiet. Even the constant arguing of the water seemed to fade to nothing as it blended with the thump of his racing heart. He wiped the sweat from his brow, his muscles turning to iron as the adrenaline fled.

"Are you O.K.?" Wes asked.

Kamal chuckled. "I'm alive, but my shoulder hurts like hell and it's going to need a little help from Lucca."

Slowly, like the dawn creeping over the horizon, the third tunnel from the right filled with light.

16

"Who's there?" the voice rattled down the tunnel.

"Is that Wes?" Abby said.

Cap answered, "Yup."

"Wes! Wes!" Knight blurted.

The reunion was short and tension-filled.

"You haven't seen Pugari and the others?" Knight asked.

Kamal and Wes both shook their heads no, but Wes said, "I heard some serious commotion coming from that tunnel." He pointed. "And I smelled, I'm not sure what."

"Kamal, how bad are you hurt?" he asked. Knight's hair was matted to his head, his eyes stung, his t-shirt was soaked through, and every muscle in his body bitched and complained, but so far, he hadn't suffered a major injury.

Kamal grunted. "It's worse than I thought. The pain was so bad before I passed out."

"And now?"

Kamal shrugged. "I need Lucca. The wound needs to be cleaned and dressed."

"Well, until that's possible is there anything we can do for you?" Abby asked.

"I've cleaned the wound with water and wrapped a clean shirt around it," Wes said. "Until we have the first aid kit…" He threw up his hands.

"What's the plan?" Cap asked. "I feel like we shouldn't stay in one place too long. When we do the things seen to home in on us somehow."

"Good point," Knight said.

Dripping water and the breeze whistling through the caves.

Knight sighed. "Cap, Wes, and I will probe the tunnel Pugari and the others used and we'll see what there is to be seen."

Kamal sat down and pressed his back to the wall and Abby handed him her water bottle.

"*Dhanyavaad*," the big man said as he accepted the bottle and drank deeply.

When Kamal had taken his fill Abby took the bottle back and held it beneath a steady stream pouring from the ceiling to refill it.

Knight and his partners left their dry bags at the interchange with Abby and Kamal and hauled only their guns and spare loaded magazines. The ammo situation wasn't dire thanks to Barbo's planning, but every time Knight reloaded his nerves jumped and his thoughts drifted to what the party would do if they ran out of bullets. He thought back to the dry karst, the trees. Perhaps they could make spears, bows, arrows, maybe even a slingshot or bolas. But those were problems he hoped to never have to deal with, though his confidence in hope was at an all-time low.

"What do we do if you…" Abby's voice trailed away as she stared at the ground.

It was a fair question. Knight said, "We should have discussed and made some kind of plan in case the party got separated."

"Hindsight and all that rot," Abby said.

"And I know what Pugari will do," Kamal said. "He won't stop until he's dead, or one hundred percent certain there are no riches to be found."

Knight nodded as he searched for an answer to Abby's question.

Cap saved him. "Use your judgment. If we're not back in half an hour, assume you need to get by on your own for a bit." He looked at Knight as if asking if he had anything to add.

Knight said, "We'll see you in less than a half hour."

"Do you want the rope?" Abby asked. The hundred-foot length was sitting atop the pile of dry bags.

"Why not," Cap said as he grabbed the line and slung the loop over his shoulder.

Headlamps off so they didn't attract unwanted attention, the trio crept into the tunnel Pugari, Lucca, Barbo, and Tank had escaped into.

The tunnel floor was flat and even, a welcome surprise in a world of perpetually cracked and slanted floors, and the passageway ran straight. The tunnel was manmade, there was no doubt of that, but time and the thick rivulets of water streaming down the walls and cascading from the ceiling had worn all the gray, black-stripped stone smooth.

As the trio walked the ceiling sprouted tiny white stalactites that dripped white mineral-rich water.

Cap's headlamp came on and the tunnel was filled with pale white LED light. "Hold up!" the big man shouted.

A low, continuous hiss carried down the tunnel like several snakes were aggrieved.

Knight and Wes joined Cap, who stood staring down into a chasm. The tunnel floor had given way, and despite the glare of Cap's headlamp, the opposite side of the hole was obscured in darkness.

Within the hole, Salamantis crawled about, but they were moving slowly, and their skin was odd-looking.

"What are they doing?" Abby whispered.

Knight didn't know. The beasts were wandering about the chamber below in a daze, the hissing murmur rising above the constant splash and drip of water.

"It looks like there are eight of them," Cap said. "And it's only ten feet or so deep."

"Any signs of Pugari and the others?" Wes asked.

The companions stared into the gap in the tunnel floor, headlamps blazing.

"There are three Salamantis corpses," Knight said.

"I see them," Abby said.

"No great mystery what happened here then," Cap said.

"The floor collapsed on Pugari, and they—" Knight's words caught in his throat like a fish bone.

In a corner of the chamber below, there was a form lying prone on the floor.

"What's that on the far end in the corner?" Cap said.

Knight pulled the Maglite, turned it on, and trained its unflinching gaze on the figure.

It was Barbo, and all will to go on drained from Knight, like sweat on a sweltering day.

Cap made the sign of the cross and said, "Why aren't they…"

"Eating him?" Knight said. "These things look different, not fully formed, if that makes sense."

"The question is, are we going to put bullets in them and follow Pugari or go back?" Cap said.

Unlike many of the questions posed to him in the last hour, this time he had an answer. "We head back. The creatures aren't after us, so why waste bullets? And we need to stick together the best we can," he said. "I'm not leaving Abby and Kamal behind."

"Plus, you heard what Kamal said, not that it was a surprise to any of us," Wes said. "Pugari will press forward without a second thought."

Knight nodded. "Let's go."

The trek back to Abby and Kamal was uneventful and fast.

"Jeez," Abby said. "You saw no other signs of them?"

Knight shook his head. "Looks as though the floor gave way and the chamber below… It was certainly disturbed… dead creatures, Barbo…"

"Both our guides are gone," Cap said. "The local authorities are going to love that."

"The question is, what the hell do we do now?" Wes asked.

Knight filled him and Kamal in on the sinkhole they'd found.

Kamal hooted. "We are saved then, yes?"

The group exchanged glances.

"Not following you," Knight said.

"All we need to do is start a fire," Kamal said. "I know we can't do that now with the rain, but as soon as it stops, we can create a barn fire and the smoke will bring help."

Excitement tickled Knight's stomach and neck. "I hadn't thought of that."

"If we can find an escarpment where it's dry, we could do that now," Kamal said.

Knight explained how he'd seen no such ledges, and even if he had, any smoke they generated would be beaten down by the storm and would go unseen. "But the rain has got to end at some point, and we'll try then."

"What of trees?" Wes asked. "Nothing tall enough to climb? Or maybe cut one down so it falls against the cliff face?"

Knight laughed. "The sinkhole walls are at least a couple of hundred feet tall by my estimation, so no, the local flora will be of no help."

"Back to the original question, then," Cap said. "What do we do? Head back to the karst? Backtrack to the main city? Explore more of these tunnels?"

"Honestly, I vote for the sinkhole," Abby said. "It felt good to not be so confined, and I think surviving there, or at least using it as a home base, makes a lot of sense."

"Any objections to heading back to the sinkhole?" Knight said. When nobody protested, he said, "O.K., then, let's—"

"Saddle up," Abby joked. "How old are you that you still use that saying?"

"Just because it's old doesn't mean it isn't great," Knight said.

The party packed up and Kamal's wound was cleaned, and a less-dirty t-shirt was utilized as a bandage. "You feel a bit hot," Wes said as he pressed his palm to Kamal's forehead.

"Infection?" Knight said.

"The wound is festering a bit," Wes said.

"If only we had some alcohol," Abby said.

"Oh, shit," Cap said, and he clapped his hands together as he unslung his dry bag and opened it, unpeeling the rolled sealed end and digging through the bag. After a moment he pulled free a metal flask with the U.S. Army logo of an eagle spreading its wings emblazoned on its front. "This was for a different type of emergency but given the circumstances. With all the commotion I totally forgot I had it. Damn, Tank could've used it on his leg."

"What is it?" Kamal asked.

"Kentucky's finest," Cap said. "Abby, give me the cleanest shirt he has."

Abby retrieved Kamal's last t-shirt which wasn't brown with rock dust and dirt. She turned it inside out and handed it to Cap, who doused it with bourbon.

Kamal clinched his teeth and closed his eyes, but the manmade no sound as Wes cleaned the wound with the alcohol-soaked cloth.

When it was done, Kamal muttered, "Thank you."

The party followed the footprints Knight and the others had made in the layer of dust and grit that covered the floor of the tunnel. Distant shrieks and bellows trailed after them, but none of the beasts sounded close. Despite this, they traveled with their headlamps off to conserve battery power and keep a low profile.

Though the party was tired, the trek seemed much faster the second time, and before long the rectangle of gray light and rain appeared in the distance.

Knight, Cap, and Abby's footprints trailed off the scree pile the tunnel opened onto, and the path Knight and Cap trailblazed could be seen running along the base of the cliff face that surrounded the jungle like a fence.

The companions dropped their bags, and Wes pulled his camp stove and set about making hot stew. Despite the overwhelming humidity and heat, Knight felt chilled to the bone from being wet for over a week, and if he didn't catch a cold, he'd be astonished. As long as he didn't catch his death, he'd be O.K. with that.

Wes said, "Any chance I can get a nip of that Jack Daniels?" Half the small flask had been used to treat Kamal's wound.

Cap said, "I'd love to take a pull myself, but..."

Knight jumped in. "Not only isn't it a great idea to dull your senses and slow your reaction time, but without the first aid kit we might need the alcohol."

Wes harrumphed. "Understood. Just figured I'd ask. Pugari has a bottle of vodka, I know that, but what good does that do us?"

Only the rain answered, its constant jibber jabbering piping "nothing" through the trees.

"Let's get some rest," Knight said. "I'll take first watch." The gray backlit sky and his watch told Knight it was still daylight somewhere above the clouds, but the team was exhausted and stressed, and Knight knew the healing powers of sleep.

Just inside the tunnel mouth out of the rain Wes, Kamal, Cap, and Abby attempted to get comfortable with water dripping on them. Abby covered herself with her rain slicker, but the others didn't bother, and soon snores were emanating from the tunnel like an out-of-tune marching band.

Knight sat in the tunnel mouth, gazing out into the rain.

The forest encroached to the edge of the sinkhole, and visibility was difficult beyond ten or twenty feet due to the dense undergrowth. A curtain of rain also obscured his view, but as he stared, an odd absence of color, a blur, marred the greenery.

Above the opaque patch, two crimson eyes stared out from the vegetation. The glowing orbs hung eight feet from the ground, but they appeared to have no body.

Knight rubbed his eyes and drew his gun. There was no sound other than the rain pelting the forest, and he strained to focus as he examined the greenery around the eyes, trying to find any discoloration that would indicate the owner of the eyes. But there was nothing but huge fern leaves, stunted palms, and a tangle of underbrush. He raised the Glock and aimed at the eyes.

The eyes stared back defiantly.

He wanted to squeeze the trigger and keep shooting until the gun clicked empty and the owner of the eyes was nothing but a pile of cracked exoskeleton, skin, claw, and blood. But he lowered the weapon. All of them needed to be smarter and show restraint if they hoped to hold out long enough to escape, and it was more than just wasting ammunition. The noise could bring all kinds of problems, and as he looked over his shoulder at his sleeping mates, he knew that was the last thing they needed.

When he turned his attention back to the eyes, they were gone.

17

Knight woke from his brief nap to the rumble of Cap and Abby who were having a spirited discussion. He sat up, rubbed his eyes, and stood. Wes was working on turning a t-shirt into an arm sling for Kamal, whose shoulder and arm had improved but still hurt the big man severely whenever he moved his damaged wing.

"So don't move it," Wes had adroitly stated. "The way I'm tying the sling should keep your arm pressed to your side, which should limit the movement of the shoulder joint."

For most people, this would hamper the flexibility and ability to fight, but Knight had no such concerns about Kamal. He believed the man would fight to his dying breath, no matter his condition. Knight had developed a new respect for the mercenary since he'd joined his tight-knit group. The way he helped the others, showed compassion... Knight knew the power and rage that roiled just beneath the surface, but he didn't think Kamal was as bad as he wanted people to believe.

"What's the big debate about?" Knight asked.

"Which way we should go," Wes said.

"What do you think?" Knight asked. As always there were four choices: straight, back, right, or left.

Wes shrugged. "The jungle looks thick, so keeping to the edge of the sinkhole, as you and Cap did, seems like the best play."

"Keep the cliff face at our backs," Kamal added.

"And we're not going back," Knight added.

"Right or left?" Wes said.

"I'll be back," Knight said. He pulled his canteen and drank deeply as he walked to where Cap and Abby stood in the tunnel mouth.

Abby said, "You look much better."

"I feel a little better." He told them about the monster in the greenery he'd seen while on watch.

"We haven't seen anything and there were no other reports," Abby said.

Knight nodded. "So what's the verdict?"

"We all agree that going around the edge is smarter than trying to fight through the jungle," Cap said. "So, we might as well go the opposite way we went the first time. Left. Since we didn't find anything the other way."

"But the vegetation is much deeper that way," Abby said.

"That's good and bad, no?" Knight asked. "More cover for us, but the going would be slower."

"And the heavy vegetation is good cover for the indigenous population as well," Abby added. "And with their camouflage abilities…" She threw up her hands.

"She makes good points," Cap said.

"I'm convinced," Knight said.

Cap nodded.

"Right it is then," Knight said.

The party of five used the trail Knight and Cap had blazed on their first trek in the dry karst, and soon the group was shuffling and climbing past the stone where Cap had rested, and he and Knight had turned around.

As they entered virgin territory, Knight said, "Has anyone seen any caves in the cliffsides?"

No response.

As the sinkhole's edge gently curved the jungle thinned to their left, the tall stone wall to their right slick with water. Rain fell in a steady stream. Knight's fingers were so pruned he didn't know if they'd ever be smooth again, and his feet chafed in his wet socks, and he felt blisters forming. His clothes were drenched through, despite his rain gear, because it was so hot and humid his sweat was almost as bad as the rain.

Knight glanced at his watch. It was 6:45 PM, November 7th. The clouds above were extra dark, and the sun, though it would have been hidden, was a distant memory. He judged most of the karst saw limited sunlight even on the nicest day of the year because of the depth of the sinkhole and the angle of the sun, but as the gloom deepened, and night thickened, Knight considered calling a halt.

The companions had gone a couple of miles at best, and the forest and its undergrowth had diminished considerably because the vegetation at the eastern edge of the sinkhole saw little daylight. Straggly bushes with tiny yellow leaves and two-inch stiletto thorns filled the ground beneath stunted palms and ferns that were a fraction of the size compared to the ones to the west.

There were no caves or notches in the cliff face. The smooth rock was gray streaked with black, and though there was minimal light, and the crew had their headlamps off to conserve battery power, shadows flitted within every crack.

"Is it time to head north?" Wes asked.

"We might miss a tunnel," Abby said.

"Not that we've got much choice here, but what's the plan beyond our basic direction?" Kamal asked. "Are we looking for tunnels? Do we want to go all the way around? We need to know what we're dealing with. We could build a shelter. Hunker down and wait for this infernal rain to stop."

Knight liked the sound of that. With a shelter as a home base, Kamal could rest, and two-person parties could explore and map the area. He wasn't eager to delve deeper, but still...

"I like that idea," Cap said. "We've got a saw, and we're all experienced in building shelters from nothing."

"We've got the foldable shovel also," Wes added.

"It would be great to be out of the rain," Abby said.

"O.K. It's settled then," Knight said. What he didn't voice was, what about Pugari and the others? Was it his responsibility to try and find them? Was Knight responsible for the entire team's safety? He shook his head. It didn't matter. He and his companions weren't prepared to fight a Salamantis horde. If they could get settled, maybe they could look, but something told him the sinkhole was a central part of the underground city, which meant Pugari and his team were bound to find their way into the karst and might have already.

The party rested, drank water, and trekked into the woods that filled the eastern section of the sinkhole. Tall Rosewood trees climbed one hundred feet into the cloud-filled sky, their trunks straight. The bases of the trees were buttressed, their bark dark gray with a rough, textured surface with vertical fissures. There were sections where the bark had peeled away, revealing heartwood, heavy purple-black wood with a fine, even texture. Oval leaves arranged in pairs ran along a central stalk creating a thick canopy, and small, fragrant flowers of pale pink sagged from the rain alongside flat seed pods that hung from many of the branches.

Beneath these behemoths were a series of stunted palms, ferns, and tightly packed bushes with yellow leaves and two-inch prickers.

Using their knives and the foldable handsaw, the party made staffs from the limbs of Rosewood trees, and they used them to bushwhack.

The companions had only gone a quarter mile or so, the sound of their hacking and crushing rising above the rain, when a musical clicking carried through the trees and slowly turned into a low-pitched wail.

Cap was on point, and he raised his fist.

The party came to a halt.

99

Cap dropped to his knee as he pointed two fingers at Wes and then pointed right. He repeated the process with Knight and sent him left. Then he indicated that Abby and Kamal should hang back.

"I don't—" Kamal started.

Cap raised his hand, palm out. "Quiet. I don't need you right now. Lay back."

Kamal wasn't the worst patient ever, but he sure wasn't the best. His restricted movement was starting to get to him, and his mood had soured as the pain level increased. The more Kamal moved, the more the scabbing wound pulled at his skin. He eased back.

Wes and Knight fanned out, guns up. Knight listened hard, trying to hear beyond the patter of the rain, but he heard nothing. He moved through the undergrowth, avoiding thorns, stones, and vines that snaked across the muddy hardpan looking for feet to trip up.

Another cooing shriek echoed through the rain and Knight froze as he gaped at the greenery ahead. He'd seen a Salamantis in full camo mode, and as he wiped the water from his eyes he stared, looking between leaves, trying to find any contrast against the wall of green and brown.

A branch snapped to his right, and he swung the Glock, safety trigger depressed, but he didn't fire. There was no blurred translucent patch that marked a camouflaged Salamantis.

Wes whistled, and when Knight looked his way, Wheat Thin pointed up into the tree canopy above Knight.

The rain chose that moment to make up for lost time, and it came in sheets, pounding the forest.

Knight looked back over his shoulder. Cap, Abby, and Kamal were still, their gazes trained on something above Knight. He looked up, rain spattering his face.

A large Rosewood tree, its trunk four feet around, stood to his left, and its dense canopy spread like a leaky umbrella above him. His eyes hurt as he stared, green leaves fading into a black cotton candy sky.

Nothing moved, the tapping of the rain and the push of the breeze the only sounds.

An absence of light appeared against the tree trunk as if the air itself had been smudged. Knight focused on the spot and noted that several tree branches disappeared two or three feet away from the trunk only to reappear a few feet down the line.

A Salamantis. Knight raised his gun and aimed.

Cap whistled.

Knight held his fire.

More smudges appeared against the rain-dappled jungle as Knight held his breath. He turned his attention back to the creature above him, but he couldn't find it.

Branches cracked and broke free, and leaves fell like rain. It was as though an invisible army of monkeys was tearing through the tree canopy. Though there was motion everywhere, Knight didn't see anything to shoot at.

A Salamantis appeared like a wraith to Knight's right, the beast peeling itself from the undergrowth as if emerging from its mother's invisible womb. The beast's color changed as it came at Knight, forelimbs extended, claws at the ready, its jaws flexing open.

Knight aimed and fired, three shots—one, two, three loud pops followed by a skin-tingling shriek that made Knight bite his lip.

The trees shook and popped, and Cap yelled something Knight didn't understand, but he caught the word "out."

Look out. The words registered and Knight dove, not heeding his direction or what lay ahead. He hit the ground hard, mud splashing his face, a tree root digging into his shoulder as he rolled and got to his feet like a boxer that's taken a bout-shaking blow and wasn't ready to stay down.

A Salamantis stood before Knight and he shot it in the head twice.

The beast's corpse hit the ground with a wet thud as its body deflated.

Knight put his hands on his knees, panting, his vision red.

As the dead creature's skin shifted to patches of green and brown, the forest fell still, the hollow shrieking ceased, and the arguing rain was all that disturbed the peace.

"Are you alright?" asked Abby as she put a hand on his back.

"I think so." Knight wiggled his fingers and toes and ran his hand across his face. Everything was where it had been. "You?"

"Fine, though I think I peed my pants," Abby said.

Cap and Wes laughed.

Kamal looked disgusted.

"Do we need to rethink our plan?" Knight asked. He was still shaken, but his heart was running at its normal rate.

"No," Cap said. "I think there's a spot up ahead where we can build our shelter."

Knight had hoped to construct their refuge closer to the center of the karst, but with the creatures able to hide so well in the thick vegetation he gave up that idea.

The companions followed Cap through a copse of stunted palms which ended at a flooded glade of trees with spiked bark that Knight didn't recognize. He thought to ask Barbo but then remembered the man was dead.

A steady waterfall poured over the edge of a sinkhole to the east, and a river, that was probably nothing more than a thin stream during normal weather, trailed into the jungle. Its banks were overflowing, and the forest was swamp-like, the water rising two feet above the base of the trees and drowning much of the undergrowth.

The area was so saturated that several of the larger trees had been uprooted, and they'd fallen across each other, creating a teepee-like pile that looked like it might fall over in a strong breeze.

When the pile was pushed, pulled, and beaten, and it didn't so much as budge, half the fellowship went about collecting branches with leaves to make a roof while the other half dug a fire pit at the center of the shelter, not that there was any dry wood.

The hours passed, the shelter was completed, and the party settled into their new digs for some rest.

Knight was awakened by Abby, and as his vision cleared, he smiled. She was beautiful, and again the thought that he'd missed the boat with her made his stomach churn. "Sleep well?" he said.

She nodded.

As Knight took up a position at the outer edge of the shelter, beneath a thick, porch-like patch of broken branches still covered in green leaves, his thoughts drifted to Abby. How she'd navigated a childhood of abuse and poverty, fought her way through public school to earn a full college scholarship, only to arrive there and realize formal education wasn't for her. Thankfully for him, the school of hard knocks had produced a brilliant, tough, and loyal teammate.

Why not a mate? asked his inner voice. Because he was emotionally weak, inflexible, and...

Sleep clawing at his eyes, his stomach grumbling, he noticed a pale light leaking through the darkness and mist. It was the glow of Knight's watch, and he saw the date was November 8th and the time of the eclipse had passed. He stared up through the tangle of greenery but saw nothing but black clouds. The beasts were as angry as ever, but the dead members of his party verified that the sleeper species had awoken before the eclipse.

Water leaked through the makeshift roof, and Knight wondered not for the first time if perhaps the eclipse had been a coincidence at some point in the distant past. A myth passed down from generation to generation and cast in stone as law, though he knew legends often had a way of coming true.

18

While exploring the sinkhole Knight and Wes found the pyramid. It appeared in the greenery so suddenly he wasn't sure what he was seeing was real. He stopped walking, clearing the water from his eyes, and Wes bumped into him, the driving rain filling the world with static.

"What's the hol—whoa," Wes said.

Vines covered the pyramid, its stones worn and rounded. Knight's first rationalization was that the structure was just a pile of stones, but the lines were too sharp, despite the decomposition of its building blocks. It reminded him of the pyramids at Giza. From half a mile away, they looked clean and newly built, but up close no stone looked to be the same size, and step-like protrusions made up the surfaces of the pyramids.

"Now that's not on the map," Wes said.

"No, it isn't," Knight said. He approached cautiously, gun up, the rain playing snare drum on his raincoat.

Knight estimated the pyramid to be fifty feet in height, with four sides. He couldn't see the capstone because it was covered in greenery, but something red hid beneath the vines. The jungle grew all around the monument, crawling up its sides, tree roots digging under the structure and pulling apart its base.

"This is old," Wes said. "Like Giza old."

The centuries had weathered the structure's façade, and the building blocks, once meticulously aligned, now bore the marks of relentless time and the elements. Beneath the vines the stone surfaces were rough, chipped, and pitted, showing a palette of muted grays interspersed with earthy browns. Each tier of the pyramid told a story of endurance, the steps now uneven and eroded. An intricate tapestry of moss and lichen filled every crevice, their greens and silvers adding a touch of life to the aged stone. Cracks ran through the pyramid's massive blocks, some deep and jagged, others fine, and most spider-webbed across multiple bricks.

"I don't see any runes or pictographs?" Wes said.

Knight pulled some vines away from the structure, but there was nothing beneath except worn rock and the tiny footprint-like lines that marked where the vine's tendrils had clamped onto the stone. "If there were any, they're long gone," he said.

The pair stood in the rain, staring up at the pyramid. There were so many crazy theories relating to pyramids—there always had been, but it had reached new heights lately.

"It's hard to believe nobody ever found this," Wes said.

"Who said it's never been found? There are hundreds of pyramids like this all over the world," Knight countered. "Let's see if we can find a way in."

Knight led as the pair stayed as close to the base of the pyramid as possible, using their staffs to push away irritating plant life and moving around thickets of pricker bushes.

Between the thwacks and cracks of the bushwacking, Wes said, "Is it me, or does the stone look a bit different than the sinkhole walls?"

Knight nodded. He hadn't noticed it prior, but now that Wes had mentioned it... "You might be right, Wheat Thin." The stones making up the pyramid were solid in color, and there were no colorful veins, no specks of quartz or fool's gold.

"Quarried?" Wes probed.

"From where?" Knight said.

Both men glanced at their feet and said nothing.

The pair had reconnoitered one full side of the pyramid and were halfway through the second when a Salamantis appeared in the vegetation ahead. Unlike in the past, Knight and Wes saw the beast, but the creature didn't appear to notice them. Knight settled behind a huge fern leaf, and Wes worked his way behind a thick Rosewood trunk.

Though the rain and gloom blurred the scene, the Salamantis could be seen clearly against the stark background of a tree trunk. The beast appeared to be sitting. Knight saw its hindlegs were folded, and its left forelimb used its claw to cycle pieces of something into its mouth.

"Do you see that? It's missing an—holy shit," Wes said.

At first glance, the creature's right forelimb appeared to be missing, but closer inspection revealed a stump protruding from the joint below the triangular head. A dark scab was the foundation of a mass of cells, a blastema, which served as the beginning of a new limb.

The developing leg appeared translucent and delicate, and an array of colors from light pinks to pale blues and greens marked newly formed blood vessels and tissues that streaked through the emerging foreleg. Tiny buds covered the stump, and Knight figured these buds would gradually elongate and shape themselves into a new leg, mirroring the intricate pattern of the original limb, because that was the process for salamanders.

"Amazing," Wes said.

"But not surprising. I wonder if—" Knight's words caught in his throat as the creature's head jerked in their direction.

The pair aimed their guns but didn't fire. Though they knew little for sure, that didn't mean Knight and his crew hadn't learned a lesson or two. The beasts occasionally left on their own when they weren't confronted, and more than once the sound of gunshots had drawn the beasts to them. So it had been decided not to fire on the creatures unless it was necessary, and any objections to this edict were met with the undeniable reality that the party was slowly running out of bullets.

A bird shrieked as the Salamantis took a hesitant step forward, head jerking about, antennas swaying, its single forelimb cycling around as it searched for a target. Its right side shifted to green as it moved, and for a heartbeat, the beast looked as though it had been cut in half.

Knight and Wes stayed still, hidden, but Knight's heart was fighting to get out of his chest. Heat spread through him, the sting of fear biting his stomach.

The creature's dark eyes shined through the gloom, the color of its skin shifting and flowing as the rain pelted the monster.

This game of chicken lasted several seconds as the Salamantis came forward and the duo aimed their guns.

Then the Salamantis disappeared as the rain picked up.

"Do you see it?" Wes said.

"Yeah... it's just inside the tree break, and... now it's gone," Knight said. He lowered his gun and looked behind him. The creatures had a way of disappearing only to circle back and attack their prey's rear flank.

The pair got low, putting their backs together, weapons at the ready.

But the Salamantis was gone.

Wes whispered, "Can salamanders only regenerate limbs?"

That was a good question, and Knight knew why his friend had asked. Could the beasts survive gunshot wounds? Would their organs grow back? Repair themselves? Was a complete headshot necessary to put a Salamantis down? He'd seen no sign of that, but still... He said, "I know what you're thinking, and we're sure as hell in no man's land here, and you've already been to the lecture about the how." He sighed. "Salamanders are renowned for their extraordinary regenerative abilities, which extend far beyond just limb regeneration. They can regenerate a wide array of body parts and organs. In addition to limbs, salamanders can regenerate their tails, including the spinal cord, nerves, and blood vessels. This ability extends to complex structures such as the lens and retina of their eyes, parts of their heart, and even sections of

105

their brain. Now, can the Salamantis do all that?" Knight hiked his shoulders. "I sure hope not."

The pair found an entrance to the pyramid on its northern side. It was nothing more than a five-foot-high, three-foot-across rectangular opening in the stone. A portico-like rock roof jutted from the pyramid and covered the entrance, but the most astonishing features were the two six-foot lizard statues guarding each side of the entrance. The guards had once held staves, but they'd broken away, and the vine-covered pieces littered the ground along with the remnants of their shields and battle helmets.

Thick vegetation covered in spider webs that glistened in the rain covered the opening like a natural door, and there were no tracks, no signs any living thing had entered the pyramid, or exited via the entrance in a very long time. A large puddle blocked the entry, and as Knight waded into it, he shined his Maglite into the maw of the doorway.

A tunnel ran away into darkness. Runes and pictographs covered the walls, but most had been washed away by the eons and the flow of water. Tiny eyes of quartz sparkled from within the stone, and the stink of stagnant water filled his nostrils.

"Cover me," Knight said, and he went to work clearing away the vines and webs. He felt the eyes of the statues on him, and his thoughts drifted to the race that had built the monument stone, the lizard statue in India. Ravel's people had discovered all this, and what must those ancient shamans have thought when they came upon this? Had the city existed? He thought so, and again the idea that the Salamantis was of another world nudged its way to the forefront of his brain.

When the entrance was clear enough to pass through, the pair checked their equipment and readied their headlamps. Knight had gotten used to not wearing the thing, but the darkness within the pyramid was thick, and though he saw no footprints, that didn't mean there weren't stormy seas ahead.

"Stay close," Knight said as he eased past the remaining vines. The cold stone chilled him as the LED lights drove away the blackness.

A tunnel ran straight into the pyramid, the floor slanting down at a ten-degree angle. Though most of the finer details had been worn away, Knight gaped at what he saw.

One pictograph depicted a large, central figure of a lizard person adorned in ceremonial attire. The lizard shaman had an elongated snout and wore a headdress made of feathers and bones. Surrounding the shaman were smaller, intricate symbols representing the four elements: earth, water, fire, and air, along with geometric patterns resembling a

106

sunburst, indicating the shaman's connection to celestial powers. Knight paused and traced the carving with his index finger. "How old do you think these are?"

Wes shrugged. "It's protected from the elements in here, usually, so who knows?"

Further down the line, there was a group of lizard warriors in a dynamic battle stance carved into the tunnel wall. The warriors wore fierce expressions, their large eyes illustrated with faded colors, and their muscular-like scales gleaming in the LED light. Each held a spear and a shield adorned with tribal designs. The scene was set in a rocky, mountainous terrain with a large lizard statue in the background.

"India?" said Wes.

Knight said nothing, though it sure did look like India. Wind whistled down the tunnel, voices from ages past issuing warnings Knight couldn't understand. He shivered.

The next ancient picture in stone showcased a community of lizard people engaged in daily activities. There were several lizard families near thatched huts with curved roofs and doors. Smaller figures played near a central bonfire, while adults were depicted harvesting crops and crafting tools.

"Here we go," Knight said.

The tunnel ended in an archway, and beyond it, a spiral stone staircase plunged into darkness. At the top of the arch was a scene of what Knight believed to be a sacred ritual. A huge Salamantis, its forelegs raised, claws on display, towered over a crowd of kneeling lizard people who were offering gifts such as fruits, carved idols, and sticks that Knight thought were probably incense, or something similar. The sky above the Salamantis was filled with dark stone, and the pictograph's borders were decorated with intricate, intertwined vines and flowers.

Wes angled his headlamp so it illuminated the final pictographs leading to the arch.

It was a dramatic scene of migration. Lizard people traversed a vast forest, a long line of crude lizard figures walking with bundles and carrying young lizards on their backs. The lizard people were dressed in flowing garments that looked too much like rain slickers for Knight's taste. In the distance, a vast ocean, and the sky was filled with birds flying in formation, along with other oddly shaped images that Knight couldn't make out.

Knight stepped inside the archway and the foul stench of decay assailed him. He shined the Maglite down the stairs which spiraled into blackness. "I wish we'd brought the rope," he said.

Wes harrumphed. "I say we head back and come back full force."

Knight nodded but said nothing. Other than the pyramid, the company had found no other tunnels leading into the karst, nor had they discovered any spot to climb out. The rain was showing no signs of stopping, and though he tried, he couldn't avoid the gut-wrenching reality that if he and his friends were going to escape their prison, they'd have to find another way.

Wes turned and headed back down the tunnel. He gazed up at the giant Salamantis, its stone antennas piercing the tunnel ceiling, its faded legs blending into the gray stone. As he left, he felt those eyes on him and heard the echo of the beast's call.

Back out in the rain, with the dark clouds filling the sky, Knight's gut eased, though he wasn't sure why. Or was he? There was something about the pyramid. Something that ate at the brain and tormented the senses. The wind chanted and sang, and again he heard voices on the breeze. They were near, and then they were gone.

Knight shook his head, pulled up his hood, and headed for the shelter.

19

The tunnel turned sharply downward and Tiger Pugari slipped in the wet grit and dust that had accumulated on the passageway floor. Tank and Lucca's footfalls and their ragged breathing chased after him, their headlamp beams bouncing over the walls behind him. Pugari's heart raced, his legs complained, and hunger pains knotted his stomach, but his mind was clear. As mud.

If he ever hooked up with Dusky, he was going to catch shit for Barbo's death. How and why were still unclear to him, but Knight would find a way to spin things so he was at fault. Of course, on an existential level, he was. The call of a statue in India holding a tablet with ancient writing on it, writing that spoke of times so long past that the urge to chase fame and adventure was stronger than a need for profit.

Now it had all gone to hell. Pugari's chest ached from running, and the hand-carved tunnel abruptly gave way to a natural cave. He paused at the interchange and waited for his companions. Water dripped everywhere, and though he knew it wasn't possible, he heard the constant rattle of the rain far above.

Soon he would have to decide what meant more to him; the adventure or the lives of his team, and perhaps his own life. What price was he willing to pay? The ultimate one? What risks would he accept? What level of collateral damage? Pugari chuckled, the rumble of his approaching companions getting louder. They were moving slowly. God, he hoped the pair wasn't carrying Barbo's corpse. That was exactly the annoying type of thing Tank might insist on. Soldiers and their ceremonies.

Did he have to decide what to do, though? Really? And if he did, did anyone need to know? Exploring unknown portions of the complex for an escape route was the same as exploring, and until he hit a literal crossroads, the topic wou—

An angry wail of pain echoed through the caves, the glow of LED light filling the tunnel Pugari had just exited.

It was then he remembered Tank's leg injury. He rushed back to feign assistance, but he only got a few feet before Lucca and Tank peeled from the darkness, the ex-soldier limping, but otherwise unharmed. Lucca looked aggrieved.

"Leave us behind next time, why don't you!" she screeched.

Anger rose in Pugari. This was what happened when you treated your workers fairly and showed them respect. They got the crazy idea that they somehow had a say. Never one to contain his rage, Pugari stepped forward and got in Lucca's face. "If you were doing your damn job, you know, checking out the path before us, we wouldn't have almost gotten killed! And as for Tank!" He turned his attention toward the big man. "Are you alright?"

Tank nodded as his gaze shifted briefly to Lucca and then to the floor.

"Whatever," Lucca said.

The trio drank water and listened, trying to discern if the creatures were pursuing them, but there was nothing to be heard except the perpetual tap and drip of water and the gentle push of the earthen breeze.

Lucca took point, gun at the ready as she eased into the natural cave portion of the passageway. The walls angled sharply inward, creating a triangular tunnel that zigzagged and lifted at random intervals.

"Look at this," Tank said.

Lucca and Pugari turned to see Tank staring at a square notch in the stone. A loop of a kind had been chiseled through the rock. "I bet there was a guide rope, like a railing here," Tank said.

Pugari searched the ground, but the rope or vine or wood, if it had ever been there at all, was gone now.

The rough-shaped walls were unadorned, and water flowed freely from many fissures and holes. They went slowly, Lucca probing the floor, Pugari and Tank stomping and testing their weight before each step. The floor looked like granite to Pugari and given the fissure they were walking through, even if it wasn't, the floor was certainly stronger than the sedimentary stone that made up the walls.

"Do you hear that?" Lucca said. She stopped and let her gun fall to her side. She was the only one with a headlamp on, and the glare of the LED light hid her face.

With their footfalls silenced, Pugari listened for the call of the Salamantis, but even the wind wasn't whispering.

Then he heard it. A gentle static, like the churning of the sea, settled just below the echo of moving water. "It's ahead. Go extra slow."

The trio inched through the cave, the floor angling down, the party using the ancient handholds to keep from sliding into blackness. A hiss, not a Salamantis, but more like a stream of pressurized water pounding stone rose above the static and gurgle of water.

Roots snaked from cracks and fissures and crawled down the cave walls, pulling apart the stone. Vines hung from the ceiling, tiny green sprouts covering the brown rope-like wood.

The sound of crashing water filled the cave, and as the trio exited into a vast grotto, Pugari and Tank turned on their headlamps.

A thin waterfall cascaded majestically from the mouth of a lizard person statue carved from the cavern's wall. The stream of water pounded a flat stone at its base before leaking into a pool. The colossal sculpture stood seventy feet tall, its detailed features almost lifelike in the dim, ethereal light filtering through the cavern. A single beam of gray light angled into the grotto, but when Pugari searched for its source, he found only darkness above.

The lizard's head, large and imposing, jutted out from the cave wall, its mouth agape in a perpetual roar, its eyes staring into the depths of the cave. Clear water glistened as it tumbled from its mouth and caught the LED light in a dazzling display of shimmering rainbow droplets. Smoothed and worn by the constant flow of water over countless years, the lower portion of the figure's mouth was almost fully eroded.

Each scale on the statue's body was carefully chiseled, creating a texture that mimicked rough reptilian skin. Its eyes were large and almond-shaped, with pupils that seemed to follow one's movements. The head was adorned with intricate patterns, possibly depicting tribal symbols or mystical runes, their meanings lost to time but hinting at the forgotten culture that once thrived in this subterranean world.

Surrounding the lizard's head, the cave walls were rugged and uneven, a testament to the natural forces that had shaped the underground realm. Stalactites and stalagmites framed the waterfall, their pointed forms resembling ancient teeth. Every surface was damp and glistening with moisture, and the constant roar of the waterfall filled the chamber as the pool at its base rippled and foamed.

"It looks deep," Tank said of the pool.

"Yup," said Pugari.

The pool was an inviting blue, its clarity revealing smooth pebbles and rocks that lined its bottom. Occasionally, small fish could be seen darting through the water. Pugari was surprised to see life in the hidden oasis. The pool's edges were lined with moss and lichen, their dark green hues contrasting starkly with the gray and brown tones of the rock.

Further out from the waterfall, the cave expanded into a vast chamber, the ceiling soaring into the gloom. The air was cool and filled with a fine mist, the humidity making the cavern feel almost alive.

The companions stood on an outcropping of stone, and roughly hewn steps led down to a natural platform beside the waterfall.

There was a wide tunnel to the left of the waterfall, and several crack-like caves spidered off the platform below. Each sound the party made was amplified and echoed through the space like an announcement of their arrival.

Pugari started down the slick steps as he said, "Careful. Break a leg in here and…" You're on your own.

"This must have taken years to make," Lucca said.

"Possibly generations," Pugari said. "As you know well, ancient civilizations, like the Egyptians, often used large projects to keep their people occupied. To give the society purpose and a reason for the leaders to spread the wealth."

"You're saying not much has changed in thousands of years?" Tank prodded.

Pugari didn't take the bait and said nothing.

A faint shriek echoed from one of the tunnels.

When the trio reached the stone platform Pugari dropped his bag and started stripping off his clothes. "I don't care if the water is freezing. I need to wash the grit off me."

"You're joking?" Lucca said.

Tank chuckled.

When Pugari was down to his underwear, he inched into a stream of water falling over a nearby stone. It was freezing, and he felt a zap of energy tweak the tips of his fingers and toes as he scrubbed at his armpits. The water felt good, and he opened his mouth and drank, the dark gray gloom above like a backlit cloud-filled sky.

He was done in moments, and Pugari and Tank kept watch, their backs turned, as Lucca cleaned herself. When Tank was refreshed, the trio found an alcove to rest. Tank could go no farther, and as Lucca cleaned his wound, she winced.

The gash was red and puffy, the telltale signs of an oncoming infection.

Lucca said, "I wish I had some of Cap's whiskey."

Tank grunted. "It's bad?"

"It's not good," she said. "On a scale of one to ten, what's your pain level?"

"Eight," Tank said.

Pugari bit his lip. Tank was the toughest—well, maybe the second toughest guy he'd ever met, Kamal holding the number one spot. That Tank would admit to being in so much pain told him it was probably worse than the man was letting on.

112

Then there was Kamal. Pugari hadn't given a second thought to the man since they'd been separated. It wasn't because he cared about the guy, he didn't, except finding someone to replace him would be time-consuming and expensive. Kamal owed him his life, and losing a person who would die for you wasn't an easy thing to replace.

"We'll rest here for a while," Pugari said. "Until Tank feels up to moving on."

Tank didn't get better and as he slipped into fever the man started muttering about how Lucca and Pugari should leave him behind.

Pugari would have done just that, but he knew Lucca would never go for it, so he didn't raise the option as a possibility.

So it was that the trio rested and slept in the dark, waiting for something to happen. Tank slipped further into a fever as his leg swelled. The waterfall rumbled, and the weak breeze played a lazy tune as the shrieks of creatures grew and faded.

Lucca and Tank were asleep, the puffing of their contentment mixing with the static of rushing water. Pugari was on watch, and he sat with his back pressed to a wall, staring out at the dark cavern from the alcove where his partners slept.

The waterfall glowed in the faint gray light that leaked from above, and his mind wandered as he tried to estimate how deep he was underground. The sinkhole, plus the climb down and the cave-in. He figured he could be anywhere from one hundred to two hundred feet below the surface. He'd been deeper than that several times. Some of the old tombs and—

Pugari bit his lower lip. The large main tunnel to the left of the waterfall was directly across from the alcove he and his companions hid in, the other crack-like tunnels spreading out on either side of their hiding place. He rubbed his eyes, hoping to scour away the mirage he was seeing.

At the center of the dark tunnel mouth, which was roughly round and rose to a height of ten feet, a light floated at the heart of the blackness.

He stood, intending to draw his gun, only to realize it was already in his hand. Pugari took several hesitant steps, and when he exited the alcove onto the large flat stone beside the waterfall he stopped, straining to see into the large tunnel ahead. The light hadn't grown or moved or changed in any way. Pugari resisted the urge to turn on his headlamp, and the impulse was so strong he put his free hand in his pocket as he strode forward.

113

The stone floor was slick, the air thick with mist. A cloud of green light surrounded him, and he tapped the face of his watch and the light died.

Pugari inched into the tunnel, gun up, his head jerking back and forth. He looked over his shoulder and couldn't see Lucca and Tank in their hiding spot. Lucca would be angry if he went off on his own... but the light. He groped forward in the darkness, the light neither growing nor fading.

A gust of foul wind pushed up the tunnel followed by a chorus of whisper-like clicks.

He rolled his shoulders and cracked his neck. Pugari couldn't take it anymore. His nerves were eating through his skin, and the heat of fear leaked through him.

A low hiss carried down the passageway.

Pugari turned on his headlamp.

The tunnel was much taller and wider than he had judged in the darkness. It was a natural cavern that had been chipped and chiseled to conform to the wishes of man, or something man-like.

Framed within the harsh stare of his headlamp, a Salamantis reared back on its hind legs, its tail straight as it pressed to the ground for balance. The creature shrieked, extending its claws as its forelegs reached out, its huge antennas flopping around as its jaws flexed open.

The Salamantis was five feet from Pugari and he blinked. He was a child, defending his sister on the playground back in elementary school, the squeak of the swings driving out the sound of a screaming teacher.

Pugari blinked again, and he stood outside a restaurant, yelling at a young woman with red hair. "Julia," he said.

Then his long-dead father was there, urging him to do something, but Tiger didn't understand. "What, Pa? What?"

"Shoot it!" yelled his father. "Shoot it!"

The Salamantis sprang.

Pugari shrieked and didn't get a shot off before the monster was on him.

20

Knight stared down the spiral staircase that led into the bowels of the pyramid, the Maglite driving away the darkness, and he noticed several things he hadn't the first time he'd visited the spot with Wes.

The steps were littered with bird droppings and chocolate sprinkle-like rodent feces, and tiny tracks of footprints trailed through the layer of accumulated dust and grit. There were no other tracks.

Abby peered over Knight's shoulder and said, "You weren't kidding." She stepped back and gazed up at the huge pictograph of the Salamantis rendered in stone.

Kamal grunted.

"Are you alright?" Wes asked. More whiskey had been applied to Kamal's wound, and he was doing much better, though his movements were still restricted, and his patience had grown thin.

"Fine," the big man said. "Are we going to get on with this, or what?"

"Only one way. Forward," Knight said.

"Not true, but..." Abby sighed. "I'm not going back to the shelter."

"I'll take point," Cap said.

Wes handed Cap the end of the rope and said, "Just give it a tug if you want us to pull you out."

Cap nodded as he tied the rope around his waist and slung his dry bag across his back. With a look back at his companions, Cap eased onto the staircase's top step, a cloud of dust billowing around his legs. He crept down the stairs, gun in its holster, his wooden staff pointed outward like a lance. The stairwell was a tight elevator shaft-like pit, and any bullet fired in the confined space would bounce around like a pinball in full play.

Next went Abby, and then Kamal. They did have their weapons at the ready, though they were under orders only to shoot as a last resort.

Knight waited as the rope played out through Wes's fingers. Water dripped and the murmurs of their companions carried up from the stairwell.

When half the rope was gone, Knight rolled his shoulders, glanced at the gray rectangle of light at the pyramid's entrance, and eased onto the first step. With the rope held loosely in his left hand, and his staff in his right, he started down, his eyes locked on his feet.

115

With each step, the air became cooler and more humid. Perspiration ran down his forehead into his eyes, his feet chafing in their wet socks. The cloud of light below grew, diminished, and then disappeared. Knight paused and looked up.

He couldn't see Wes where he anchored the rope at the top of the staircase, but his headlamp's blinding light leaked down the stairwell. "How much rope do you have left?" Knight yelled.

"About ten feet, but I think they reached the bottom because no rope has played out in the last thirty seconds."

Or Cap left the tether behind, but Knight kept that thought to himself as he turned his attention back to the stairs.

A shriek from above echoed through the tunnel and down the spiral staircase.

Knight looked up, the rope still in his hand, but it didn't move.

Another shriek, and then a single gunshot.

Knight dropped his staff and drew his gun as he bounded up the steps.

There was yelling from below, but Wes had gone silent above.

When he reached the top of the stairs Knight inched his head over the lip of the tunnel floor.

LED light filled the space. The end of the rope lay on the floor, and Wes's long shadow fell across the far wall. A headless Salamantis was sprawled at the top of the stairs.

Wheat Thin stood at the center of the tunnel, the history of the ancient race that had built the pyramid staring at him with stone faces. At the far end of the passage, a crowd of creatures clustered at the entrance, their claws clicking, eyes shining, antennas scraping on stone.

Knight took several steps forward.

Wes turned and yelled, "What are you doing? Go! I'll hold them off."

"Leave them," Knight said. "We can defend the stairs better than the tunnel."

"Look how they don't want to come in here... See that? I'd swear the big guy at the front is holding the others back."

Knight strained to see what Wes described. A knot of beasts surged forward and fell back as if unsure how to proceed.

"Come on. Leave them," Knight said. He considered throwing in, "That's an order" but decided against it. He'd never heard anyone utter those words and not be an asshole.

Wes didn't need to be told twice. He backed up, never taking his eyes off the fist of monsters filling the tunnel entrance.

116

When Wes reached Knight, he bent and picked up the rope without taking his eyes off the monsters.

Despite Wes's retreat, the creatures still hadn't advanced, as if the pyramid was hallowed ground.

"Go," Wes said.

Knight stared at the churning beasts.

"Go!" Wes yelled, then added, "Please."

Snapped from his amazement, Knight headed back down the steps, taking them two at a time.

Light blossomed below and above, and the calls of his companions echoed in the confined space. The staircase wound down and down. Twenty steps. Forty. Sixty. Knight stopped counting when he hit a hundred. The spiral stairs were a marvel of engineering and craftsmanship, each step the same height, their rough time-worn surfaces like natural stair treads. His knees protested, his mouth was dry as paper, and though he didn't hear the creatures above, he didn't dare pause, even to take a sip of water.

The rope began steadily running down the stairs as if someone below was reeling it in. Knight came around a turn and found Cap waiting, the loop of rope in his hands, his face painted with a torn expression of worry. "What the hell took so long? I thought you bit the donut."

"Company arrived," Knight said.

Wes arrived, panting and out of breath. "What... are... wait... for?" he asked.

"You," Knight said as the pair descended the remaining steps and found the rest of the party huddled in the dark, Cap standing guard.

The small antechamber was unadorned, and the only exit was a narrow, almost inconspicuous cave. Cap took point again, this time with his gun in his hand.

As the party filed into the cave, the cool, damp darkness grew thick with the scent of earth and stone, and the persistent sound of running water filled the tight space. The passageway was smooth and sinuous, and there were no side passages.

After a hundred feet or so the cave branched into multiple corridors, each with unique characteristics. Using the Maglite, the companions examined the tunnels, trying to determine which route to take.

Some passages were wide and expansive, their ceilings soaring high above like the nave of a grand cathedral and adorned with stalactites that hung like nature's chandeliers. These stalactites sparkled faintly in the LED light, their crystalline structures reflecting a myriad of colors.

On the ground, stalagmites rose to meet them, creating columns that seemed to support the weight of the world above.

"It's like a labyrinth," Abby said.

Kamal grunted.

Other tunnels were much more claustrophobic, with walls that pressed in close and ceilings so low that the travelers couldn't walk upright in them. These narrow corridors wound and twisted unpredictably, and the rock was rough and jagged. In some places, the walls were adorned with delicate formations of flowstone, their rippled surfaces resembling frozen waterfalls cascading down the rock face.

"I guess we should just pick one," Cap said.

"I don't know," Knight said. "A pair could explore, anchor the rope here."

"What good will that do?" Abby asked. "We can see farther than a hundred feet."

"Good point," Knight said.

"We can always backtrack," Kamal added.

Knight pointed to one of the larger tunnels.

Wes took a turn on point, and the party continued, their headlamps blazing through impenetrable blackness.

The air got colder and more humid, a stark reminder that the companions were traveling down, not up. An unusual silence took hold as the sound of water diminished, but it was there, always disturbing the peace like an unruly dog.

Knight and his companions wandered about for hours, returning to their point of origin where the tunnels branched several times to reorient themselves. He was beginning to think Abby's proclamation that the caves were a maze was an understatement. A maze had a way out, a prize at its center, and Knight was beginning to doubt either of those existed in the current labyrinth.

The maze was filled with evidence of the massive geological movements that had shaped the underground world. Fault lines and fissures ran through the rock, their presence marked by abrupt changes in the terrain. In some places, the floor was a jumble of broken stone, the result of seismic activity that had fractured the rock and created new passages. These areas, where the Earth's crust shifted and heaved, added to the maze's complexity, creating new pathways, most of which led nowhere.

The party entered a broad chamber with many inflows, and they stopped to rest.

"Anyone need—" Wes's voice broke off as it boomed through the chamber like he was speaking through a bullhorn.

"A resonate chamber," Abby said.

"A what?" Kamal asked.

"Occasionally, pockets of trapped air within the rock create resonant chambers where even the slightest sound is amplified and distorted," Abby said.

The companions moved on.

Knight was surprised to see non-Salamantis life in the maze. Tiny, eyeless creatures adapted to the perpetual darkness scuttled along the walls and floors, and delicate fungi and lichens clung to the damp surfaces, drawing sustenance from the minerals in the rock and the moisture in the air.

"Are we lost?" Wes asked.

"No," Abby and Cap answered at the same time.

"We can still go back," Abby said.

"For what?" Cap said.

Knight sighed. He had no interest in wandering around lost until he died of starvation or was gutted by a Salamantis. At the same time heading back to the shelter and hoping that the rain would stop soon sounded like no plan at all. Not that wandering around in the dark was, but at least they were doing something.

The party plowed forward, and time slipped away, the companions growing more irritable, brittle, and tired.

Hope grew when the natural tunnels were left behind and the company trekked through a maze of hand-carved tunnels that made sudden turns and often backtracked on each other. But exploring these tunnels was easier because they were short and contained few natural obstacles like cave-ins and pits.

Wes disappeared around a turn and as the darkness peeled away, he screamed.

The head of a huge reptile, a dinosaur of some type, peered down at the party from the shadows above. Under the glare of the LEDs, the white flowstone looked gray, and if the sculpture had glowing eyes Knight would have soiled his pants.

The great beast had been molded from a huge splash of flowstone that poured off one of the chamber walls. As if emerging from the stone itself, the dinosaur appeared alive, the flowstone's translucent, milky hues contrasting with the rough, fossilized texture of the dinosaur frozen in the embrace of geological artistry.

As the headlamps drove away the gloom the heart of the maze was revealed to be a vast cavern that appeared to defy the confines of the earth.

"Kill your headlamps for a second," Cap said.

One by one the headlamps went dark, and as Knight's eyes adjusted, he saw bioluminescent fungi clinging to the damp walls which glowed with a soft, ethereal light. The fungi, thriving in the nutrient-rich environment, emitted a gentle, bluish-green luminescence that highlighted the intricate details of the cavern's formations. The ceiling rose to an impressive height, disappearing into darkness, while the floor was a mosaic of rock dotted with pools of crystal-clear water that mirrored the stalactites above.

Massive columns of flowstone and calcite rose from the ground, their surfaces smooth and polished by centuries of mineral deposits. The walls of the chamber were lined with shelves and ledges, each one a masterpiece of nature's artistry and adorned with delicate draperies of flowstone that resembled frozen curtains in mid-sway.

"Incredible," Abby said as she turned her headlamp back on and pulled her water bottle.No other passageways terminated at the chamber, and at the center of the cavern, covered in drips of melted stone, there was a gold pyramid. Knight judged the structure to be fifteen feet tall at its apex, and the gold appeared real. Though it was smooth and worn, and flecks of gold surrounded the pyramid like snow, there were no bare patches of stone, which told Knight the pyramid wasn't gold-plated or painted.

"Somewhere Pugari's ears are ringing," Kamal said.

That got a laugh that echoed through the cavern until it was consumed by the sound of running water.

There were rectangular blocks of stone, like pews, around the pyramid as if a crowd had once assembled before it. Closer inspection revealed that the pyramid was indeed made from gold bricks, their mortar joints worn away by the elements and time. There was a gold door with a tiny round hole, and the stop symbol, which the party hadn't seen in some time, was skillfully etched into its center.

"There's something in there," Cap said as he closed one eye and stared into the keyhole-like opening.

"Let me see," said Knight. Within the hole, there appeared to be a stone button that could only be accessed by using a finger or a stick or rod.

"An old school lock," Cap said as he stuck his finger in the hole to press the button-like stone within.

Knight grabbed his arm and pulled it back.

As if the Salamantis horde was somehow in tune with the happenings in the central chamber, a series of cackle-screeches carried into the cavern.

"They must have followed us from the karst," Kamal said.

Knight nodded. "Let's open it up."

21

Knight had a pocketknife with a plethora of tools packed into its casing, one of which was long enough to poke the rock button within the keyhole on the golden pyramid's door.

Abby, Kamal, Wes, and Cap watched eagerly as Knight pushed the screwdriver into the opening and wiggled it around.

At first, nothing happened.

Knight pushed, jerked, and thrust the tool into the hole.

A crack burst from within the pyramid and slowly the door began to rise as the sound of stone rubbing stone filled the cavern. When the doorway was open, Knight thrust his head through the opening, his headlamp filling the space beyond with LED light.

There was a counterweight of stone and the mechanism was primitive when compared to the combination lock that had protected the underground complex. "It's just a stone rod that releases the weight when removed." Knight stepped into the pyramid.

The space was empty save for a narrow shaft at the center of the floor, and about it, there were three stone lizard statues, palms out as if containing whatever was in the narrow hole.

"Careful," Abby said as Knight stepped forward and peered into the shaft. It was four feet around, and if there had been a ladder or rope providing access it was long gone.

Knight's headlamp beam disappeared into darkness. "Hand me the rope," he said.

"Do you really think it's a good idea to just drop down there? You don't—" Abby stopped talking when Cap put up a hand.

"Give him a minute," Cap said as he handed over the rope.

Knight took one end of the rope and handed the other end to Cap. Then he dropped his end into the hole and played the rope out through his fingers.

Abby snickered and said, "I get it now."

When the end of the line hit the bottom of the shaft the rope went slack.

"How many feet would you say we have left?" Knight asked.

Cap used the spread of his arms to measure the remaining line, and said, "We've got about forty-five feet."

"Damn," Knight said.

"What am I missing?" Wes asked. "We've got a hundred feet of rope?"

"Right," Cap said. "And if we tie it off on one of the statues, how will we retrieve the rope when everyone is at the bottom?"

"Oh," Wes said.

"We drop ten feet," Abby said matter-of-factly. "The folks at the bottom can help those..." She looked at Kamal. "The folks at the bottom can help the athletically challenged among us."

"Will that work?" Cap said.

"If we loop the rope around one of the statues, that means the double length will reach about forty-five feet into the shaft," Knight said. "Plus the lengths of our bodies."

"And we drop the rest of the way," Wes finished.

The sound of dripping water filled the pyramid, and when nobody spoke Cap went to work preparing the rope for the rappel into the shaft. The big man said, "Everyone listen up. I'm going to twist the line together, but if you notice it slipping, let me know."

Harsh breathing filled the small pyramid, the party shuffling about as Cap worked. He looped the rope around one of the lizard person statues, and then roughly ten feet out from the anchor began loosely twisting the line together, making it one. When he was done, he tied the end and tossed it into the pit. "Who's first?"

"I'll go," Knight said. "I can help everyone except you two." Knight pointed at Cap and Kamal. "You dudes are too heavy."

"I'll go last," Cap said.

Knight holstered his gun and grabbed his dry bag, the cylinder of his mini-scuba tank ringing when it grazed one of the statues.

"Wait!" Abby said.

Knight froze with his back to the pit as he prepared to drop into the hole.

Abby was staring at the open doorway. "Should we close the door?"

Cap nodded as he squeezed through the assembled and examined the counterweight system. "I can close it," he said. "But..."

"But what, Cap?" Knight said. "Spit it out."

"Do we want to?" Cap said. "Yeah, it will keep the creatures from following us, but it would slow our escape should one be necessary."

Knight nodded.

"And what about Pugari and the others?" Kamal said. "What if they're behind us?"

"Pugari and Lucca are smart folks. They'll figure out the lock the same way we did," Abby said.

"If they have time," Kamal countered.

"Leave it open," Knight said.

To that, nobody had anything to say.

"See you at the bottom," Knight said as he pushed off and began his climb.

The shaft walls were smooth and unadorned, and there was nothing natural about the hole. Though smooth, Knight saw the chisel marks of the ancient workers who had excavated the pit. But why? That question just wouldn't leave him be.

As the rope slipped through his fingers, and the scent of moisture and must assailed him, his mind wandered, and he recalled the dwarves in The Lord of the Rings opining about delving too deep into Moria and releasing a horrific evil. Is that what the ancient race that built the complex had done?

The rope ran out and Knight dangled from its end, his headlamp jumping around and illuminating the floor below. It looked like more than ten feet, but there was no turning back. He took a deep breath, relaxed like he was getting sucked under a wave while surfing, and dropped.

Knight hit the stone floor, rolled, and came to a stop against a wall. His ankles screamed, and his calf muscles ached, but as he got to his feet and stretched the pain eased. He looked up and saw Cap's face staring down at him.

"Are you alright?" Cap yelled.

"Fine." He didn't tell his companions that Cap's calculation had been off a bit, and it was more like a fifteen-foot drop, minus the length of one's body.

Next came Abby, and Knight was able to break her fall.

Wes went slowly and helped Kamal, who struggled to lower himself with his hurt wing still in a sling. The rope squeaked and twisted under the strain of the two men, but when they dropped to the floor, they were both unharmed.

Cap made fast work of his climb, and as he untwisted the rope so he could retrieve the line he said, "There's only one way?"

"Looks like it," Abby answered.

The fellowship was packed into a ten-foot by six-foot stone chamber that looked to be part natural and part manmade. A narrow crack in the bedrock was the only exit, and etched crudely into the stone all around the thin cave mouth were hexagons with a hand palm out at their center.

Cap looped the rope over his shoulder and drew his gun.

Harsh breathing filled the space as Knight worked himself into the crack. It was tight, but the cave beyond opened up, and though he had to bend over, he was able to walk.

LED light blazing, the narrow gash in the bedrock looked to have been helped along by something other than nature. As the companions worked their way through the cave, some sections had clearly once been so narrow that nothing bigger than a rat would have gotten through had these narrow areas not been widened. There were also spots where shaped rocks had been placed like paving stones to fill gaps in the floor.

The sound of crashing water grew.

Cap said, "What do you figure all that gold is worth?"

Knight harrumphed. "The find is sure to be preserved and studied, and I doubt the pyramid will be moved, and if it is, it'll go in a museum, not to a smelter."

"If we get out of here to tell our tale, you mean," Kamal said.

The tunnel had no tributaries, and the group went on in silence, the roar of water growing.

A splash of water washed over Knight's boots, and he stopped walking.

The tunnel ahead was flooded.

"Great," Wes said.

"Come on. Maybe it's not that deep," Knight said.

Wishful thinking was kin to hope, and the party had only gone twenty feet before they were knee-deep in water and the LED lights revealed the reality that the passageway was flooded to its ceiling.

"There's a natural dip in the tunnel," Cap said. "Probably caused by eons of flooding and the stone in the area must be more porous than the rock surrounding it."

At that moment Knight could have cared less about geology.

"We've still got mini-scuba kits, right?" Kamal said.

"Two and they're more than half empty and we don't know how far we'll have to go," Cap said.

"In the dark," Abby added.

Knight nodded solemnly. The flashlight and the headlamps weren't waterproof, and they'd have to be stowed in the dry bags.

"Third time's the charm for our rope," Cap said. "I'll go first and check things out." He dropped his dry bag and waited.

Knight opened his bag and gave Cap one of the two mini-scuba kits which he'd carried all the way from Antananarivo.

"We're already drenched to the bone so there's no sense in stripping down," Cap said as he stowed his headlamp and gun, tied the rope around his waist, and accepted the small cylinder with the regulator at its top from Knight. He slung his dry bag over his shoulder and clipped the mini-scuba unit to the rope via a carabiner. "I'll only use oxygen if I have to," he said.

Knight nodded.

Cap waded into the dark water up to his neck before looking back, giving the crew a thumbs up, and disappearing beneath the surface.

Tiny waves closed out on Knight's legs as he stared into the gloom. A minute slipped away. Two. Three. Knight's skin began to crawl as if covered with imaginary ants. Throughout the entire ordeal underground, he'd never once thought about what he would do without Cap. But now, as bubbles popped and snapped on the surface of the water, he began to despair.

Five minutes later Cap emerged from the water, panting, the mouthpiece of the mini-scuba in his mouth. The rope was still tied around his waist and as he pulled the mini-scuba's mouthpiece free he said, "It's far. Forty feet, easy." He handed the mini-scuba to Knight, who noted that the gauge on the cylinder read one-quarter full.

"Did you notice any air pockets up toward the ceiling? Any openings at all?" Wes pressed.

"Nothing," Cap said. "But don't sweat it. We can share."

And that's exactly what the team did.

Cap and Wes went first, sharing a scuba unit, and when they were through the watery clog, they anchored the rope, which Kamal, Abby, and Knight used to make fast work of their swim while sharing the remaining tank of air.

When all five members of the party were on the opposite side of the flooded section, they drank their fill as they ate power bars. The sound of crashing water drowned out all other sounds, and the air was so thick with moisture it left a cool coating on every surface.

Headlamps blazing once more, Cap leading, the companions pushed on, the cave becoming nothing more than a natural crack in the foundation of the Earth.

To Knight's surprise and delight, the tunnel angled upward, and the party found themselves slipping and sliding in the wet muck that coated the floor.

After trekking for half an hour, the companions reached a vast chamber where the cave terminated. A thin waterfall flowed from the mouth of a huge lizard person statue carved from the rock, the water landing on a flat stone at the base of the waterfall before continuing into a pool. The colossal sculpture, standing seventy feet tall, had detailed features that appeared lifelike in the dim light filtering through the cavern.

Stalactites and stalagmites surrounded the waterfall, and every surface was wet. The constant roar of water filled the cavern, and the pool rippled and foamed from the crashing water as a column of gray

126

light angled into the grotto from the darkness above. A broad natural tunnel lay to the left of the waterfall, with several narrow cave-like fissures branching off a stone platform. Every sound the party made echoed through space announcing their arrival.

"Look at these," said Cap. The big man dropped into a catcher's crouch as he traced the floor with his index finger.

Bootprints trailed across the cavern floor to the large natural tunnel to the left of the waterfall.

"Hello! Anybody there?" called Abby.

There was no response except the echo of her own voice.

"The prints could be Pugari's," Kamal said. "Lucca's feet are smaller, and Tank would be dragging his wounded leg a bit."

"Let's find out," Cap said.

Soaked to the core, fingertips shriveled like dried prunes, Cap walked toward the large tunnel mouth, gun up as he followed the single track of footprints.

Knight and the others fell in beside him, and as they left the waterfall behind and entered the tunnel the coppery scent of blood filled Knight's nostrils, his vision dancing from being in the dark for so long.

The bootprints led into darkness, and as the companions delved deeper the shriek of a Salamantis trailed after them.

"There's something there," Cap said.

Knight strained to see, and as his headlamp peeled away the darkness he squeaked.

A dark form lay on the floor before them.

Abby screamed.

Knight rushed forward, danger forgotten.

The walls and floor were splattered crimson, though the blood had dried and looked black under the stare of the LED lights. A dry bag had been torn open and its contents scattered about, and what remained of Pugari's mutilated body lay sprawled on the stone floor.

22

Knight knelt beside what remained of Pugari's corpse, a sense of dread settling over him like a dark shroud. The once muscular frame of his employer was a twisted, slashed-up, broken mess, his brown face frozen in a mask of agony. His arms were missing, and broken bone, gristle, and blood leaked from the stumps. The corpse's legs were bent at unnatural angles, and what skin remained was torn and mottled with bruises.

The stench of death and decay filled the air, a sickening mixture of viscus fluids, sweat, and despair. Bile rose in Knight's throat, and the metallic tang of blood and the sourness of death filled his mouth as he bit the inside of his cheek. He reached out and touched Pugari's face, and the skin was cold and clammy. Knight stared at the pool of blood on the floor and the splatters on the wall and the red blindness of anger seeped over him.

Abby turned away, her hand covering her mouth.

Kamal stepped closer, a grim expression painted on his dark face.

"We need to stay focused," Cap said. "The Salamantis that did this might still be lurking nearby. Clearly, the creatures haven't finished with this... kill."

Another surge of hot anger and fear fought for control of Knight's thoughts. Their team had been reduced again, and the unity they'd forged now seemed fragile, shattered like Pugari.

The contents of Pugari's dry bag were scattered about the tunnel, and his gun was on the floor beside his body, un-fired.

As Wes collected the items and stuffed the Glock in his waistband, he said, "The thing must have caught him unawares. It doesn't look like he put up much of a fight."

"No, it doesn't," Knight said.

The wide natural tunnel had been molded by something other than time and water continued into darkness.

"What are we going to do..." Kamal pointed at his boss's corpse.

Knight hiked his shoulders and said, "There are no stones to cover him and no way to bury him, and burning... We've had this discussion before, unfortunately."

"We're just going to leave him?" Kamal said, but the big man didn't sound very upset. All the fight appeared to have drained from him, and he leaned to the left like a sinking boat, his wound pulling him down. "I'm... free."

Knight said nothing. In a shadowed stretch of waiting, he'd come to know Kamal and the man's story haunted him. It was a horror of Kamal's own making, yet somehow darker than Abby's.

Born in the slums of Mumbai to impoverished parents, Kamal had turned to thievery because survival left him no other choice. He'd ended up in the infamous Tihar prison, where Pugari found him and offered a deal he couldn't refuse: freedom in exchange for a lifetime of servitude. Knight suspected Kamal had never imagined that it would be Pugari's death, not his, that would end their bargain.

"Should we go back and look for Tank and Lucca?" Cap said.

Knight looked back over his shoulder. "I didn't see any other tracks coming in here, did you?"

The murmur of running water and the faint whistle of the breeze filled the cave.

Cap said, "There was only one set of tracks."

"But we didn't search the surrounding alcoves and tunnels," Knight said.

"It's clear what happened, isn't it?" Abby said. "When we all got separated Pugari ended up on his own somehow. As to how he got all the way down here..." Abby threw up her hands.

"Regardless," Knight said. "We have to go back and give the grotto at least a cursory inspection."

"And when we don't find anything?" Kamal asked.

Knight pointed past Pugari's corpse down the tunnel.

"Fair enough," Wes said. "I'll start back and—"

A cacophony of braying and shrieking rang through the cave and the tunnel mouth that led into the cavern with the waterfall filled with glowing eyes. The darkness ahead appeared free of menace.

"So much for heading back," Wes said. He took point, gun ranging back and forth as the tall man eased into darkness, his headlamp pushing away the blackness.

Cap didn't wait for orders and followed.

"*Om Namo Narayanaya*," Kamal said as he bent and closed Pugari's eyes.

The Salamantis horde cautiously worked their way into the tunnel, claws scraping on stone, the hiss and clicks of their breathing carrying down the passageway.

"We need to go... my friend," Knight said. He put a hand on Kamal's shoulder and the big man nodded and got to his feet.

"See you in another life," Knight said. Then he turned from Pugari's corpse and followed Wes and Cap without looking back.

Abby waited with Kamal, but Knight had only gone a few feet before he heard their footfalls and labored breathing behind him.

The creatures shrieked and argued as they bounded up the tunnel.

Knight looked back, his headlamp painting the scene in garish black and white. The Salamantis horde was closing quickly as the knot of beasts fought their way forward, the creatures crawling over one another and fighting for position, their jaws snapping, antennas flopping wildly.

Heart pounding in his chest, Knight clenched his jaw as he broke into a run. The others followed suit as the cave widened and plunged steeply downward. There were no bootprints here, but the vertical slashes that marked the passage of the Salamantis were everywhere, and the companions slipped and slid in the thin coating of damp muck that covered the cave floor.

As the fist of creatures drove down the tunnel their echoing wails and snarls grew louder, their claws clacking against stone.

Cap called from further ahead. "Knight, what do we do? They're almost on us."

Knight's mind ranged through his limited options. The tunnel behind them was blocked by the horde, and the darkness ahead was unknown. He spared a glance over his shoulder and what he saw gave Knight the answer. The beam of his headlamp revealed a field of eyes and teeth twenty yards behind him.

"Stand your ground!" Knight yelled as he skidded to a stop, turned, planted his feet, and aimed his weapon at the charging creatures.

The rest of the fellowship did the same, and soon Knight's ears were ringing with the thunder of gunshots.

Smoke and grit filled the tunnel as the Salamantis horde surged forward, their guttural shrieks exploding through the cave. Monsters crumbled as exoskeletons cracked and shattered, bullets tearing through the creatures' long bodies. The monsters climbed over their dead, but as the beasts went down their corpses blocked the passageway and slowed the horde's advance.

Knight's Glock clicked empty, and he slipped in a new magazine, chambered a round, and continued firing. Aiming precisely wasn't necessary.

The wave of creatures filled the cave, a breaking mountain of teeth, claws, and powerful snake-like tails. As he fired, sweat dripped down Knight's back, each shot reminding him the party now had one less bullet.

When the pile of Salamantis corpses fully clogged the tunnel the knot of creatures was momentarily impeded. The beasts dug through their dead, trying to slip through every gap in the tangle of Salamantis bodies.

"That's enough," Knight yelled. "Let's make like a tree."

The fellowship didn't need to be told twice.

Cap led, followed by Wes, and soon the group was bounding down the tunnel again, the calls of the Salamantis horde fading.

The passageway gave way to a cavern so vast that the ceiling was lost in shadow. In the center of the cave stood what looked to be a gnarled tree with branches that twisted and reached out like skeletal fingers. Its leaves were a sickly shade of gray, and there was no sound save for the constant rush and murmur of water running down the walls. The air was thick with the scent of damp earth and something else, something metallic and acrid that made Knight's eyes water. Knight stared open-mouthed, unable to wrap his noodle around what he was seeing.

Cap approached the tree cautiously, gun up.

The tree bark was covered in strange markings, symbols that seemed to writhe and shift as if alive.

A chill leaked through Knight, and when the distant call of a Salamantis tore through the chamber he looked back, but the tunnel mouth was dark.

"Be careful," Wes warned, his voice low and urgent. "There's something not right about this."

"You think? A tree three hundred feet underground," Abby scolded.

Cap, unable to resist the pull of curiosity, reached out a hand, hesitating only for a moment before touching the gnarled bark. The moment his fingers touched the odd tree he recoiled. "It shocked me," he said.

A low rumble filled the cavern, growing louder and more intense with each passing second. The ground beneath their feet trembled, and loose rocks skittered across the floor and a stalactite broke free.

The spear of stone landed on a section of the giant tree, which broke apart like paper mâché. Leaves shattered, the shards falling like rain as branches cracked and broke, their log-like forms crashing to the cavern floor and exploding into projectiles of flying stone.

Knight dropped and covered his head. The ground steadied as he was pelted with pieces of the stone tree. Dust filled the cavern as Knight pushed to his feet.

Abby shuffled forward into the cloud of dust as she coughed.

"What the hell was that?" Wes said. "An earthquake?"

"I don't think so," Cap said. "But…"

"Yeah," Knight said.

"It's petrified," Abby yelled through the dusty haze.

"Is that possible?" Knight asked. "We're damn deep here, no?"

Abby said, "Petrification turns wood into a stone-like substance, but it takes a very long time. The process usually begins when a tree dies and falls, becoming buried under sediment such as volcanic ash, mud, or sand. But there are many examples of standing trees being petrified when a sinkhole, or karst, caves in or is buried by water rich in minerals, especially silica."

"I've seen the painted desert," Cap said.

"Great example," Abby said as she wiped drool and dirt from her chin.

"The mineral-rich water makes French Toast," Cap said.

Abby chuckled, and it was a welcome sound. "The mineral-rich water flows through what remains of the tree, and over time the water deposits silica and other minerals in the wood's cellular structure. As the organic material of the wood decomposes, it's replaced by minerals that create rock-like formations that retain the intricate details of the original wood."

"You think this was a sinkhole?" Wes asked.

"No," Abby said. "We're too deep. But maybe this entire section of bedrock dropped in the distant past."

"Because of excessive water erosion?" Kamal said.

"Possibly," Abby said. "I think—"

She was cut off by a Salamantis call that carried from the passage the party had just exited.

There was only one other passable tunnel that terminated at the odd space, a thin crack that a human could barely fit through, and with one last look at the petrified tree, Knight ran, his dry bag slapping his back, his muscles protesting from lack of rest.

Lucca came awake with a start. The waterfall thundered, and she thought she heard the faint echo of a scream. She nudged Tank and said, "Wake up."

Shrieks and wails filled the cavern and the tapping of scuttling claws on stone rose above the hum of moving water and the static of the waterfall.

"They're coming!" Lucca yelled as she inched to the edge of the alcove she and Tank hid in.

Tank rubbed sleep from his eyes as he tried to get to his feet. He grunted and slid back onto his butt, his wound reminding him who was in charge. "Where's Pugari?" he sputtered.

Lucca rocked back like she'd been punched as she looked around, but she saw no sign of Pugari.

A Salamantis horde burst into the cavern, the creatures pouring from the tunnel and down the steps Lucca and her companions had used. Beasts also appeared in the large tunnel mouth straight ahead, their glowing eyes cutting through the gloom.

"Can you walk?" Lucca said.

"Do I have a choice?"

"There's always a choice," she said. "We could try and hold them off, but…" Her voice trailed away as she stared into the gloom and tried to count how many creatures she saw, but they were moving too fast and shadows danced in the gloom.

Tank used the wall for leverage and pushed to his feet. "What about Pugari?"

Lucca hiked her shoulders but said nothing.

Tank grabbed his dry bag, tossed Lucca her bag, and said, "Which way?"

Several caves trailed away from the central chamber on both sides of the alcove, and Lucca went left. She had no reason and saw nothing indicating that the tunnel she chose was any different than the others. It was the closest and with a field of glowing eyes bouncing across the chamber there wasn't time for planning and risk management.

Tank fell in behind her, groaning and struggling, but the cave she chose was too narrow for two people to walk abreast so she couldn't help him. The waterfall and the calls of the beasts faded as the partners battled on and the cave widened.

"Do you think he's alive?" Tank asked.

The partners both had their headlamps off and Lucca felt her way through the darkness, using the light sporadically for very short durations to map the path ahead. "I don't know," she said.

It was slow going, and the partners were forced to rest frequently because of Tank's injury. His fever was the same, and he was still hurting, but the little sleep he'd gotten had brought color to his face and he claimed he felt better.

The sound of water had fallen to a low hum when the duo slipped from a narrow cave into a chamber where many tunnels converged. A main tunnel trailed away straight ahead, and to the right and left there were other tunnels of various sizes. But none of that was what made Lucca want to scream with joy.

There were bootprints in the dust that covered the floor of the chamber, and they were fresh.

"These prints have to be from our group," Lucca said as she went about studying the various types of prints. "At least five people were here. Maybe more."

"And it's easy to see which way they were going," Tank said between gasps of pain.

Footprints trailed down the main corridor into the room where the tunnels converged. The chamber Lucca and Tank had just entered.

From there things got more difficult, but Lucca probed several tunnels and found backtrack trails of prints, and after much trial and error Lucca identified the tunnel she believed her lost companions had taken.

"And lookie here," Tank said.

There was a staff of wood lying on the floor, its bark stripped off, its end gnawed to a point. "I'll wrap a shirt around the end and make a crutch."

"Hurry," Lucca said. "I want to catch up to them before..." She smiled at Tank but knew he couldn't see it in the darkness. Before you can't go on. She drove the thought away.

23

The party squeezed into the cave, Cap leading the way, rock biting their skin, but the stone was slimy and wet, and even Kamal was able to get through. Headlamps illuminated the dark passageway, which was nothing more than a crack in the bedrock. The calls of the Salamantis horde chased after them, but even the smallest of the beasts that Knight had seen couldn't wedge through the tunnel he and his companions had just squeezed through.

A puff of air chilled Knight's face, the sound of rushing water growing as the group eased their way forward, moving around outcroppings and navigating a floor that shifted and lifted like an amusement park ride.

The cave ended abruptly at a drop off where another large crack cut vertically across the party's path. Roughly hewn steps trailed down into the chasm, and water leaked into the crack from many points along the fissure's length. Ahead the cave appeared to peter out to nothing.

No discussion was needed, and Knight didn't insult his companions by asking. At this point, the group was in too deep, and heading back, which all would agree was the smartest thing to do, was such a distant reality Knight wouldn't spend a moment's thought on it.

Though Knight couldn't help but wonder if the rain had stopped above. He glanced back at Kamal and found the man watching him.

"If anyone wants to hold post here and wait for us, that would be fine," Knight said.

Nobody spoke.

"O.K. then," Knight said.

Headlamps and Maglite blazing, the party descended the narrow steps and soon found themselves in another tunnel. The passage had been meticulously excavated, and a series of petroglyphs and ruins covered the walls. Many of the images were similar to the carvings at the pyramid's entrance, and they appeared to tell the story of the race of beings who had once called the massive underground complex home.

The sound of crashing water filled the passageway as the fellowship exited into a vast cavern, unlike anything Knight had ever seen.

Knight and his companions stood at the edge of a vast body of water reminiscent of a large lake or bay. The shoreline was eroded and irregular, and it was made up of soft golden sand and scattered shells, the remnants of creatures from ages past. Miniature waves crashed without pause, creating a deep and melodic sound that chanted through the vast grotto. A breeze blew off the water and dusted Knight's face with fine sand as he gazed in wonder.

The huge chamber was bathed in a soft, blue light as if the sun had set and the moon had risen simultaneously. Knight breathed deep, the air crisp and clean. The scent of earth mixed with water pervaded the air, and there was a hint of ozone, like the smell after a thunderstorm.

Constant electric light resembling the aurora borealis filled the sky-like ceiling of the cavern. The pseudo sky appeared to be composed of a conglomeration of nebulous vapors that stirred with constant motion that created an unusual light, and yet it was not like the sun because it gave no heat.

Electricity crackled and hummed, filling the air with a perpetual, low buzzing. Jagged wavy streaks of blue and white spidered over dense clouds that concealed the cave's roof. The phenomenon produced an astonishing play of light and shade, and beams of the odd glow knifed through the gloom like mana from heaven.

At the center of the vast lake, an immense structure of flowstone towered over the chamber. It was a colossal formation of rock with a wide base that disappeared into the water. The obelisk-like structure had been carved and smoothed at its middle, only to widen at its top where it disappeared into the odd clouds.

The party stood on a small expanse of beach. All the cavern's sides were made up of jutting headlands and massive cliffs weathered by crashing waterfalls that spilled into the huge underground bay from hundreds of points like a giant strainer.

"Wow," Abby said.

"You can say that again," Wes said.

"Wow."

"Is what we're looking at... possible?" Cap said. "The light I mean."

Knight shrugged. "If I hadn't seen it with my own eyes I'd have said no, but..."

"Let's see what there is to be seen," Cap said.

The party walked along the edge of the subterranean lake, towering rocks to their right, stacked like colossal steps. From these rocks, countless waterfalls cascaded down, eventually turning into gentle streams that flowed into the lake. Wispy clouds of steam rose sporadically and drifted over the boulders, indicating the presence of hot springs that also flowed into the massive reservoir, providing heat in this damp, dark, cold place.

Tiny waves lapped gently on the shore, the sound echoing through the cavern like a heartbeat. Knight said, "Is it me? Or is it very quiet in here?"

"Yeah," Cap said. "Where are the beasties?"

Knight led the group up a thin path to a steep outcrop atop which there was an odd forest. The trees were tall and straight, with branches reaching up like the top of an umbrella. The wind that dusted Knight's face with sand didn't affect the trees, and they remained motionless as if frozen or petrified.

"They're huge mushrooms," Abby said as she rushed past Knight. "I've never heard of mushrooms this big, but the Lycoperdon giganteum can reach nine feet in circumference."

Kamal's eyes widened as he looked up at the towering fungi. "These are fifty feet tall!" he exclaimed.

Hundreds of massive mushrooms covered the top of the cliff, their thick caps blocking out most of the light. Beneath their canopy, darkness ruled, and there was no underbrush. The air was thick with a damp, earthy scent and the ground was soft under the party's feet, as if they were walking on a sponge. The towering fungi pulsated with life, the gills on the underside of their vast caps rippling with each passing breeze.

As the fellowship left the mushroom forest, they were greeted by more wonders that challenged what Knight thought he knew of science and nature. Huge ferns, their leaves dark green, and a variety of mosses clung to the stone walls. There were no full-grown trees, but here and there stunted palms fought for life under the odd light created by the phenomenon that dominated the roof of the cavern.

"What does this place remind you of?" Wes said.

"Nothing like this has ever been documented," Knight said. "Though I believe you're right. It was theorized somewhere by someone..." Knight's nerves were a jumble, and his long-term memory was offline.

Abby said, "Photosynthesis, the process by which plants convert light energy into chemical energy, requires specific wavelengths of light, primarily from the visible spectrum. While some organisms can thrive in environments with minimal light, such as caves or deep-sea habitats, they often rely on alternative energy sources like chemosynthesis or bioluminescence."

"And yet." Wes pointed at the sky.

"We're not sure what we're looking at," Abby said.

As the slash-like prints of the Salamantis began appearing in the grit and sand that covered the ground Knight's thoughts turned to the question of why wasn't the cavern filled with the creatures?

Knight called a halt when the party had circumnavigated a third of the great lake. With the waterfalls grumbling, the wind whispering warnings, and the lap of the lake stroking his nerves, the tension in Knight's stomach and neck eased as he ate.

Wes dug out the binoculars and went to work studying the flowstone obelisk at the center of the lake. "You should check this out, boss."

Wheat Thin handed the field glasses to Knight, who pressed them to his eyes.

The structure looked more obelisk than flowstone, though the entire monument appeared to have been chiseled from a huge column that was created when a massive stalagmite met a stalactite and the two became one. There were no symbols or decorations on the side Knight could see, but there were openings of all sizes and shapes. The obelisk's surface was pocked and perforated, creating a latticework of openings like a giant beehive. These openings ranged in size from snake holes to large apertures that could accommodate larger creatures. Light filtered through the perforated surface, casting delicate, lace-like shadows on the water's surface and walls.

The lake's expanse rippled as its water reflected the obelisk above as it tapered away into the clouds. This reflection created the illusion of an endless monolith, stretching infinitely into the depths below. Its base was rooted in a small island of stone covered in a thin layer of luminescent moss, its soft, greenish glow spilling over the water.

Knight gave the binoculars back to Wes and said, "Saddle up. We need to find a way to get a closer look."

When the party had gone halfway around the base of the lake, the tall cavern walls still disappearing into the clouds, a waterfall crashing on the boulders behind them, the companions found a bridge that spanned the lake and ended on the rock island supporting the flowstone obelisk.

The bridge was a marvel of nature and craftsmanship, blending seamlessly into the subterranean environment. Its main pathway was constructed of cut stones hewn from the same rocky bed that formed the cavern. Though the blocks were irregularly shaped, they were meticulously fitted together like a puzzle. Along its edges, the bridge was lined with rough-hewn railings, carved to mimic the natural flowstone of the cave's formations.

What truly set the bridge apart were its supports. Instead of manmade pillars or columns, the bridge rested upon massive stalagmites that rose from the lake, their rugged and textured surfaces covered with milky flowstone. They were varied in height and girth, some towering upwards with sharp, needle-like tips that met stalactites, while others were rounded and squat, their tops smoothed by the ages. Knight thought the bridge looked like it had grown out of the cave's natural formations, each stalagmite unique, their surfaces adorned with intricate patterns of mineral deposits that glistened in the LED light.

"Wait here," Knight said. "Abby, with me. You're the lightest." Knight inched onto the bridge, probing and jumping, but the way ahead was solid.

The bridge was only wide enough for a single person, and the span curved gently, following the natural contours of the cave as the pair advanced. Knight gazed over the balustrade into the abyss of dark water that rippled below, the faint breeze stirring the flashing dark clouds as the bioluminescent fungi clinging to the bridge shimmered and cast fleeting shadows across Knight's path.

So it was that the pair didn't realize the crest of the bridge was missing until they came upon it. The empty gap was at least thirty feet. Way too far a jump for a man or Salamantis.

Knight dropped into a crouch and trained the Maglite on the broken edge where the fitted stones had fallen away. "There are chisel marks all along the edge. Do you see them?"

"I do," Abby said. "You're saying the bridge was intentionally razed?"

Knight said nothing. It was obvious why the bridge had been destroyed.

"How are we going to get across?" Abby asked.

He smiled, the warm glow of pride and love leaking through Knight. There was no question of whether they should cross. It was a foregone conclusion that they were close to the end of the line and there would be no stopping now. What that might mean scared Knight more than he wanted to admit, but without fear there is no greatness. "Don't worry," he said. "I've got a plan."

24

Sales wasn't Knight's bailiwick. Wheat Thin often told him if he showed a little more enthusiasm and wove a bit of fiction and hope into his tours, Badlands Dinosaur Adventures would be more successful. But when he felt strongly about something and was certain that his path would lead to the prize, Knight was as persuasive as a politician after a disaster during an election year.

The fellowship arrived at the gap in the bridge and joined Knight and Abby. The newcomers looked dubious.

"We need to do a Tyrolean traverse, but it's going to be a challenge getting our rope anchored on the opposite side," Knight said.

"Is our rope strong enough? Long enough?" Kamal asked.

Knight nodded.

"How can we help?" the big man asked.

"Go find me a rock," Knight directed, using his hands to illustrate the size—about half the size of a football. He scanned the area, searching for the perfect candidate. "Preferably with a hole in it," he added, gesturing with his fingers to indicate the desired size, which was big enough for their rope to fit through.

Kamal and Cap went in search of a stone.

"Abby and Wes, you can help me," Knight said.

Wes and Abby worked in perfect tandem, uncoiling the one-hundred-foot climbing rope and carefully laying it out on the bridge.

Meanwhile, Knight fashioned a makeshift pole by tying together the two remaining wooden staves carried all the way from the sinkhole. After some adjustments and measurements, he ended up with a roughly ten-foot pole.

"Pass me a carabiner," Knight instructed. Abby handed him one, and he snapped off the gate, leaving a flattened hook. He then attached it to the end of the pole.

Kamal and Cap returned with a stone, about twice the size of a softball, but it had no holes.

"Will this work?" Cap asked as he lifted the stone.

"Perfect," Knight said as he exchanged the hook-pole for the rock and explained his plan to his partners.

"What else?" Kamal asked.

"Nothing," Knight said. "You and Cap are the heaviest, so you're done. Give Wes the pole."

Cap grunted but nodded as he handed the makeshift device over.

With cautious steps, Wes tested the remnants of the bridge for stability. The stones held up under his weight, and as he inched to the edge of the broken span, Abby followed him.

When he got to the gap Wes lay flat on his stomach, extending his hook-pole over the treacherous break. Eighty feet below the water was a dark void, and the lake shimmered in the odd electric light that leaked over the cavern.

Abby held Wes's long legs and braced her feet in a crack that ran across the bridge's deck.

Knight secured the stone to one end of the rope and swung the rock like a bolas as he planted his feet and widened his stance for maximum power. He launched the rock across the open span, aiming for one of the gaps between the carved flowstone railing spindles that clung to the remains of the bridge.

The rock fell short. He drew in the line and retrieved the rock, his heart beating so fast his eyelids were vibrating.

His next throw also fell short, and frustration bubbled inside Knight, spreading through his body like a fever. He gritted his teeth and redoubled his efforts.

On his nineteenth toss, his arm rubber, the stone hit the balustrade with a crack and bounced between two thick spindles, the rock plummeting toward the lake and drawing the rope through Knight's fingers. He waited a three count before gripping the rope tight.

The line went taut, the rock bounced up and then swung over the lake, the dark blue light casting a long shadow on the rolling water.

Wes missed snagging the stone on its first pass, and the group was forced to endure five seconds of silence and waiting as the rock swung like a pendulum and came back toward Wes. He almost got it the second time, but it bounced off the hook, kicked to the side, and appeared to lose momentum.

On the fourth swing, with the stone barely making it far enough, Wes jerked forward, extending the pole out as far as he could.

Abby tugged on his legs and pulled him back, but Wes was determined, and he thrust out the pole and caught the rope on the carabiner hook.

From there it was easy to tie the ends of the rope together with the loop around a strong railing spindle. Wes was the first to use the rope crossing, and one by one the adventurers inched across the chasm like ants, the rope sagging under their weight.

Cap was the last one across and as the five companions dusted themselves off the distant calls of the Salamantis rang through the cavern.

"Let's go," Knight said as he drew his gun.

Wes and Abby led as the fellowship crossed the remainder of the bridge, and Knight breathed a sigh of relief as he stepped onto land.

The island the monolith was rooted in rose from the water like a lonely stone turtle, its rocky surface covered in a thin layer of moss. The soft, greenish glow of the moss spilled over the island and cast a gentle light on the lake.

Waterfalls pounded stone and the distant calls of the creatures got louder and more frenzied. The party climbed boulders and sections of snowdrift-like slabs of flowstone as they worked their way to the monolith, their feet glowing green from the moss.

As the fellowship drew closer to the formation, wind gusted over the lake, streaming through the holes in the obelisk, and the monolith hummed with a melodic vibration that rattled Knight's bones.

"Look over here," Abby yelled.

On what Knight believed to be the northern side of the obelisk, there was one hole larger than all the others at the structure's base, and around its edge were symbols and images the party knew well, all except for one.

The pictograph showed lizard people, their reptilian forms depicted in fine detail, each scale and claw rendered in stone. They stood in a solemn procession, their bodies slightly hunched as if bearing great weight, and above them loomed a black sun. A Salamantis horde surrounded the lizard people, but there was no sign of battle. Large hexagon shapes with a hand palm out at their center were chiseled across many of the pictographs.

"Is that a reference to the eclipse?" Kamal asked as he pointed at the odd pictograph with his good arm. He still wore the sling, which was so dirty the original color of the t-shirt used to make it was no longer discernable.

The cacophony of taunting beasts carried through the cavern.

"It appears to be," Abby said. "But there are no date markings, no indication that detail the eclipse cycle. No star charts and such."

"So they had no idea why the sun went dark or when. What does that mean?" Wes asked.

"I don't know," she said. "But the more I see, or rather, don't see, I think the eclipse has nothing to do with the sleeper species awakening. Knight is right. There was a coincidence one time, and the ancients turned it into myth. At least that's where my money would be."

"But you have no real proof of that," Kamal said.

"Look around," Abby said. "Do you see anywhere sunlight could affect this place?"

Kamal gazed up at the odd aurora borealis sky and said nothing.

Knight appraised his team. They were dirty, hungry, dehydrated, and rundown, and they each had an array of bumps and bruises that would have sidelined most professional athletes. He shined the Maglite into the large opening and darkness consumed the LED light.

The obelisk towered above the party, resembling a narrow beehive with its porous and pitted surface. Its honey-gray stone glinted in the electrical light, casting shadows that danced across the moss-covered ground and seeped onto the still waters of the lake and the rocky walls of the cavern.

Wisps of mist engulfed the obelisk's base as Knight reached out and touched the rough stone. A faint vibration thrummed beneath his fingertips, and a low hum filled the air as everyone stepped back.

Creatures poured from tunnels all around the cavern, as if the Salamantis horde was controlled by one mind. The beasts bunched up on the shoreline of the lake, and none of the creatures ventured into the water.

Blue beams of light sparked from the undulating clouds, and Knight and his team watched in horror as the cavern was inundated. Creatures scaled the walls, crawled over stones, and tore through the mushroom forest and surrounding vegetation like locusts.

But still no Salamantis ventured into the dark waters of the lake.

"They're afraid of water? How ironic," Abby said, her eyes jerking around as she tried to track all the monsters at once.

A weak snicker escaped Knight's lips.

"It makes sense, really," Abby said.

"How?" asked Cap. He had his gun up, but it wasn't aimed at anything.

"As easy as the Salamantis might perceive water as its birth, they could also see it as an ending," Abby said.

"Their death?" Knight asked. Then he realized how stupid his question was and added, "If they die."

"Right," Abby said. "If water is somehow associated with their long sleep, fear of it seems like a reasonable reaction."

Like ants looking for food, the creatures swarmed the bridge, the beasts mounding over each other as two of the creatures tumbled off the broken span into the lake. The monsters hit the water hard, where they struggled for a few seconds as they tried to stay afloat before sinking like stones.

An eager Salamantis probed the length of rope that still spanned the gap, testing its strength. The brave beast stepped off the bridge onto the thin double line and fell into the drink and drowned like its mates.

Knight plunged into the obelisk, his companions on his heels.

Lucca burst from the tunnel, tumbled down a rocky embankment, and landed face-first in water. It wasn't deep, and she flipped herself over and crab-walked into deeper water.

A flurry of creatures burst from the tunnel like yellow jackets streaking from their hive, but the horde pulled up short when it reached the water's edge. The beasts climbed and crawled over each other, their claws screeching on stone.

Lucca backed further into the dark water as the beasts hissed and shrieked at her. She was in a vast cavern filled with a huge primordial lake. At its center, a column of flowstone streamed from the water and pierced the nebulous clouds that emanated an unearthly light. She raised her gun and aimed it at the tunnel mouth she'd just exited. Her nerves crawled. Tank had been right behind her.

Gunshots blazed from the tunnel, the glow of a headlamp painting the tunnel mouth gray. Then Tank was there, gun blazing as he tore through a knot of beasts and lurched from the cave.

Lucca got to her feet, her legs and arms scraped and bleeding from her fall. She raised her Glock, which was soaking wet and dripping, and she prayed it would fire.

Her prayers were rarely answered but on this day they were. The gun boomed and bullets smacked into the advancing Salamantis horde.

Tank half stumbled, half rolled down the scree pile of stones that led to the lake, Lucca picking off creatures and clearing his way, bullets ricocheting around, sparks flying, gun smoke filling the air.

Lucca smiled as Tank limped toward her.

A flash of movement above Tank drew Lucca's eye as a Salamantis peeled from the side of the cavern like a wraith, its skin changing color as it moved.

Tank swung his weapon around.

Lucca aimed and fired, but it was too late.

The Salamantis leaped from its perch, claws out, tail waving, jaws flexed open revealing needle-sharp teeth.

Tank screamed and fired as the monster hit him, but the shots punched into the stone floor. A sickening wail echoed through the cavern along with the sound of crunching bone and tearing flesh. Tank disappeared under a mound of creatures, the man yelling and screaming as he was torn apart.

Lucca fired, her shots taking down beasts, but she stopped when she realized she might hit Tank. As blood splattered stone Lucca thought that might be a good thing, but still something stayed her hand. Her feet were cemented to the lake bottom, tiny waves rolling across her legs, her muscles cramping with dehydration.

The creatures pushed aside by the fray spotted Lucca and advanced to the water's edge, but no further.

Lucca turned away from Tank. There was nothing she could do for him, and when his screaming fell silent, she made the sign of the cross, though she didn't believe in God. She stalked further into the dark water and didn't look back.

When the water reached her shoulders, she floated on her back, staring up at the odd lights that filled the sky, the glow filling the huge cavern with a blueish-white light. She balanced her dry bag on her stomach as she carefully opened it and stowed the gun before resealing the bag. Then she slung it over her shoulder, twisted onto her stomach, and stroked through the dark water toward the obelisk at the center of the lake, the creatures shrieking behind her.

She lost herself in her swim as she recounted her recent journey and questioned her relationship with Pugari for the thousandth time. If they got out of this she was quitting, and she'd never have to see the slug again.

Her life had been a series of pitfalls; some she'd managed to escape, others had swallowed her whole. After a failed relationship and the death of her mother, she resigned from the police force and drifted across the globe, picking up private security jobs. That's when she met Pugari. He was charming at first: fair, generous, even likable. But by the time she realized she was working for a dirtbag, it was too late. She was in too deep, cornered by the choices she'd made, complicit in more than a few of his dirty dealings.

What did any of it matter now? Pugari might be dead.

Lucca didn't know how much time had passed, but her arms ached when she found herself swimming beneath a thin bridge carved from the flowstone that made up the cavern. A climbing rope spanned a broken section of the bridge, and a thrill of excitement burned the tips of her fingers and toes.

With a new sense of urgency, she swam on. When she realized her face was wet not only from the splash of lake water but also from her tears, she pushed away thoughts of what might be swimming in the depths below her and swam harder.

25

Knight lurched to a stop. "Did you hear that? Was it a scream? Gunshots?"

"The wind," Cap muttered, and the guy had a point.

As the party's headlamps battled the darkness, a gentle breeze drifted through the open holes, slits, and crevices of the towering obelisk and brushed Knight's skin. The wind carried the faint scent of water and ancient stone, and the eerie melody made Knight's skin prickle.

A short narrow tunnel led to a vast room that resembled an ancient audience chamber, and the air grew cooler and damp, the scent of earthen stone strong. The ceiling soared high above, supported by massive flowstone columns intricately carved with serpentine patterns and symbols of reptilian lore. Their surfaces sparkled with traces of mica and other minerals that caught the severe LED light.

The floor was a smooth expanse of stone tiles, each meticulously placed and polished, though now they were covered with a coating of dust and grit and the slash marks of the Salamantis were everywhere. Geometric patterns decorated the floor tiles, and along the room's perimeter, there were low stone benches that provided seating for the audience that might once have gathered to witness grand ceremonies or debates. The benches were carved with scenes of daily life and mythological tales, depicting the lizard people in various activities, from hunting and gathering, to worship and ritual. Knight noted that the benches were several feet away from the cavern walls. To accommodate tails?

Mutilated Salamantis corpses littered the room, and blood covered the floor and splattered the columns and stone accouterments. Many of the creatures were missing limbs, though even in death Knight saw the regeneration process still at work. Bloody stumps were forming into blastema, and gashes and holes were filled with the white scab-like process of cellular dedifferentiation. The stink was like a fish store's dumpster.

"What happened here?" Kamal asked.

"A frenzy would be my guess," Abby said. "Most likely upon waking."

At the far end of the chamber, a grand dais rose from the stone like a natural formation. It was the focal point of the room, and it was accessed by a series of wide, shallow steps. Behind it a colossal bas-relief stretched across the wall, depicting a pantheon of reptilian deities in a dynamic tableau of power and reverence. The deities were rendered with an astonishing level of detail, their scales, claws, and eyes so lifelike Knight envisioned the creatures stepping out of the stone.

A series of ingeniously designed sconces and braziers, placed at strategic intervals along the walls and columns, revealed a level of intelligence that wasn't present in other areas of the subterranean complex. These fixtures were crafted from stone and appeared to have been designed to hold candles or pools of bioluminescent algae. Shadows danced and flickered, the party's headlamps creating an ever-changing play of light and dark that made the carvings move.

Knight had been trapped in darkness so long, his circadian rhythm had unraveled. Exhaustion clung to him, and a rising wave of anxiety blurred the edges of reality, shadows began to take shape where nothing existed. He shook his head, trying to steady himself as he drew in a deep, shaky breath.

The murmurs of the fellowship echoed through the hall as if the chamber had been engineered to carry sound with perfect clarity. Even the softest whisper could be heard from one end of the room to the other.

Throughout the vast hall, niches and alcoves pitted the walls, and Abby paused to stare at a broken statuette on the floor that appeared to have fallen from one of the alcoves. She touched it, and the piece crumbled, a puff of dust rising from its remains as if there'd been a tiny explosion. Many of the nooks had piles of rubble in them, some of which had precious stones and shards of gold within.

"These niches would have displayed statues and idols, along with other sacred items," Abby said.

Knight nodded. "Most ancient cultures created effigies representing revered ancestors and legendary figures, and many of the statues I've seen were adorned with precious stones and metals, their eyes often inlaid with gems. We touch nothing," he said. Knight's gut told him that was the right thing to do for several reasons, some of which were anchored in reality and some that weren't.

"I've got a little battery left on my cellphone," Abby said. "Do you want me to document this place? Take some pics?"

The scream of a Salamantis broke the stillness and it was answered by several others.

"Do it fast," Knight said.

Despite the age and isolation of the chamber, it was remarkably well-preserved, and it appeared protected from the water that flowed through the rest of the underground complex. The chamber was dry as a popcorn fart, and the stonework was solid, the carvings on the walls and pillars sharp and clear. Though the air was musty, it was free from the smell of mold, and only the rotting Salamantis corpses and kicked-up dust poisoned the air.

Knight felt like he was standing in a place of great significance, created by a civilization whose history and culture were still shrouded in enigma. Every surface, every detail, told a story, and his mind spun with the possible history of the beings who had once gathered here.

A loud beep echoed through the room. "Phone's dead, but I got the good stuff," Abby said.

There were staircases sculpted from stone on both sides of the dais. One plunged downward, the other headed up.

The party paused before the dais, Knight's light deprived mind conjuring a lizard shaman preaching to a room full of subjects.

"What did you mean before when you said frenzy?" Cap asked. The big man hadn't spoken in some time.

Abby said, "I was thinking of bees. Frenzies often begin with a sudden, heightened activity within the hive or a specific area, as if an invisible signal has been sent through the colony. In the case of bees, this frenzy can be triggered by various events, such as the arrival of a new queen, the discovery of an abundant food source, or an intruder threatening the hive. In the case of the Salamantis, I believe the trigger is waking from their long sleep."

"Great," said Kamal.

"What doesn't make sense..." Abby paused as she looked around at the Salamantis corpses littering the floor. "Usually, within the organized chaos of a frenzy, there's a sense of urgency and purpose. Worker bees communicate through rapid, intricate dances, sharing information about the location of nectar or the need to defend the hive. Guard bees become more aggressive, their movements sharp and deliberate as they patrol the hive's entrance and perimeter. Foraging bees hasten their collection of nectar and pollen, flying in and out of the hive." She paused again to let her statement sink in, before adding, "What we never see with bees is cannibalism, or bees attacking and killing each other."

"Have you ever heard of anything like this?" Cap asked.

Abby and Knight snickered.

"There are many examples," Knight said. "Sharks for one. During feeding frenzies, sharks can become so aggressive and competitive that they bite and kill each other."

"Add piranhas to the list," Abby said. "They'll turn on each other even when food isn't scarce."

"Stress, environmental factors, and food supply play a role," Knight said. "Rats can be cannibalistic under high-stress conditions, often leading to fatal encounters."

"And don't forget chickens," Abby said.

Wes laughed and said, "Chickens? Like, cluck cluck?"

"In crowded conditions or under extreme stress, chickens will engage in cannibalistic behavior known as "pecking," where the animals peck each other to death," Abby said.

The roar of a Salamantis killed the discussion and everyone looked to Knight.

He was so tired of making decisions his head hurt, but as he considered his options the local fauna once again decided for him.

A Salamantis appeared on the staircase leading up, the LED lights painting its tall shadow on the wall. The beast's triangular head jutted out, its forelimbs cycling around, its claws scratching stone as it moved.

Knight surged forward and bounded onto the steps that went down, his companions falling in behind him.

The monster screeched.

Knight broke into a jog, and then a run as he took the steps two at a time.

The stairs emptied onto a platform with four tunnels winding through it. Knight didn't pause; he ran into the central tunnel, the footfalls of his companions beating the ground behind him, dust filling the air.

Headlamps lit the interior of the ancient obelisk, where whispers echoed in every shadow, and the countless tunnels of various sizes wound and twisted like the delicate holes in a chunk of Swiss cheese, each passage a secret. The stone walls were cool to the touch, their surfaces often etched with pictographs that danced and shimmered in the flickering LED light which cast long, ghostly shadows along the tunnel walls as the fellowship fled.

Several of the passageways opened into chambers, some vast and cavernous, others intimate and cloistered, each space unique yet interconnected, like the synapses of a giant, sleeping brain. Most of these rooms were empty save for piles of sand and debris, the remains of items that once decorated the spaces.

Knight burst into a chamber containing a pool of crystal-clear water that reflected the ceiling's ornate carvings, creating an illusion of depth. The pool rippled gently, disturbed only by the flow of water from above, a reminder of the world outside and the rain. Judging by how wet the stone was around the inflow, Knight figured that the stream of water had been much stronger recently. Around the pool, stalactites and stalagmites reached out like fingers, their surfaces glistening with minerals that created a subterranean rainbow that defied the darkness.

All the tunnels were natural in origin, their walls smooth and curved, shaped by time and the wind that wove through the obelisk. Some passages were narrow, and the party was forced to squeeze through tight spaces, while other caves gave way to wide, airy tunnels where the ceiling disappeared into the darkness. The acoustics in these spaces amplified the smallest sounds; a footstep, a whisper, the rustle of fabric—into a symphony of echoes that blended with the incessant breeze, creating broken music that was eerie and enchanting.

As the party fled deeper, the tunnels became more treacherous, with sudden drops and narrow ledges that appeared out of the darkness. Yet, despite the danger, Knight felt a sense of awe, a feeling of being on the brink of discovering something profound, something that had been hidden from the world for millennia.

The group came around a wide turn and found a dead-end. It wasn't common for a tunnel the group had traveled to lead nowhere. Some passages had backtracked on each other, but it was only the second passage they'd discovered without an outflow.

A cacophony of yelling and arguing creatures carried up the tunnel.

Knight reached the end of the passage, the natural wall before him smooth and dry.

It was then Knight noticed he no longer heard the faint static of moving water.

When the entire fellowship stood at the dead-end, Knight said, "Let's head back to the—"

"Knight!" Cap was at the rear, and he started firing before Knight saw the cause of the man's dismay.

A Salamantis horde blocked the party's retreat, but the creatures moved slowly, like they were in a daze, almost as if they were sleepwalking.

Cap's shots took down the two creatures at the front of the pack, but the others didn't seem to care. They came forward like shuffling zombies, several rows deep as they pressed down the corridor.

"They look... lethargic," Kamal said.

"They could be ectothermic," Abby said. "Meaning their body temperature depends on the environment. In cooler temperatures, maybe their metabolism slows down, making them sluggish."

The hum and muffled arguing of the creatures pushed down the passageway as the creatures got closer.

150

"But that's not what I think it is," Abby said. "Bees near the end of their life cycle often move more slowly as they approach natural death."

"Or hibernation?" Wes asked.

Abby hiked her shoulders.

The tunnel ahead was clogged and the party put their backs to the wall that blocked their forward progress.

"O.K.," Knight said. "We've only got one option. Lock and load."

Lucca crept into the dark maw of the obelisk like Sam Gamgee sneaking into Minas Morgul, hunched over, beaten, and silent. Her quarry's footprints trailed through the dust, drips of water from her swim pelting the ground. She was cold, and the gun in her hand felt overly heavy.

The huge chamber stretched into the distance and its fineries slowed her progress to a crawl, her weakening headlamp beam revealing epic pictographs and the trail left by Knight and the others.

She made her way through the room and stopped before the grand dais, staring up at the pictogram that loomed over the ancient stone stage. It all reminded her of her church back home.

The Catholics sure did know how to put on a show. The pageantry, the clothes, the hats, the incense, the drinking of the blood of Christ. As she stared at the lizard shaman who stood arms raised and thrust out, snout turned up, she saw a priest telling people to do as I say, not as I do.

Yet still Lucca felt the urge to kneel and say a prayer, but whatever God the ancient lizard shaman prayed to had forgotten this place long ago.

Gunshots carried up from a staircase to the left of the dais and it jerked Lucca from her reverie. She scanned the floor and saw the bootprints of her fellow travelers disappear down the same steps.

She jumped down the stairs, moving as fast as she could, her breathing coming in ragged bursts, her wet clothes chafing against her skin, her weary muscles protesting.

More gunfire as she ran through the twisting tunnels. There were spots where the footprints of her companions backtracked over one another, but she ignored them. The sound of shots being fired was unmistakable in the confined space, and she had no doubts about what direction she should go.

Her headlamp suddenly grew extra bright, and the LED light pushed far down the tunnel. The light grew dim and grew bright again before sputtering out, its battery finally giving up the ghost.

Lucca was plunged into impenetrable darkness, and it was then she noticed that she no longer heard the faint roar of the waterfalls outside the obelisk. She groped on in the dark, using the walls as feelers, following the distant sounds of gunshots and turmoil. She nearly fell several times as she slipped, got her feet caught in cracks, or tripped over raised sections of the tunnel floor, while the walls angled inward above her.

She squeezed from a particularly narrow tunnel and spilled into a passageway filled with a cacophony of yelling, shrieking creatures, and the pop and crack of gunshots. There was a cloud of light to her left, and Lucca pulled the magazine free from her Glock and checked it for the thousandth time.

At last count, she had eight bullets left. There was already a round in the firing chamber, and she slammed the magazine home as she pushed to her feet and ran toward the fray.

26

The fellowship had their backs to the dead-end wall, and when Knight's gun clicked empty, he yelled, "Cease fire!"

The nearest dead Salamantis was fifteen feet away, and beyond that frontrunner there was a scattered field of corpses that blocked the tunnel. Beasts fought and clawed to get through the pile to no avail, but the maggots churning in Knight's stomach didn't slow. They were trapped.

"Do you hear that?" Cap said.

Gunshots and squealing creatures echoed down the cave from beyond the clog.

Forelegs burrowed through the top of the pile as the creatures began pulling away the remains of their fallen brethren.

Pop pop. Two fast shots and the cycling arms fell still.

Knight looked around at his companions. Nobody had fired.

"Hello," Knight yelled.

"Knight?" It was Lucca. "Knight!"

A series of emotions fought for control of Knight's flagging body; joy, anger, worry, concern, and then disbelief. He yelled, "Lucca?"

Lucca didn't respond but only laughed.

Twenty minutes later, the companions had managed to dig away some of the Salamantis corpses and create just enough room for the fellowship to wriggle through.

It was Knight's worst experience to date in the subterranean dungeon. Viscera and blood leaked through the pile onto him as he squeezed past a crushed Salamantis, its abdomen open, its head half gone. Claws, broken bones, and chunks of cracked exoskeleton rubbed and scratched him as he fought through the dead creatures. When he squeezed out on the other side, he felt like he'd crawled through a sewage pipe.

As the party dusted themselves off, cleaned and loaded weapons, and buttoned up their gear Lucca told her tale from the moment of the breaking of the fellowship to the present. "When Tank died... was murdered, I figured it was safer to stay in the water. So I swam to the island, saw your rope, your footprints, and I followed."

"Pugari is dead. Did you know?" Kamal asked.

Lucca's eyes strayed to the floor, and she said, "No."

With the recounting of the dead done, feelings filed away for later, and thoughts of giving up buried deep beneath a mental callous where healing would never occur, the companions backtracked up the dead-end tunnel and found a new route.Wes and Kamal led, followed by Lucca and Abby. Then came Knight with Cap watching their backs. Nobody spoke. What was there to say? What they would do when they got to the end of the road was a question for another time.

Knight was lost in his thoughts as the group trudged on, each new passageway plunging further downward. The air held a crisp chill, and the faint gurgle of water and the push of the wind were the only sounds. Air currents pressed through the lower tunnels, and they were surprisingly strong. Knight figured it had something to do with the narrowing of the tunnels, which would increase the atmospheric pressure. Barometric pressure decreased with increasing altitude, so he had to assume the reverse was true. Also, he knew weather patterns could affect things, and who knew what types of odd weather the electrical cloud cover in the cavern could produce?

Wes called a halt when the passageway ended at an organ-like chamber, the big main space pocked by hundreds of holes of varying sizes. But that wasn't what caught the attention of the fellowship.

An archway lay straight ahead, its dark maw fixed within the jaws of a giant stone Salamantis head. The triangular head and its two antennas leapt from the stone, and sharp teeth hung like icicles, the beast's dark eyes staring forward as if guarding what lay beyond.

Long stone legs arched across the walls, the Salamantis's narrow body surging from the stone.

No orders were needed. Cap took point and plunged into the Salamantis mouth.

The short passage ended inside an alcove of stone that looked out upon a vast cavern unlike any other, a sanctuary carved from the living rock. Its entrance, a wide and low cut channel in the stone, was worn by centuries of water flow, and its straight path contrasted starkly with the round cavern. The cavity's walls resembled a gigantic beehive. Countless hollows and depressions dotted the surface, each one varying in size and depth, giving the cavern an almost organic appearance as if it had been painstakingly carved by the meticulous work of ants. Or the Salamantis.

Abby murmured, "The main hive."

The party stood in one of the hollows, which was roughly eight by ten feet in size.

Sweat dripped into Knight's eyes as he stared. The hive's ceiling arched gracefully overhead, forming a nearly perfect dome. Every sound reverberated, creating an eerie echo that stroked every nerve in Knight's body.

Like veins, narrow outflows were scattered throughout the hive that led away from the main chamber, each one winding its way into the dark unknown. Some were wide enough for a person, or something bigger to pass through, while others were mere slits, impassable to all but the smallest creatures.

LED headlamps filled the darkness, creating patterns on the pocked walls, highlighting the intricate textures, and casting shadows that danced as the light shifted. In the deeper recesses of the cave, where the LED light barely reached, darkness hung heavy, yet the gleam of the slimy substance coating everything defied the blackness.

Knight turned on the Maglite, but it didn't help much. He panned the light around, searching for… what he wasn't sure.

Wes let loose with a scream that turned into a bellow. He pointed and Knight shifted the beam of the Maglite.

A Salamantis was motionless within one of the nooks that filled the sides of the round hive. A thick, almost translucent slime, like clear concrete, held the beast in place, its eyes closed. Spidery veins of various colors sprouted from the walls of the creature's protective cocoon and found their way through the thick slime and pierced its body.

"One that didn't wake," Abby said.

Water poured into the chamber from a large hole in the ceiling, but like the other water inflows Knight had recently seen the flow appeared to be significantly diminished. Drips of water also leaked from most of the empty nooks, as if they had recently been filled with water.

Knight noted the dormant creature still in its cocoon was dry.

Kamal groaned and fell onto his butt.

Abby rushed to help him. "He's exhausted and his wound has gotten worse. He needs to rest."

Kamal opened his mouth to protest, but a stern look from Abby made him think better of it.

Knight inched to the open end of the alcove and peered over the edge. The slimy substance that coated everything was plastered all around the nook's opening, as though something had broken free. He turned the Maglite on the notch where the group hid.

Garden hose-like veins hung from the ceiling and walls, their white flesh free of color. A dark liquid dripped from several of the veins.

"What now?" Cap asked. "I don't see any gold."

"Not of the traditional type, anyway," Abby said.

All heads turned toward the woman.

"I'm guessing the biological gold down here might be very valuable," she said.

"I see," Lucca said. She put her finger beneath one of the dripping veins and it turned black. She wiped her digit clean and added, "This stuff… It's blood? Whatever, and that," she said as she strode across the alcove and touched the slime. "And whatever that is. This stuff keeps them alive for hundreds, maybe thousands of years. You're telling me the big brains couldn't use the stuff for something?"

"A fountain of youth?" Wes said. He sounded mesmerized, but perhaps it was his exhaustion and hunger.

"You're saying we should take samples?" Knight said. "That'll take time."

"What's the rush?" Cap said as he glanced at Kamal.

"How are you feeling, Kamal?" Knight asked and to his surprise he got an honest answer.

Guys like Kamal were trained from birth that showing weakness of any kind is bad, but Knight figured the big man had spent too much time with him and his group and their ways had rubbed off on him. He said, "Not too good, boss."

Knight pursed his lips. Though he hadn't given it any thought, with Pugari gone he was officially in charge.

Despite the decreased inflow, the sound of crashing water filled the hive, making it difficult to talk. "Huddle up," Knight said.

The fellowship crowded in tight.

"Wes and I will get the samples. Abby, do we have containers that will work?" Knight asked.

Abby nodded.

"O.K. Abby, take care of Kamal's wound while Lucca and Cap take inventory of our remaining supplies."

Nodding heads and murmurs of agreement.

Headlamps were turned on, water and food were consumed, and then Knight went to work with two plastic water bottles. He and Wes collected the black blood-like liquid streaming from the veins and the plentiful slime that coated every surface.

He didn't know how much time had passed because when Knight consulted his watch, he found its glass face broken.

The party took turns sleeping, and the rest helped Kamal greatly, and soon the man was pestering Knight to move on.

Move on. But to where? The hive was the end of the line, no debate was needed there. And there would be no rescue if they stayed three hundred-plus feet below ground. He'd made up his mind to propose backtracking to the dry karst when Cap pulled him aside.

"Did you notice it's not as loud in here anymore?" the big man asked.

He hadn't, but he did now as Cap's voice carried through the hive.

"That stream of water isn't what it was," Cap said.

Knight walked to the open end of the alcove and stared out into the darkness, his headlamp peeling away the blackness. The inflow of water leaking from the hole in the hive's ceiling had diminished to a strong trickle.

"Maybe it stopped raining," Cap said.

"Maybe."

Knight took a second turn sleeping and when he woke, he found his companions in the midst of a serious debate. He kept his eyes closed, listening, but it wasn't much of a debate because the group had few options. Stay or go back. Then he realized he could hear his companions whispering from ten feet away and he sat bolt upright.

"You're awake," Abby said.

The sound of flowing water was nothing more than a faint trickle.

"We've been talking," Wes said. "We think we're ready to head back."

Knight looked toward Kamal, who nodded.

A hollow silence consumed the hive, and Knight heard the breathing of his teammates for the first time in a long time. He vaulted to his feet, bolted to the edge of the nook, and turned on the Maglite.

The flow of water from above was nothing but a drip, and it made no sound that Knight could hear.

In the newfound silence, the wind meandered through the round, flute-like hive, conjuring a symphony like the gentle exhalation of the Earth. The peaceful melody transformed from a whisper to a song as the cave became an instrument, the initial notes delicate and airy, reminiscent of a distant flute playing in a grand concert hall.

As the song gained momentum, the pitch rose, and the melody became more intricate. The hollows on the walls started to sing, each contributing a unique tone. Some cavities produced high, clear notes that pierced the air like a bird's call, while others emitted deeper, richer tones that vibrated the stone.

Knight thought of Close Encounters of the Third Kind. Specifically, the ending when the aliens played their odd music, their song not just a random assortment of sounds but a carefully orchestrated piece of music conceived to communicate. But Knight didn't think that was the purpose of this song.

The melody ebbed and flowed, swelling to fill the cavern, then gently subsiding into a murmur. Ever the masterful musician, the wind adjusted its tempo and intensity, exploring every nook and cranny of the cave. Lower, more hollow notes emerged, harmonizing with the higher pitches to create a rich tapestry of sound. These deeper tones pounded through the hive, their vibrations felt as much as heard, adding a primal element to the song of the Salamantis.

As the wind picked up, the song reached a crescendo, the air moving at its peak speed, producing a powerful sound that filled the entire cave. The notes blended in a harmonious yet tumultuous symphony, the high-pitched whistles intertwining with the deep, resonant booms as the cave walls vibrated with the energy of the music.

"When the rain stops, they sleep!" Abby yelled.

Knight licked his lips and rolled his shoulders. "And to sleep they'll come back to the hive. Get your stuff together. It's time to make like a tree."

27

The first Salamantis tentatively poked its head from one of the many passages that led into the hive, as if the beast had been hanging around waiting for the call. With a squeak that echoed through the chamber, the eager newcomer secured a location in one of the alcoves, its ruby eyes glowing in the darkness.

"Is it musical chairs?" Wes asked.

"What?" Kamal said as the man winced and he put his hand over the wound on his shoulder.

"You didn't play musical chairs when you were a kid?" Knight said.

Kamal stared at Knight like he had four heads.

"Kids game," Abby said. "But it's brutal reality, really."

"Brutal?" Cap said. "That's a bit of a stretch, no?"

"Can someone just tell me what we're talking about?" Kamal said.

Lucca sighed loud and hard. "You have a circle of chairs, one less than the number of people playing the game. Music is played, and then the players must try and get one of the seats when the music stops. The player left standing is out of the game, a chair is removed, and the process repeats until one person is sitting on one seat."

"If not brutal, certainly a life lesson," Abby said. "When I was a kid, I remember hitting the floor, crying. My friend pushed me. My friend!"

The song of the Salamantis ran through the cavern, the wind twisting through the many passageways and holes, the series of booms, squawks, and whistles so close to orchestrated music it made Knight's skin prickle. Flute music was usually soothing, but the cacophony that played the caves like a saxophone rubbed the nerves raw with sudden changes in volume and pitch, almost as if the sounds were an odd language.

"But to answer your question, Wes, who the hell knows?" Knight said. "If new creatures are born each cycle, it's possible there might not be enough..." He looked out on the pocked walls of the hive. "There might not be enough spots for all of them and it could be first come first served."

"And the early arrivals, like our guy there, might have to defend their spot," Cap said. The creature that had crawled into its cocoon hadn't moved or made a sound.

"We don't know how many of them there are," Abby said. "What their life cycle is. Shoot, we're not sure what they eat when humans aren't on the menu. Has anyone seen a single creature drinking water?"

To that, nobody had a response, and the companions went about packing their gear and tending to their guns.

"What's the ammo and food situation?" Knight asked. They had plenty of extra guns, but they weren't much use without bullets.

Cap said, "We've got grub for four days thanks to our reduced force, and one hundred and twenty-three rounds, which I distributed evenly amongst us. Everyone has a full fifteen-round magazine, one in the chamber, and a few stragglers."

"Who got the extra three rounds?" Kamal said.

Cap smiled. "Me."

"Knight," Wes said. He was keeping watch at the edge of the alcove, staring into the darkness of the hive beyond, his headlamp off.

"We're out of here in five," Knight said as he pressed to his feet and joined Wes.

More creatures had worked their way into the hive and were taking alcoves just as the first beast had.

"Yeah, we need to get out of here," Knight said.

"Not yet," Wes said. "Give me the Maglite. I'm going to risk some light."

"Make it fast," Knight said as he handed over the flashlight.

"Look at the top of the hive. Where the water was flowing in," Wes said. He pointed the Maglite at the top of the hive, turned it on for three seconds, and then killed it.

In that flash Knight took a mental picture that he studied in his mind's eye as blackness pressed into the alcove, his eyes adjusting to the abrupt changes in light.

"Did you see the thick flow of slime dripping from the hole and coating the walls?" Wes said.

Knight felt the others behind him, so he chose his words carefully. "It looks like it's going to take a long time for the stuff to coat the entire hive, but yeah, I saw it."

"The creatures likely won't all come at once," Abby said. "It could take days."

"And what happens when it starts raining heavily again?" Kamal asked.

"That... stuff appears to be filling holes like caulking," Knight said.

"And the water will be blocked," Cap said.

"Or redirected," Abby said as she turned and stared at one of the vein-like hoses hanging from the alcove's ceiling.

A screech carried through the cavern and that was the fellowship's cue to sling their bags and move out. They followed their own footsteps and encountered moderate resistance as they backtracked, always driving upward. Shrieking and braying carried through the subterranean passages, but the beasts the party encountered were slow and mostly unresponsive unless confronted, which was often necessary to continue.

"I'm not surprised by the lack of heavy traffic," Knight said. "Not only did the song just start, but remember the lake, the broken bridge."

"You're saying they can't get into the obelisk?" Cap said, his voice laced with hope.

"Not necessarily," Abby said. "There could be access points above."

Knight recalled the stairs on the opposite side of the dais in the great hall that went up.

Without the constant sound of moving water, the song of the Salamantis took center stage. The flute-like music lulled Knight into a false sense of peace, only to jar him from it with booms deeper than explosions and high-pitched shrieks that went through him like the sound of fingernails being dragged over glass.

The companions ran out of luck when they reached the obelisk's main audience hall. A steady stream of creatures screamed and argued as they fought for position in the hall, as if unsure which way to go, the faces of the stone lizard people staring down at them with distant eyes and blank expressions.

Creatures poured from the stairs on the opposite side of the dais.

Cap fired and Wes fell in behind him as the two men blazed a trail across the vast chamber toward the exit.

Knight thought to stop them but didn't. If there was a way for the creatures to get into the obelisk above, that meant there was a way out, but the lake seemed like the safer route.

Lucca grabbed his arm as she surged forward and Knight followed, gun up as he selectively took out beasts who took notice of the group and decided they wanted to play.

Abby was at the center of the fellowship, helping Kamal, whose wound was still a hinderance.

Outside the odd aurora borealis-like light painted the cavern in a creepy blue glow, the luminescent moss covering the stones coloring their feet green as the company struggled over boulders. The bridge loomed ahead, the party's rope crossing still in place over the gap.

There were no beasts about, though there were still many creatures creeping around the edge of the lake, many of which were probing the bridge. Despite the cover of the lake, Knight figured there were too many of the beasts to attempt an escape that way. His thoughts drifted

161

back to the creatures streaming into the audience hall from the stairs that led up.

Knight said, "What's the plan, Cap? We swim?"

"To where?" Abby asked.

Knight took a moment to examine the lake's shoreline with the binoculars, but with only the odd glow from the clouds, their remaining three functional headlamps and one flashlight, he didn't see much. What he did see was getting into one of the tunnels along the lakeshore would require a swim, and probably just as much fighting as taking the stairs to the top of the obelisk. The difference was one was known, the other unknown... but maybe that was good. When he explained his thoughts to the group, he got only one comment.

Cap said, "Since we're not currently under siege, I think I should retrieve the rope." He looked up at the tall obelisk molded from flowstone.

"Agreed," said Knight. "Make it so."

Knight, Abby, and Kamal retreated and put their backs to a boulder.

Cap took control of the rope retrieval, and Lucca and Wes stood guard as he worked.

A collection of four creatures stood at the edge of the bridge's broken span, catcalling, scraping their claws on the broken stones, their tooth-filled jaws snapping at the air.

Cap held his Glock steady in his right hand as he fired four kill shots, the triangular heads popping and spraying nasty fluid over the remains of the bridge. Two of the corpses fell into the lake, and the other two collapsed onto the remains of the bridge.

A crack of violent white lightning illuminated the cavern, and for an instant, all the creatures froze as if caught in the glare of a giant flashbulb.

Cap tugged the rope and pulled the knot across the span as the loop cycled around the busted balustrades. When the knot arrived, he untied it, and with Lucca's help, he quickly spooled the rope before tossing the line over his shoulder.

When the group was together again there was no need for further discussion.

Knight rolled his shoulders, cracked his neck, and checked his gun... again.

"I'll take a turn on point," Wes said.

"I've got the rear," Cap said.

"Everyone stay tight," Knight said. "I don't want anyone getting separated from the group." What he left unsaid was, because there'll be no backtracking this time.

When the party reentered the obelisk, there was a steady stream of beasts flowing around the dais. The creatures moved as if in a trance, their triangular heads bent low as their fiery eyes stared at the floor.

The team covered each other, firing selectively as they worked their way across the chamber, following the path beaten into the dust-covered floor from the party's two prior trips through the grand hall.

Wes was the first to arrive at the dais, and he fired methodically, bullets punching into Salamantis heads, the creatures crying and wailing as life left them. He took position to the right of the stairs that led up and began firing up into the stairwell, clearing a path. When Wes was satisfied, he ushered the group forward with a wave of his hand and Cap took point as he bounded up the steps.

Next came Abby and Lucca, who supported Kamal on both sides.

"Let's go!" Knight yelled as he mounted the steps.

A human wail of pain cemented his feet to the bottom step as Knight looked back.

Wes had been driven back and was surrounded by a Salamantis horde. He fired, steady shots, most of which hit their mark as bullets ricochetted and sparks flew.

The knot of creatures surged, climbing over one another.

Then Wes was gone, swept under the fist of monsters.

Knight screamed, his throat burning as he squeezed the Glock's trigger as fast as he could, picking off triangular heads like he was playing a video game, his vision blurry with sweat and red with rage.

28

Lucca grabbed Knight's arm as he surged forward.

Knight ripped his arm free and looked at Lucca, rage heating his chest.

"He's gone," Lucca said, her dark eyes meeting Knight's.

The flow of creatures had eased as more beasts mounded atop Wes, and the *pop* and *crack* of gunshots carried down the stairwell.

Knight's stomach burned, his gaze jerking between Lucca and the horde of creatures pressing against the dais. Not that he didn't care about his other teammates who had been lost on their little foray, but Wheat Thin was like a brother. They ran... had run, Badlands Dinosaur Adventures together. Wes had helped him take an idea and make it a business, and now he would never see him again.

"Come on, Knight," Lucca said. "We don't want to fall too far behind."

Knight met no living creatures on the stairs, the glow of LED light leaking through the stairwell along with the occasional gunshot. After climbing fifty steps he reached a landing where he found his companions. Like below, the chamber marked the convergence of a knot of tunnels, the natural caves randomly twisting through stone.

Cap stood before three passageways that turned upwards, and as beasts appeared within their dark maws, he shot them. A steady flow of creatures was coming from above, and this both stoked and soothed Knight's raging nerves.

"Which one?" Cap yelled as a Salamantis peeled from the darkness, its color shifting as its claws cycled forward. The ex-soldier tapped the beast in its triangular head without taking his eyes off Knight.

"Let's hope last time is the charm," Knight said as he sniffed the center tunnel. Blood, rot, and something else... The righthand tunnel turned sharply up, too sharply. "We've been to the bowels of this instrument, now let's try and find the mouthpiece," Knight said as he darted into the lefthand tunnel.

The floor was smooth and sandy as if it had been filled eons ago to create a better path, and the rough surface made it easier to climb. There were sections where the incline became so steep the party had to crawl, and progress slowed.

Like the lower section of the obelisk, the monument was filled with chambers big and small, some showing signs of ancient habitation, others bare.

"Shiiittttt!" Knight screamed when he came around a bend and found no wall separating him from a tumble to the stones at the base of the obelisk.

Cap grabbed the back of Knight's shirt and pulled him back from the precipice, but Knight's dry bag swung off his back and fell into the abyss. He reached out to grab the bag, slipped, and teetered on the brink before toppling off the pathway.

Knight twisted and clawed at the edge, stone and sand falling into his face.

Then Cap was there, his red face framed above him as Lucca and Abby held the big man's legs.

Kamal kept inquiring beasts at bay as Knight was hauled back onto solid stone.

"That was too close," Knight forced out between breaths.

"You almost bit the donut," Abby said, and then the companions were laughing, and the sound echoed through that forgotten place only to be beaten down by the ragged melody of the Salamantis.

The vast cavern was filled with blue light, and it was much brighter so close to the glowing clouds. As Knight gazed down at the broken bridge, he estimated the company was two hundred feet above the base of the obelisk. All the waterfalls were nothing but silver trickles.

Though one side had broken away and was open, the passage the company had been following looped back into the obelisk. Cap led the group down the tunnel, and they came to a steep section that heaved up in a series of step-like natural breaks in the foundation stone. He stopped his climb halfway up, and Cap perched on a flat stone and helped the rest of the party.

Knight took point, the Maglite peeling away the darkness, the walls free of ornamentation. The song of the Salamantis shrieked and bellowed through the passageways, and beneath its constant call was the shrieking and arguing of the creatures.

A Salamantis dropped from the ceiling, the color of its skin shifting as it moved.

Knight skidded to a stop but didn't fire. The things had been moving slowly and he wanted to see if the—

The monster launched itself at Knight in a flash of claws and teeth.

Knight fired twice, and the beast crumbled at his feet, the remains of its head, viscera, and blood spilling over the slanted stone floor.

"Well, that one wasn't moving slow," Cap said.

Knight said, "Abby, sounds like you might be right about all that body warmth stuff."

"Ectothermic," Abby said.

The fellowship pressed on, backtracked, and argued, but there was one constant in their madness. They were going up. Steadily.

Twelve dead creatures later, the party arrived at a bridge that spanned a narrow chasm created when the obelisk was split, most likely from the inflow of water through its center. Like the bridge that led across the primordial lake, the center span had been knocked out. But as if the God of the lizard people were looking down on the companions the broken section was only ten feet wide, and the explorers leaped over it with ease, though the rope was utilized as a safety line.

Kamal squeaked with each step, and when he jumped across the span he landed with a muted scream and tumbled to the ground.

Knight worried that was it, and Kamal wouldn't get up, but the big man was tough as stone, though his wound had begun to fester. They had run out of whiskey some time ago, and there was nothing to clean the cut with. Though Abby used water, it was most likely filled with microbes, some of which Knight was certain wouldn't be good for an open wound.

Beyond the bridge, there was a natural triangular cave mouth decorated with all the symbols Knight now knew well. The Maglite melted the darkness, and Knight held his breath. He had good spatial awareness, and if his racing heart was right, the fellowship had reached the pinnacle of the obelisk.

The cave beyond the opening slanted steeply upward, and there were small sets of steps carved into the ancient stone where the floor heaved and pitched. One person could walk single file, the passageway nothing but a slit in the stone and no more than three feet wide.

With the song of the Salamantis leaking through the tower, the party exited the tunnel onto the obelisk's top tier, which was a majestic open-air pavilion made of finely sculpted flowstone.

Dark clouds churned above, and blue and white streaks of light illuminated the dark clouds. The curved supports that arced overhead caught the blueish gloom like a sundial and cast long shadows across the intricately patterned floor. Time had worn away the carvings that once adorned the arched columns, but faint traces of intricate designs still clung to the stone like ghosts of the past.

The pavilion was open to the elements, though from the ground the obelisk had appeared solid. Knight's stomach tingled with nausea as he panned the Maglite over the spidery tangle where the curved supports met at the zenith of the open dome. At the confluence, a stalactite speared from the clouds and melted into the top of the open dome where the supports met.

Knight thought the entire structure resembled an upside-down funnel, with thin, widely spaced columns along the sides. Where the supports met Knight saw what looked to have once been a Salamantis carved into the stone, but the ravages of millennia had reduced its features to whispers.

A flash caught Knight's eye. He swung the Maglite and the light disappeared. "Turn off your headlamps," he said as he killed the flashlight.

There were only two headlamps left working and Abby and Cap killed them.

A column of white light. Light! Real light, not the cold bone marrow-chilling blue pseudo light that clung to the air or the jarring soul-sucking LED light, but real light knifed through the gloom and painted a circle atop what looked to be an altar.

At the center of the flowstone rotunda, a large, circular platform dominated the space. Carved from a single block of white stone, it was stained black from what appeared to be the blood of an age long past. The surface of the altar was sloped slightly inward, directing the flow of sacred liquids toward a shallow channel that ran off the edge of the obelisk.

Knight pictured a blood waterfall as he stared, his stomach twisting, his feet rooted to stone.

Around the altar, the floor was made up of large, flat stone slabs, their surfaces uneven. The slabs looked to be cut from a red stone Knight had yet to see anywhere beneath the surface of Madagascar. Each piece fit snugly against its neighbors, creating a solid, unyielding foundation, and Knight wondered at how the giant cuts of rock had been transported to the top of the obelisk. In some places, the floor was cracked or chipped, but despite the damage, it still appeared smooth.

The view was a panorama of sparkling stone, the lake below reflecting the cavern's many hollows and headlands. But as the remaining members of the fellowship crowded around Knight the companions couldn't pull their gaze from the column of natural light piercing the altar like a spotlight.

Cap rushed forward and Knight thrust out his arm and stopped him.

"Slow. Careful. There could be…" Knight wanted to say traps, but the group had yet to encounter one, so he said nothing.

The sound of metal scraping on metal carried over the rotunda as Cap reloaded his Glock and eased forward, his headlamp's beam bouncing around. When he reached the large white stone table he tentatively reached out and broke the stream of light.

Nothing happened. No giant stone fell from the ceiling. The floor didn't collapse, and no darts shot from the arched support columns.

"When the sun disappears from the middle day sky," Abby said.

Knight and the others joined Cap, and Knight tried to follow the path of the beam of light, but it disappeared into the blackness above. He shined the Maglite up into the shaft that bore through the stalactite, the base of which was the focal point of the arched beams, a creature carved into its face.

A round shaft pocked with holes of various sizes ran away into blackness. Several creatures worked their way down the inside of the stalactite, but the beasts froze under the glare of the Maglite like spiders caught in the middle of the carpet when a light came on. Their glowing eyes stared down at the party, and Knight and the others stepped back until they could no longer be seen by the creatures.

"Let's do a fast search," Knight said. "See if there are any other doorways."

"Got it," Cap said.

"I'll go with you," Lucca said.

Abby and Knight helped Kamal find a place to sit where he could rest for a few minutes. Knight didn't like how the guy looked; bloodshot eyes, red cheeks, trembling hands, his forehead hot to the touch, and worst of all, Abby said all these signs plus the thin dark lines spidering from the red swollen wound all indicated an infection. Abby met Knight's eye. No words were needed. Abby was telling Knight that Kamal couldn't go much further.

Knight licked his lips and nodded. The remains of the first aid kit were stowed in Abby's dry bag, but what Kamal needed was a strong antibiotic and there were none to be had.

The reconnoiter of the pavilion didn't take long, and Lucca and Cap returned to find Abby, Knight, and Kamal drinking water and eating.

"Anything?" Knight asked. He was sullen and couldn't get Wheat Thin's face out of his head. If he survived, he'd have to tell the man's mother, and his chest ached with the thought.

"There are no other exits, and there are no stairs on the exterior of the obelisk," Cap said.

The pungent scent of urine wafted over the rotunda.

"What's that smell?" Kamal asked through his haze.

"Sorry," Lucca said. "I couldn't hold it anymore."

With that, the group fell silent.

Knight sipped water as he stared at the thin beam of light piercing what he believed to be a sacrificial altar, his thoughts a jumble of impossible ideas. Going back served no purpose, and as he gazed upward into the shaft above the altar, he thought maybe they could climb one of the supports arcing over the pavilion, and then use the rope to climb up the shaft. The chill of worry ran through Knight, and his gaze shifted to Kamal.

"So what now?" Lucca asked.

Cap, having read Knight's mind, dropped the length of rope onto the floor and said, "Now, we climb."

Nobody spoke as they stared at the column of white light and the shaft above.

"Kamal," Knight said.

The man looked up, his face red with fever.

"We need to get you out of here," Knight said. "Otherwise…"

Kamal nodded.

"Do you think you can climb? With help, of course," Cap asked.

Kamal struggled to get up, and when Abby tried to help him, he gently pushed her away. The big man pushed up to one knee, swayed, got to his feet, and said, "I can climb. Or I will die trying."

29

As was the custom, Cap free-climbed ahead of the group. He scaled one of the support beams that arced over the rotunda and hammered the largest piton he had into the rock at the base of the hollowed-out stalactite above the sacrificial altar.

The click of a carabiner snapping onto the piton rang over the hall as Cap secured the rope around his waist before starting his climb up the shaft.

Like a bug under a klieg light, Cap made his way from hole to hole, opening to opening, as he climbed up the shaft. After ten minutes he faded into darkness.

Several tense minutes passed before the steady hum of the song of the Salamantis was broken by gunshots. Bullets ricocheted around the shaft, and three creatures crashed onto the sacrificial altar, their exoskeletons breaking apart, blood and guts splattering stone.

Then Cap was there, backlit by the column of white light as he glided down the rope like a spider descending on a strand of silk. He landed amongst the creatures he'd dispatched, and said, "It ain't gonna be easy, but it's doable. We're going to have to run multiple pitches."

"For those of us who haven't climbed Everest," Lucca said.

"A pitch is like a run or a section," Cap said. "Meaning we're going to have to rig and unrig our setup multiple times because we only have one hundred feet of rope, limited carabiners, and I already used the largest piton and getting it out might not be possible."

"What are you saying?" Knight said.

Cap's eyes shifted to Kamal. "We need to check what gear we have, and…" He took a pull from his water bottle and licked his lips before continuing. "I'm in charge. If I give a command, you move. No questions. No committees. No discussion groups. Failure to act swiftly will most likely lead to your death. Are you all agreeable to this?"

Even Kamal made no sound.

"I know you all have climbing experience, and you're looking up at the shaft and you're seeing all those pocks and hollows and openings. You're thinking there are plenty of spots for a foothold, or to grip onto, and you can rest in the larger crags along the way." Cap took another pull of water and shook his head. "Everything is coated in flowstone and as slippery as river stones."

Kamal coughed, but the rest of the party gave no sign.

"Because the rope is only one hundred feet long, we'll only be able to climb fifty feet per pitch. I'll be the lead climber and Knight, you'll be the anchor. Once Abby and Lucca are up, you'll attach the rope to Kamal, and I'll use myself as a counterweight to lift him. Questions?"

The sound of dripping water, the scuttling claws of the creatures, and the song of the Salamantis carried over the rotunda.

"Make sure your binger is locked onto the rope," Cap said. "If you fall, don't struggle. Knight and I will have you. Since the rope is already set, we'll all haul Kamal up to the start of the shaft because climbing the beams would be very difficult for him. Ready?"

The rope still hung from the piton at the base of the shaft, and Kamal clamped on and gave a thumbs up.

With Cap as the anchor, the team hoisted Kamal, and when he reached the top, he untethered himself and dropped the rope down into Knight's waiting hands.

"Should we haul Lucca and Abby up?" Knight asked. "They're much lighter than Kamal?"

Cap shrugged, and Knight and Cap helped Abby and Lucca climb to Kamal. When they were done, their three companions staring down at them through the gloom, Cap and Knight climbed one of the arched beams and joined their teammates.

The fellowship rested for a few minutes at the base of the stalactite that flowed into the top of the open dome, the arched beams like melted candle wax. A beam of light still raced from the top of the shaft and cut through the gloom below.

Several creatures appeared in the shaft above, and Cap dispatched them before starting his free climb, one end of the rope around his waist. The man was a spider, and because there were plenty of holes and alcoves, he made fast work of the first fifty feet. Seconds later one end of the rope slithered down to Lucca.

Knight's brow wrinkled. He hadn't heard the tapping of the rock hammer, so he knew Cap hadn't used one of the remaining pitons to create the belay station. He called, "What's the rope anchored on?"

"A gap in the rock," Cap yelled. "Now, let's go, and knock it off with the stupid questions."

Lucca climbed, but as before Knight and the others helped her.

Abby was next, and with Knight acting as the belayer and managing the rope from the group's starting point, she was up in moments. Then Cap belayed back down to Knight as he hauled the injured Kamal up to where Abby and Lucca waited.

Then it was Knight's turn, and though the rock was slippery, his hands took a beating as his fingers searched for handholds, his momentum buoyed by Cap's constant tension on the rope.

When Knight reached the others, Cap again free-climbed and joined his companions. "Fifty feet," said Cap as he gazed upward and took a pull of water. The entire process took twenty-five minutes.

The gunshots from Cap's probe of the shaft brought more creatures, and a spotter was added to the climbing rotation. Over the following two hours, the party repeated the climbing sequence, hauling up Kamal, Cap resetting the lines, and using pitons when needed as the team took turns dispatching any Salamantis brave enough to venture into the party's cloud of light.

They were resting after their seventh pitch, the top of the shaft still lost in blackness, the beam of white light splitting the darkness down the middle, when Abby said, "Should we go back?"

Cap snickered.

"The shaft is getting narrower," Abby said. "You see that, right?"

"I do," Cap said.

So had Knight and his stomach gurgled with the idea that the shaft might just peter out. But the beam of light running down the center of the shaft hadn't wavered, so Knight pushed the idea away and said, "It's too late to go back."

The gentle hum of rushing water began to drown out the call of the Salamantis after the eleventh pitch. Though the sound made Knight's skin prickle with memories that superheated his stomach and made his skin feel sunburned, it also brought him hope. His muscles ached, and he was exhausted, and he'd lost...

"We've climbed over four hundred feet," Cap said. "But it looks like we've almost reached the top."

The Maglite revealed a rough stone ceiling with thousands of tiny stalactites. None of the ancient spikes dripped water, but the echo of a gurgling stream filled the shaft and the song of the Salamantis was nothing more than a whisper.

With the grim determination of a group that had been through too much to give up or fail, the fellowship climbed another hundred and fifty feet, and at the start of the fifteenth pitch Cap yelled, "I'm at the top."

Cap anchored the line, and one by one the party climbed onto a scree pile of jagged stones that slanted upward to a pool fed by an underground river. There were no signs of Salamantis here, and the party holstered their weapons for what felt like the first time.

The banks of the river were wide and steep in spots, but only a trickle of water ran down the center of the sandy riverbed. Shadows danced as the column of light knifed from a hole in the ceiling.

Knight's heart sank. Without heavy excavation, the fellowship could no longer trace the light's path.

Cap's headlamp chose that moment to give out, and a large section of the pool fell dark. Abby's headlamp, the last one still alive, and the Maglite kept the darkness at bay, but it didn't take light to see there was only one direction to go.

The pool was shallow, and as the companions waded into it Knight saw there were many holes in its bottom that allowed water to drain into the obelisk.

"There's probably plenty of places like this," Abby said as she turned her headlamp on where the river streamed from a cave mouth. "It's perfect for us."

"Come again?" Lucca said.

"See the soil between the stone? Like mortar?" Abby said. "We're close to the surface. I'd guess within a hundred feet."

Knight nodded and followed the stream into the darkness, the flashlight illuminating the narrow, spiderweb-infested cave, the sandy bottom of the river sparkling under the harsh LED light.

The tunnel widened, narrowed, pitched, and heaved, but Knight didn't think they were making much upward progress. Occasionally he thought he heard birds singing and the rustle of leaves or the gentle drumming of rain, but when he stopped and listened hard, he realized the sounds were a mirage.

A hiss carried down the tunnel.

Knight came to a halt. "Do you hear that?" he whispered. Knight drew down and so did the others. So much for holstered weapons.

A deep rumble, like a low growl, broke the stillness and two eyes appeared in the dark water ahead. But these weren't the eyes of a Salamantis.

Knight's mind spun through the possibilities and none of them were good.

Cap came up beside him and said, "Let me take a look, boss." When Knight didn't respond, he added, "O.K.?"

Knight looked back into the darkness at the faces of Lucca, Abby, and Kamal. They all stared at him. The next move was his. The next move had always been his, even when the party was eleven strong and led by a shaman and a big-dollar adventurer with questionable morals. He nodded and eased aside and let Cap pass. He would come to regret the choice moments later, though the decision probably saved his life.

As Cap inched forward, he raised his gun, aimed, and put two bullets between the cold eyes.

A wail echoed through the tunnel, followed by a splash of water as a mid-sized crocodile thrashed out of the darkness, spasming in its death throes.

With the gunshots still ringing through the cave, a second, much larger croc wriggled through the shallow river and launched at Cap, narrow jaws open wide, conical teeth lining the inside of the beast's mouth.

As Cap struggled to aim his gun he fired, and the bullets punched into the cave wall and rock splinters flew.

The crocodile clamped down on Cap's leg and thrashed its head, pulling the big man to the ground.

Knight and Abby stood in shocked silence, and it was Lucca who acted first.

The croc's jaws chomped on Cap as the big man screamed and fired his gun, bullets ricocheting around the cave, sparks flying like fireflies.

Lucca got in close and shot the croc in the head three times.

Knight's ears rang, and all at once, everything fell still: Cap's wailing, the croc's growling and thrashing, all gone. Only the faint song of the Salamantis remained, pulsing beneath the steady heartbeat of the Earth.

Cap's torn-open body lay on the ground like a deflated balloon, the man's eyes staring at the ceiling, his killer's powerful jaws still locked on his midsection.

Lucca bent and closed Cap's eyes.

Knight screamed and let it all out; the rage, the frustration, the anguish, and the sorrow. He'd lost two close friends on this forlorn quest, and he wasn't sure he'd ever be able to scrub Wheat Thin and Cap's blood from his hands.

The screech of a Salamantis carried from the tunnel ahead.

Knight raised his gun and started forward, but Abby stepped in his way. "They're gone, Knight. And you can't bring them back, so sacrificing your life serves no purpose."

"Purpose? Purpose? Look around, Abby," Knight said.

"The crocs may have trapped several creatures," she said. "We have no way of knowing how many of them there might be."

A smile crept across Knight's face, and he said, "I don't care." Then without another word, he continued following the stream which he knew would either lead to redemption or doom.

174

30

As the fellowship followed the dying underground stream the Maglite wavered and dimmed. Knight's heart thumped, sweat stinging his eyes as thoughts of feeling his way through the stygian darkness took up prime position in his cortex. The light burst back to full strength, and the tunnel was once again revealed in stark black and white, the thin river shimmering and the mineral-rich sentiment of the stream bed sparkling.

Reading the situation, Kamal said, "Maybe you should give the flashlight a break. Abby's light is weak, but we can manage."

The idea had merit. Knight thought maybe the Maglite had just given the party a huge warning. The creatures didn't fear the light, but they certainly didn't like it, and it was much easier to shoot when you could see what you were shooting at.

Knight turned off the Maglite and as his eyes adjusted, he saw no glowing eyes in the darkness. Cap's broken body filled his mind's eye, and Knight gritted his teeth in frustration. He should've foreseen the trouble with the crocodiles. The beasts crawled all over northern Madagascar, and they loved underground water sources and subterranean lairs. Cap should've known, too. They all should've known.

The stream died and the tunnel began to narrow, the ceiling pressing in on the party, and they were forced to crouch to continue onward. Cracks and side passages appeared, and the composition of the cave walls shifted from solid stone to a mix of huge rocks and pebble-filled soil, and roots hung from the ceiling like greasy hair.

Tiny creatures were everywhere; ants, spiders, and beetles of various colors and sizes called the underground realm home. A sharp hiss carried down the tunnel and the remaining four members of the fellowship stopped short and bumped into each other.

Kamal squealed.

The high-pitched hiss was unlike the crocodile's calling card, and relief flooded through Knight when the flashlight revealed a massive cockroach. Distinguished by its large size, the Madagascar Hissing Cockroach was native to the island of Madagascar.

"*Gromphadorhina portentosa*," Abby said.

The beast was five inches long, its tough exoskeleton a dark, glossy brown. Forelegs cycled around, and though the roach was wingless, its notched legs looked powerful. The bug hissed louder, and it reminded Knight of a Poodle barking at a Doberman.

Abby said, "The hissing is unique to this species and is produced by expelling air through small openings called spiracles located on the bug's abdomen."

Knight took two fast steps forward, pointed the Maglite directly at the creature, and turned it on.

The massive insect scuttled away into a crack in the wall.

A Salamantis shrieked, and the call was answered by two others, but to Knight's surprise, the calls sounded like they'd come from the tunnel behind him.

Knight killed the flashlight and pressed on, the shrieks of the creatures filling the cave as it shrank to a six-foot high by three-foot-wide crack that was more dirt than stone.

Ahead, a field of thin rays pierced the darkness like spotlights shining through a strainer.

"We're close," Kamal said.

Knight could feel it also. The hum of the land, the sound of birds, the rustle of the forest. "We can try and dig out," he said.

"We've got no idea how deep we are," Abby said.

"Could be ten feet or fifty," Kamal said.

"Only one way to find out," Knight said. "Give me the shovel."

Lucca dropped her dry bag and pulled out the folding shovel, one of the few tools the companions still had in their possession. She handed it to Knight, who unfolded it and locked the blade in place.

A Salamantis peeled from the blackness, its skin shifting color, its eyes gleaming, jaws extended as its claws searched for flesh.

Knight swung the shovel with everything he had, and it connected with the beast's head.

The creature shrieked and reared back on its hindlegs.

Abby fired, the sound deafening in the confined space.

Knight swung the shovel again but only hit air.

The monster's head exploded in a burst of blood, brain, and bone, spattering the dirt wall as its body crumpled to the ground.

Ears ringing, Knight turned on the Maglite.

A knot of creatures clogged the tunnel behind the party, their hungry eyes rolling wildly, antennae twitching, limbs churning like they'd been flipped onto their backs and were scrambling to turn over.

"They're trapped here," Lucca said.

"The damn crocs," Knight said. He beat himself up again over his lack of foresight. Crocs in northern Madagascar. Shoot, it wasn't even worthy of a question on Jeopardy. He shined the flashlight into the tunnel ahead, wiping away the daggers of natural light. Knight shifted the flashlight beam, and the rays of light reappeared.

Knight turned his attention back to the horde, which was inching up the tunnel toward its prey.

"They look a little... shellshocked," Abby said.

With all eyes on the Salamantis knot rolling down the tunnel, a beast appeared behind the group, and Lucca didn't see the creature until it was too late.

A cackle-bark shriek blasted through the subterranean passage as the Salamantis surged into the cloud of LED light, its eyes ablaze as its foreleg pierced Lucca's right side, the claw at its tip slicing into flesh.

Lucca screamed, blood spurting from a wound just below her ribcage. She doubled over and hit the ground, her wail fading to a gurgle of pain.

Abby fired three times at point-blank range and turned the beast's head into green and brown oatmeal. Before the monster's corpse hit the floor, Abby was at Lucca's side, raising the woman's head and resting it on her dry bag.

Knight aimed his gun and the flashlight at the approaching fist of creatures. "How bad is it?"

"Bad," Abby said. "But she might make it if..."

If. "We need to get out of this tight space. We're sitting ducks here," Knight said.

Kamal and Abby waited, and Lucca moaned.

"Take Kamal as deep into the tunnel as possible," Knight said. "And take this." He handed her the shovel. "If you see an opportunity, don't hesitate. Try and dig out. But be careful. You don't want to get buried under a cave-in."

"What are you going to do?" Abby asked, her voice cracking.

"Stay here with Lucca and hold these things back," Knight said. What else was there for him to do?

Abby opened her mouth to protest, thought better of it, and pressed her lips together.

"Take this," Kamal said as he handed over his gun. "There's eight bullets in the mag and one in the chamber."

Now it was Knight's turn to open his mouth but not speak. He nodded as he accepted the gun.

Abby handed over her weapon as well. "It's almost empty. Six bullets left, I think."

Knight stuck the weapon in his waistband.

Abby hugged Knight as she shot a final glance at Lucca. Then she wrapped Kamal's arm over her shoulder, crouched lower, and eased forward into the dark tunnel, the shovel raised like a sword.

When Abby and Kamal were out of earshot, Knight said, "If they reach us we're done for."

Lucca didn't respond. Her eyes had fallen closed and though Abby had used a t-shirt as a bandage to try and stop the bleeding, a fresh trail of blood ran from the wound and puddled on the floor.

Knight shook the woman and yelled her name.

Lucca came lazily awake, her eyes staring at something Knight couldn't see.

"You've got to stay awake. Please, Lucca," Knight pleaded.

Though it was barely a movement, Lucca nodded.

Catcalls ranged down the tunnel, and three creatures separated from the horde and were bouncing through the cave, using all their appendages, even their forelimbs which gave the appearance that the creatures were running on all six of their legs.

Knight placed the blazing Maglite on the ground and strode straight toward the beasts, a Glock outstretched in each hand, yet he didn't fire. He waited, his muscles screaming for rest, his stomach a knot of pain. When the three leaders were twenty feet away, the glare of the flashlight peeling away the darkness, Knight fired. Six shots. Three from each gun like an old-school gunslinger.

Two Salamantis heads popped, and their owners stumbled and crashed to the floor in a tangle of legs and antennas. The third beast took two shots to the abdomen and lost two legs before it stumbled to the ground, its corpse coming to rest at Knight's feet.

But he wasn't finished. Rage surged through Knight. It was time to end this. Now.

He looked over his shoulder, but Knight couldn't see Lucca in the darkness. What he did see brought a surge of hope that stoked his anger and built his confidence, a dangerous brew.

A wide column of light, like a door had been opened, illuminated the tunnel beyond where Lucca lay hidden in shadow.

Knight charged the remaining creatures, firing as he went, bullets cracking exoskeletons and severing appendages. When Kamal's gun clicked empty, he dropped it and pulled Abby's weapon.

Dead creatures clogged the tunnel, their twisted bodies stacked like discarded refuse. A tremor rippled through the earth, followed by a deafening crack, like the splintering of an ancient tree, that echoed through the cave. The beasts froze, halting their climb over the mound of their fallen kin.

There was a moment of silence, and then a loud rumble, as if the Earth itself was being rattled.

With a chorus of shrieks and wails, the creatures turned tail and ran.

A smile crept over Knight's face, and he let the guns fall to his sides.

Another loud crack, and the tunnel ceiling crumbled. Dirt, stones, roots, and bugs poured into the cave from directly above and behind Knight.

There was no time to think, to plan, to consider the pros and cons. Knight dove and avoided a huge boulder as it crashed into the tunnel. He pressed to his feet like a surfer and ran for his life, rocks and dirt falling all around him.

A stone landed before him and Knight cut to his right to avoid it, but he slipped and went down hard. His face smacked stone, tiny stars dancing before his eyes.

He saw the party standing around the karst filled with water, the underground city, and one by one the faces of the dead flashed before him; Barbo's curious eyes, Volana's dark hair splayed around her bloody face, Pugari's sinister grin, Wheat Thin's geeky frame, Tank, and Cap.

Debris fell onto him, and Knight heard Wheat Thin's voice. It was so clear he thought he was losing his mind. "Run, boss! Run!" screeched his number one from beyond.

The urging was enough, and Knight rolled over, spit out dust and grit, and got to his feet. Rocks, uprooted plants, and earth filled the tunnel behind him, blocking the way. He didn't want to die here. Alone. Tears welled in Knight's eyes as he clawed at the cave-in, calling his friends' names.

When only the calls of the Salamantis carried on the damp breeze, he sprinted down the tunnel, leaving the chaos of the cave-in behind, clinging to the desperate hope that his companions hadn't been buried alive.

31

Joseph Ravoahangy Andrianavalona Hospital, Antananarivo, Madagascar
10:19 AM EAT, eighty-three hours later

Abby and Kamal sat in a private waiting room at the Hôpital JRA, Abby marinating in the news that Lucca was going to make it, and possibly without permanent injuries. She was resting comfortably, and though Abby didn't know the woman well, she cared more than she was willing to admit. Stressful situations create strong bonds, and she and Lucca would remain friends regardless of where life's path took them.

Kamal sat beside her, his arm still in a sling, but his wound had been treated, and he was given the proper drugs and was on his way to a full recovery. The big man's transformation from enforcer to righteous tough guy suited him well, and they'd agreed to work together in the future.

The waiting room was beat, even for a hospital. There were no prints hanging on the walls and no water cooler. The table's nasty laminate was chipped and missing in spots, and the chairs were a mismatch of soldiers that had survived upgrades all around the hospital. It was where they put people who were being detained but hadn't come to terms with it yet.

Abby knew this because when she'd ventured from the room to go to the bathroom, she discovered a Malaysian police officer casually sitting by the door playing with his phone. The young man hadn't followed her physically, but he had with his eyes, and Abby was certain that if she'd tried to leave the floor, he would have radioed his backup and Abby wouldn't have gotten far. Because their mission into the jungle was unsanctioned, the U.S. Embassy in Antananarivo had been little help.

When the cave-in occurred, the companions had only been ten feet below the surface of the jungle. Abby was able to create a controlled cave-in, and she and Kamal climbed into the dull, drab grayness using the dirt pile and found that it wasn't raining. After helping Kamal, Abby retrieved Lucca, who had been hanging on by the thinnest of threads. Turned out that the three survivors weren't far from the flooded karst where the fellowship had abandoned their ATVs and much of their equipment. So it was that the three companions found their way out of the jungle eighteen hours after the cave-in. Had it taken longer, Lucca most likely would have died.

With the list of dead including three locals, one of which was missing but presumed dead, the Malaysian authorities were skeptical of Abby and Kamal's story. Abby's phone was buried with her dry bag, and the pair had no proof other than their account of the events that had led to the deaths of six people, possibly eight. It put Abby and Kamal in a difficult position, and had it not been for them pressing so hard for a rescue mission, Abby believed they'd be in a jail cell pending an investigation, and there'd be a guard outside Lucca's door.

As it was, the pair was waiting for the local police chief who would inform them of their fate and listen to their request.

Kamal sniffled as the faint hum of elevator music leaked into the room.

Abby hugged herself. "It's cold in here," she said.

"I don't think I will ever be warm again," Kamal said. "I think it might be—"

The door lock clicked, and the door swung open.

Chief Adriana Lamgihonie wasn't what Abby had expected. When Abby was informed of the meeting, she'd assumed the woman would be an ancient bureaucrat, wrapped in the safety blanket of the law. A person concerned only with making her path as easy as possible as long as that path led to the right thing for Madagascar.

The chief appeared to be none of these things. She was a local, and young. Abby pegged her at no more than forty, which, in a country like Madagascar, was considered young for a prominent position of power, especially for a woman.

She dropped a file on the desk, old school, forgetting that everyone in the real world used datapads or their phones. The chief's eyes shifted from Abby to Kamal as she smiled and sat down before the pair.

"I'm sorry for your losses," Chief Lamgihonie said.

Abby and Kamal both nodded in unison and said thank you.

"I know you are both worried about your friend, so I'll get right to it. I read the file, heard the stories, your accounts..." She paused and looked them both in the eye. "You have to understand. I must be skeptical."

It was a question and Abby answered it. "No worries," she said. "If I hadn't been there, I wouldn't believe any of it."

"From what I can see, you're asking the Malaysian government for assistance, and to let you traipse back into the jungle. Assuming your entire story is true, how does that make sense?"

"Because I believe he is alive," Kamal said. "Mr. Knight."

Silence filled the small room, and Abby heard the distant murmur of voices and the push of air hissing from the vent above her head.

"Listen," Chief Lamgihonie said as she leaned back in her chair, exasperated. "If it were up to me, I would allow it. There's nothing you can damage up there, but of course, I can't say that officially." She stood. "Do you have any more questions?"

"So that's a no?" Abby said.

The chief sat back down. "You've filed your request with the Ministry of Culture and Heritage. Yes?"

"I have, but..." Abby licked her lips, beat back her temper, and said, "If you read the accounts in the statement, you know there were two locals down there with us, three if you count the shaman, and they're missing."

"We're looking into that," the top cop said.

"Knight was alive the last time we saw him," Kamal said.

"Before the cave-in, you mean?" said Chief Lamgihonie.

"Yes," Abby said.

"Our people have scoured the site. All they found was an empty tunnel and a cave-in, like you described. They used metal detectors and dogs. They found nothing. I'm sorry."

"You don't care about the dead down there?" Kamal said.

"We do," the chief said. "A team of Malaysians will attempt to follow your path and as the bodies are discovered... if the bodies are discovered, they will be exhumed and brought to the surface for proper burial."

Again, silence reigned.

"Anything else?" Chief Lamgihonie asked.

"So, you totally don't believe the monsters part of the story?" Kamal said.

This made the chief sigh long and hard. "I believe it. But until one appears topside..." She threw up her arms.

Abby understood. The media saturated, conspiracy loving inhabitants of Earth didn't believe anything unless they saw it. If there wasn't a picture, it didn't happen.

"That's it then," Abby said. "You're telling us to leave our friend to die?"

Chief Lamgihonie shook her head vigorously. "No, no, no. Give it a little time. You'll get an official decision very soon, and in the meantime, we'll be searching the jungle."

"He's not in the jungle," Kamal said.

"Again, I'm sorry for your loss," the chief said. "I'll ensure that your paperwork gets processed as quickly as possible. I would expect a response within the next forty-eight hours, but my guess is your request will be denied. So go home."

"What if we don't?" Kamal said. The implication was clear; will you make us leave the country or stop us if we go into the jungle?

"As the three of us sit here right now you're not a suspect in any crime," the chief said in her stern voice. "When Barbo, Volana, and the shaman's... if their bodies are discovered, and it's determined that they were somehow killed in any way other than an accident, you, Kamal, and Lucca would immediately become suspects." She let that hang out there as her strongest warning. "Go home, Ms. Rent, Mr. Kahn. I'll contact you immediately with any new findings."

But Abby didn't go home and neither did Kamal. They stayed in town, visited Lucca, and pressed the local police and government officials for action.

32

As promised, thirty-four hours later an email hit Abby's mailbox. Kamal and Abby were in Abby's room, and the big man lounged on her bed drinking coffee.

"It's here," Abby said as she sat before her laptop which rested on the hotel room's writing desk.

Kamal pushed up from the bed and stood over her shoulder.

There were several PDF files attached to the email and they were titled: Environmental Impact Assessment Report, Cultural Sensitivity and Community Engagement Evaluation, and Monitoring and Assessment Plan. The Prime Minister's Office, the Ministry of Environment and Sustainable Development, the U.S. Embassy in Antananarivo, and the UNESCO World Heritage Centre were cc'd. The message read:

Republic of Madagascar
Ministry of Culture and Heritage
Office of the Minister
Case Number: MCH-24-007

To: Ms. Abby Rent, Mr. Kamal Kahn, and Ms. Lucca Naropa
From: Dr. Ralison Razafindrakoto, Minister of Culture and Heritage
Subject: Request for Search and Rescue Mission on Heritage Grounds

This memorandum addresses the formal request submitted by the aforementioned U.S., British, and Indian citizens for a search and rescue mission on heritage grounds located at and around Tsimi's Tear. The request detailed an urgent need for intervention due to the perceived threat of an unknown sleeper species, the possibility of survivors, and the structural integrity of the cultural artifacts at the site.

The area holds significant historical, cultural, and spiritual value for the people of Madagascar. It represents a critical component of our national identity and heritage. The Ministry of Culture and Heritage recognizes the importance of preserving such sites and has consistently supported measures to safeguard them.

Upon thorough review and evaluation of the request, several key considerations have led to the decision to deny the proposed search and rescue mission at this time.

The primary justification for the proposed search and rescue mission was to locate Lucius Knight, A.K.A Dusty, who was lost on an unsanctioned expedition to the site, and to recover the bodies of Malaysian citizens Narivony Ravelonarivo, Matheus Barbo, and Volana Copra, as well as visitors Wesley Eakin, Richard 'Cap' Kingsbury, Tommy 'Tank' Bullond, and Tiger Pugari.

However, the detailed investigation by our expert team, in collaboration with international heritage conservation specialists, local authorities, and the military, found no conclusive evidence supporting the claim of an urgent threat that necessitates immediate intervention.

The proposed mission includes extensive activities that could potentially disrupt the delicate ecological balance of the area. The site's flora and fauna, which are integral to its historical and cultural context, must be preserved. Our environmental impact assessment indicated that the proposed interventions could cause irreparable harm to these natural elements and the subterranean sites that have allegedly been found.

In addition, as per Malagasy Law No. 94-007 on Cultural Heritage Protection and the UNESCO World Heritage Convention, to which Madagascar is a signatory, there are stringent regulations protecting heritage sites from any activities that could degrade their value, and approving this request may set a concerning precedent for future activities in other heritage sites.

The area is not only a historical site but also a living cultural and spiritual center for local communities. Any intervention must be approached with the utmost cultural sensitivity and in close consultation with these communities. The proposal did not include a comprehensive plan for community engagement, nor did it adequately address the potential cultural ramifications of the proposed activities.

This denial does not imply a lack of commitment to this issue. In this regard, the Ministry of Culture and Heritage acknowledges and appreciates the dedication of the aforementioned, and moving forward, all relevant agencies will increase the frequency and scope of monitoring activities at Tsimi's Tear and the surrounding area to ensure any emerging threats are promptly identified and addressed as the newly discovered heritage sites are investigated.

The preservation of our national heritage is a shared responsibility, and it is through collaborative efforts that we can achieve sustainable and meaningful outcomes. The Ministry of Culture and Heritage remains committed to working with all stakeholders to protect and celebrate Madagascar's rich cultural legacy.

Should you have any further questions or require additional information, please do not hesitate to contact my office.

Sincerely,

Dr. Ralison Razafindrakoto
Minister of Culture and Heritage
Republic of Madagascar

Abby slammed her laptop closed.

"In my country that is called a *Babugiri*," Kamal said. "That email is nothing more than a way of telling us that the powers that be in Madagascar don't want an American, a Brit, and an Indian crawling over the area, especially with Narivony Ravelonarivo missing and Barbo and Volana dead, and their deaths being an open investigation."

"An American, a Brit, and an Indian walked into a bar," Abby said.

Kamal chuckled.

Abby said, "They don't want us poking around. We'll see about that."

Four days later, as Abby, Kamal, and several locals crept through the jungle, thick plumes of black and white smoke billowed above the treetops, curling through the canopy and spreading like a stain across the forest. When the helicopters arrived, they discovered that the fire causing the smoke was in a dry karst not far from Tsimi's Tear.

Other Severed Press novels by Edward J. McFadden III: TRAGIC (#1 Amazon Bestseller Tag), HOWLER, Purgatory Beach, Time's Claws, Landfill Lizards, CRICS, Terror Lake, Predators & Prey, Wolves of the Sea (#1 Amazon Bestseller Tag), Fortune's Cypher, Crimson Falls (#1 Amazon Bestseller Tag), Hell Creek, Barracuda Swarm, The Cryptid Club, Dinosaur Red, Drop Off (#1 Amazon Bestseller Tag), Jurassic Ark, Keepers of the Flame, Throwback, Sea Tremors, Primeval Valley, Shadow of the Abyss (#1 Amazon Bestseller Tag), Awake, and The Breach (#1 Amazon Bestseller Tag, Amazon #1 Hot New Audio Release Tag). His other novels include: Crypsis, Just Beneath the Skin, Terror Peak (#1 Amazon Bestseller Tag), the Theo Ramage Thriller series: Quick Sands, Sandbagged, and Too Much Grit, and Dogs Get Ten Lives, The Black Death of Babylon, and HOAXERS. Ed lives on Long Island with his wife Dawn, their daughter Samantha, and their cats Snoop and Skittles.

 SEVEREDPRESS

 facebook.com/severedpress
twitter.com/severedpress

CHECK OUT OTHER GREAT CRYPTID NOVELS

SWAMP MONSTER MASSACRE
by **Hunter Shea**

The swamp belongs to them. Humans are only prey. Deep in the overgrown swamps of Florida, where humans rarely dare to enter, lives a race of creatures long thought to be only the stuff of legend. They walk upright but are stronger, taller and more brutal than any man. And when a small boat of tourists, held captive by a fleeing criminal, accidentally kills one of the swamp dwellers' young, the creatures are filled with a terrifyingly human emotion—a merciless lust for vengeance that will paint the trees red with blood.

TERROR MOUNTAIN
by **Gerry Griffiths**

When Marcus Pike inherits his grandfather's farm and moves his family out to the country, he has no idea there's an unholy terror running rampant about the mountainous farming community. Sheriff Avery Anderson has seen the heinous carnage and the mutilated bodies. He's also seen the giant footprints left in the snow—Bigfoot tracks. Meanwhile, Cole Wagner, and his wife, Kate, are prospecting their gold claim farther up the valley, unaware of the impending dangers lurking in the woods as an early winter storm sets in. Soon the snowy countryside will run red with blood on TERROR MOUNTAIN.

CHECK OUT OTHER GREAT BIGFOOT NOVELS

THE BEASTS OF STONECLAD MOUNTAIN
by **Gerry Griffiths**

Clay Morgan is overjoyed when he is offered a place to live in a remote wilderness at the base of a notorious mountain. Locals say there are Bigfoot living high up in the dense mountainous forest. Clay is skeptic at first and thinks it's nothing more than tall tales.

But soon Clay becomes a believer when giant creatures invade his new home and snatch his baby boy, Casey.

Now, Clay and his wife, Mia, must rescue their son with the help of Clay's uncle and his dog, a journey up the foreboding mountain that will take them into an unimaginable world...straight into hell!

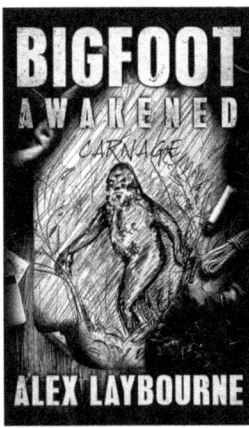

BIGFOOT AWAKENED
by Alex Laybourne

A weekend away with friends was supposed to be fun. One last chance for Jamie to blow off some steam before she leaves for college, but when the group make a wrong turn, fun is the last thing they find.

From the moment they pass through a small rural town they are being hunted by whatever abominations live in the woods.

Yet, as the beasts attack and the truth is revealed, they learn that despite everything, man still remains the most terrifying evil of them all.

 SEVEREDPRESS

 facebook.com/severedpress
twitter.com/severedpress

CHECK OUT OTHER GREAT CRYPTID NOVELS

RETURN TO DYATLOV PASS
by J.H. Moncrieff

In 1959, nine Russian students set off on a skiing expedition in the Ural Mountains. Their mutilated bodies were discovered weeks later. Their bizarre and unexplained deaths are one of the most enduring true mysteries of our time. Nearly sixty years later, podcast host Nat McPherson ventures into the same mountains with her team, determined to finally solve the mystery of the Dyatlov Pass incident. Her plans are thwarted on the first night, when two trackers from her group are brutally slaughtered. The team's guide, a superstitious man from a neighboring village, blames the killings on yetis, but no one believes him. As members of Nat's team die one by one, she must figure out if there's a murderer in their midst—or something even worse—before history repeats itself and her group becomes another casualty of the infamous Dead Mountain.

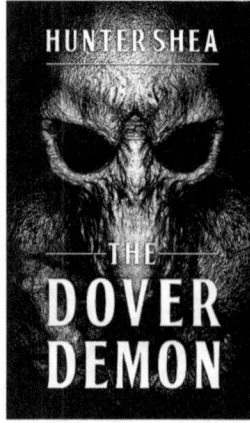

DOVER DEMON
by Hunter Shea

The Dover Demon is real...and it has returned. In 1977, Sam Brogna and his friends came upon a terrifying, alien creature on a deserted country road. What they witnessed was so bizarre, so chilling, they swore their silence. But their lives were changed forever. Decades later, the town of Dover has been hit by a massive blizzard. Sam's son, Nicky, is drawn to search for the infamous cryptid, only to disappear into the bowels of a secret underground lair. The Dover Demon is far deadlier than anyone could have believed. And there are many of them. Can Sam and his reunited friends rescue Nicky and battle a race of creatures so powerful, so sinister, that history itself has been shaped by their secretive presence?

www.ingramcontent.com/pod-product-compliance
Lightning Source LLC
Chambersburg PA
CBHW071513170626
46811CB00007B/2835